I grew up without a home – what was it, the south, Pittsburgh? – and by my mid-twenties the anxiety had grown palpable. My most potent memories were southern, but the inherited memories were of my parents' Canada, especially Montreal, where they had met and life had taken an improbable turn for both of them. But by 1966, when I moved my family to Montreal, my parents had divorced, my father was in Mexico, my mother had returned to Winnipeg, I had married a woman from India, and I didn't know where I'd come from or where I was going. Montreal provided the answer.

I re-entered a world I had never made, Montreal, and determined I would become the son I might have been, and would assert authority over an experience I could and should have had, but never did. Confusion remained, but at least I would be the French and English son of befuddlement, the crown prince of Canadian identity.

Books by Clark Blaise

A North American Education (1973)

Tribal Justice (1974)

Days and Nights in Calcutta (1977)
(with Bharati Mukherjee)

Lunar Attractions (1979)

Lusts (1983)

Resident Alien (1986)

The Sorrow and the Terror (1987)
(with Bharati Mukherjee)

Man and His World (1992)

I Had a Father (1993)

*Here, There and Everywhere:
Lectures on Australian, Canadian, American and Post-Modern Writing* (1994)

If I Were Me (1997)

Southern Stories (2000)

*Time Lord:
The Remarkable Canadian Who Missed His Train* (2001)

Pittsburgh Stories (2001)

The Selected Stories of

CLARK BLAISE

Volume Three

Montreal Stories

With an Introduction by
Peter Behrens

The Porcupine's Quill

National Library of Canada Cataloguing in Publication Data

Blaise, Clark, 1940–
The selected stories of Clark Blaise

Introduction to v. 3 by Peter Behrens.
Contents: v. 1. Southern stories – v. 2. Pittsburgh stories – v. 3. Montreal Stories.
ISBN 0-88984-219-1 (v. 1). – ISBN 0-88984-227-2 (v. 2) –
ISBN 0-88984-270-1 (v. 3).

I. Title. II. Title: Southern stories. III. Title: Pittsburgh stories.
IV. Title: Montreal stories.

PS8553.L34S68 2000   C813'.54   C00-932402-X rev

1   2   3   4   ·   05   04   03

Published by The Porcupine's Quill,
68 Main Street, Erin, Ontario NOB 1TO.
www.sentex.net/~pql

Readied for the press by John Metcalf; copy edited by Doris Cowan.

Represented in Canada by the Literary Press Group.
Trade orders are available from University of Toronto Press.

We acknowledge the support of the Ontario Arts Council
and the Canada Council for the Arts for our publishing program.
The financial support of the Government of Canada
through the Book Publishing Industry Development Program
is also gratefully acknowledged. Thanks, also, to the Government of
Ontario through the Ontario Media Development Corporation's
Ontario Book Initiative.

 Canada Council
for the Arts

Conseil des Arts
du Canada

ONTARIO ARTS COUNCIL
CONSEIL DES ARTS DE L'ONTARIO

 Canadä

Contents

Introduction

These stories speak to the whereness of who and what I am.
– *Resident Alien*

Montreal functions like an (unreliable) heart within the body of Clark Blaise's *oeuvre:* a treacherous, indispensable organ at the centre of his fiction. The writer, so far, has spent just thirteen years consecutively (1966–78) in the Paris of North America. (With its brick tenements, multiplicity of nineteenth-century churches and urban funk, Montreal physically – spiritually, perhaps – resembles Brooklyn, even Dublin, more than it does the City of Light.)

Thirteen years. Not a lifetime, but longer than any place else in an accomplished, peripatetic career. Born in Fargo, North Dakota; raised in Florida and Pittsburgh; the son of a French-Canadian father from the Megantic/Maine borderland and an English-Canadian mother from Manitoba, Blaise found home and exile, all at once, in Montreal. The city is his Dublin *and* his Trieste. The bipolarity of Mo'ray-al/Munntreeall – electrified him. If the city had not existed, he would have to invent it, as Faulkner would have invented north Mississippi. Of course, this is exactly what each writer did, but both needed to ground their imaginations to the touch of actual earth (or asphalt).

If Blaise characters are certain of anything, it is the significance of place: they usually attempt to explain themselves by giving sets of geographic coordinates (and never simple ones).

Leaving the United States, crossing a border to settle in a city whose fault lines doppleganged his own, was a crucial act for a writer who was already exploring geography as metaphor and motive. In the Montreal stories, Blaise investigated fluid, broken identities, and the terrors and instructions thereof. He sited these on working-class French Canadian streets of the East End; on Hutchison Street 'with the Greeks moving in'; and just west of downtown, where 'someday Montreal will have its

Greenwich Village and these short streets between St. Catherine and Dorchester will be its centre'.

These stories have as protagonists watchful, self-reliant boys, ambitious young professors or middle-aged writers, the latter two imaginable as those boys, two, three or four decades later. I should mention that they all seem part of one unfolding story: Blaise's short fiction has a unity and coherence that make each collection read like the latest instalment of a novel being published, in many volumes, over the lifetime of the writer.

The collection includes two 'chameleon boy' stories set in Montreal in 1950s, a city locked in an icebox. 'Drab ... the interiors and streets, the minds and souls and conversations of east-end Montreal. One big icy puddle of frozen-gutter water, devoid of joy, colour, laughter, pleasure, intellect or art.' (You cannot call Blaise a booster.) The chameleon boys watch their identities (French/English, American/Canadian, Montreal/Florida) spinning like citrus in a slot machine after the handle has been cranked. They are utterly uncertain which combination is going to turn up next, and some version of this helpless, chancy, bleakly funny situation comes up repeatedly in Blaise. The mythology of borders is this writer's medium. He uses it to investigate our terms of existence on this planet, the nature of the lease.

In 'North', a family flees Pittsburgh, routed in their attempt to establish American lives. Arriving in Montreal, they camp out in a relative's East End flat. Québec is still under the wet blanket of *Duplessisismo*. A boy who had thought himself soundly American discovers, to his horror and fascination, that he is, in Montreal, someone else.

This chameleon, whether he happens to be a native ('I'm Dreaming of Rocket Richard') or a transplant ('North') exists hyper-aware of parental failure, of the doom and slide in life, which is, in Blaise, always associated with the crossing of borders. In 'I'm Dreaming of Rocket Richard' the narrator's alcoholic French-Canadian father gets one weak shot at success American style when his brother-in-law considers hiring him to run one of his Florida dry-cleaning shops. Crossing borders, heading south or north, is as an action as electric, misunderstood and consequential in Blaise as getting married is in Richard Yates, or commuting by train in Cheever, or sex in Philip Roth.

'Unhousement' is the *echt* Blaisean word. ('Memories of Unhouse-

ment' is one of the superb, startling, nonfiction pieces in *Resident Alien*.)
Seen from one angle, Clark Blaise, like Jack (Ti-Jean) Kerouac, is a diaspora writer. Their specific diaspora – the emigration of millions of
French Canadians from Québec and Acadia to the United States – is otherwise almost completely absent from the literature and consciousness
of English Canadians and Americans, even those living within twenty
miles of the Quebec/New England border.

Like Jack Kerouac, Blaise, a French Canadian born in the United
States, is writing a world that is restless, fluid and on the move. Like
William Faulkner, Blaise has myth clenched between his teeth and is
technically capable of digging very deep into one plot of ground.

The oddness of a Kerouac/Faulkner juxtaposition suggests Blaise's
singularity, his essential unlikeness to other North American writers
operating in English. All he has in common with his contemporaries –
Munro, Carver, Dubus and Yates – is that the stories are unmistakably
his and could not have been shaped, or imagined, by any other writer.

His first collection was called *A North American Education*, but Blaise
often reads like a European. Perhaps it is the weight of the past on his
present. With his rapt awareness of the social and geographic nexus
framing character, he does recall another American expatriate, Henry
James. In its deliberate and daring instability of form (is this memoir or
fiction?) Blaise's 1970s work anticipates writers like W. G. Sebald. The
chameleon-boy stories especially suggest the influence of French New
Wave cinema, which Clark Blaise would have absorbed as a graduate
student and cinephile at the University of Iowa Writers' Workshop in
the early sixties.

'I'm Dreaming of Rocket Richard' always pairs in my mind with
Truffaut's 'The 400 Blows'.

Blaise's watchful, shape-shifting boys, ambitious professors, and
weary middle-aged writers typically experience sudden, violent
geographic transplantation. Pittsburgh to Montreal ('North'); Montreal
to Florida ('I'm Dreaming of Rocket Richard'), Montreal to India
('Going to India'), upstate NY to Montreal ('Translation'). The signal
events in these lives are border crossings, often sudden ones, and usually
('North'; 'Going to India') happening at night.

Blaise people are refugees, always, whether they travel in beat-up Plymouths and Greyhound buses ('I'm Dreaming of Rocket Richard';

'North') and carry dubious citizenship credentials ('Translation'), or are armed with respectable passports, credit cards and return tickets ('Going to India'). The chameleon boys pore over road maps in the back seat. The professors cannot sleep on their intercontinental flights.

In 'A Class of New Canadians', Professor Norman Dyer, a transplant from the US, pauses to consider the window of an elegant Sherbrooke Street men's shop (the same establishment where, I seem to recall, P. E. Trudeau used to buy his spiffiest outfits). Mentally fondling Montreal's cosmopolitan glamour, he congratulates himself for his connoisseurship in selecting such a city. Hubris. Meanwhile, his English-as-a-second-language class can hardly wait to quit the place, to them a churlish backwater, a port of entry. *Everyone mixed together and having no money. It is just a place to land, no?* As soon as they grasp sufficient English, they aim to move on, preferably to the US, hoping to launch authentically North American futures.

In the other young professor stories, the narrator and his wife, academics, are also ambitious emigrants in a freshly post-Catholic Montreal, which seemed in its hectic, modernist heyday (1961 to 1970) as thrilling as New York, with as much to say to the rest of the world. The young professor glories in his gifts for teaching, for styling, for marrying well. But look out. Bugs breed under the gorgeous rug ('Extractions and Contractions'), leeches fester ('At the Lake'); cars break down in the middle of night ('He Raises Me Up'). These are the fictions where Blaise perfects a pellucid, almost documentary style. The reader senses a writer pounding at his own life.

> In a certain season (the late winter) and in certain areas (those fringes between the city core and the river that makes it an island) Montreal is the ugliest city in the world. Despite its reputation, its tourist bureaus, most of the island of Montreal will break your heart.

More than any other North American city – except El Paso, Texas? – the proximity of frontiers juices up Montreal's peculiar energy. And apart from boundary lines on maps, this is also a city where English and French have historically sought to maintain invisible, well-policed borders, physical and mental, between themselves.

Take away Montreal's various borderlines and you have ... a big Quebec City?

Fifty minutes from the United States, the same from the Province of Ontario, Montreal (like Belfast, Nicosia, Jerusalem) happens to be crisscrossed by internal boundaries separating communities that do not see themselves as sharing a common fate, or even dwelling within the same country. (The most dispiriting thing about Montreal is not active animosity along the borderlines, but how weakly the language groups are interested in each other. Amongst other losses, this means that the best writers, French and English, are rarely translated. How tiresome that not one of Clark Blaise's books – works by a major writer, dealing with affairs crucial to Montreal life – has ever been published in French in Québec!)

In tourist guidebooks, going back to my 1910 Baedeker, St. Lawrence Boulevard is always named as the line separating French and English, even though the adjacent streets seem always to have been a multilingual borderland: Irish/English on Jeanne Mance Street; Yiddish on St. Urbain Street; Ukrainian and Greek on Park Avenue and Hutchison Street, Portuguese and Central American Spanish on de Bullion Street. There are cleaner examples of the spatial/linguistic divide – the Montreal West–Ville St. Pierre frontier, say – the point being that for anyone interested in borders and crossings, Montreal is a case study. So the city was a natural for Clark Blaise. In his stories, the international line forty-five minutes south of Peel and St. Catherine hums with the same invisible, palpable energy that the Blackfoot and Sioux picked up along the Medicine Line – the United States/Canada border east of the Rockies, where a few stone cairns sited along the forty-ninth parallel radiated enough juju to stop the US Sixth Cavalry in its horse tracks, like those flagged lines that zap trespassing dogs with an streak of electric pain.

Montreal used to be awfully good at mixing things up. In what other city could you buy a fresh-killed chicken at a *Notre Dame de Grâce Kosher Meat Market*? And where else would leading figures in an assertively *francophone* nationalist movement bear names like Johnson, Ryan, and O'Neill?

(Pundits contrast the city's polyglot character with the supposedly *pure laine* hinterland of Québec, but cities are always distinct within nations, and in precisely this style. Dissolving the heavy, dreary union of blood and soil, splitting the atom, releasing energy, goosing the race – this is what cities do.)

A Blaise character, whatever his age, is usually a new boy in a new place. If he is not, he must behave like one. He is compelled to mix things up, taking a degree in the US but a job in Canada, a wife in Montreal but an extended family in India. He must wear his Bruins jersey to games at the Forum.

In several of these stories a French-Canadian father and English-Canadian mother are trapped in an incomprehensible marriage. (The current usages – Québécois, Anglo – would be anachronistic to the 1950s and '60s settings and sound too self-integrated, too stable, to be quite real for the Blaisean world; they don't trail messy, bloody roots, as the double-barrels do. In Blaise, every identity has a hyphen buried somewhere.)

There is rarely a scene where the parents address each other. The mother confides in her son; the father confides in no one. There is no physical violence, simply because the parents are not close enough to hate each other. We sense a separation coming, but it's not going to do either partner any good; divorce will only emphasize their individual limitations.

So Blaise – born in North Dakota! – dishes up the primal Canadian situation. He gets to our heart of darkness, and beyond. In the tension between mother and *père* twitches the nervous compass needle of being human in the late twentieth century.

These stories have been profoundly influential in the literature of our country. Like Mahfouz's Cairo, Mistry's Bombay, Price's northern New Jersey, Blaise's various Montreals belong to the world, not merely to readers who happen to give a damn about the spiritual condition of the Great White North. His obsession with the spatial and spiritual geography of our corner of North America intensifies rather than limits his range, which is why these stories would work powerfully translated into Finnish or Urdu (or French!). Blaise – through his teaching but more importantly, through the strangeness and hectic beauty of his Montreal work – was one of the portals by which, sometime around 1975, English-Canadian writing stepped into its place in the sun. He demonstrated to a generation of writers that fiction which read like a painfully intimate conversation amongst ourselves could at the same time be speaking to the world.

Peter Behrens

Peter Behrens, a Montreal native, lives in Maine. He is the author of *Night Driving* (short stories).

North

In the beginning, my mother would meet me at the *'Garçons'* side of Papineau School. She might have been the tallest woman in the east end of Montreal in the early fifties. I was walking with my friend Mick. I was thirteen, and he was older but smaller. From the neck up he looked twenty. He was in my cousin Dollard's class. He had discovered me on the first day of school, standing by the iron gate looking puzzled. 'Take the garkons,' he had advised, under his breath. *Garkons* was an early word in my private vocabulary. In the beginning, I had to trust strangers' pronunciations, or worse, my own.

'You're not one of them, are you, eh?' I liked that; *them* – it sounded science-fictiony. How could he tell? Getting no answer, he went on, 'My old lady, she ups and marries this Frog. What's your story?'

My story? Same old story, too preposterous. Until the week before, I'd been Phil Porter, content but lonely, riding the airwaves of Pittsburgh, attaching rabbit-ears to our apartmenthouse chimney, pulling in seven channels from adjacent states. All I said to Mick that first day was, 'My name's Carrier, but I'm not French.'

'Me too. Bloody Fortin. All the Fortins in my family are English and all the Sweeneys are French. Funny, eh? Where you from – the States? Vermont?'

Pittsburgh rang no bells for Mick Fortin. He only knew the cities that sent us tourists – Burlington, Plattsburgh, and half of Harlem, plus the cosy loop of the old N H L. 'Do you have a job yet?' he asked me, and I feared for a minute that a job was required in this new world of the French eighth grade, like my pens and tie and white shirt for school. Mick was too ignorant, too solicitous, too eager with his confessions to be trusted. He promised me a job in the spring, down along St. Catherine Street, passing out peep-show leaflets to the Yanks. 'You've heard of Lili St. Cyr, eh?' I hadn't, but nodded. 'All you gotta do is say, "C'mon'n see her! Lili St. Cyr's younger and sexier sister!" All the girls down there call themselves St. Cyr something, Mimi or Fifi. The Yanks, they eat it up.' In the beginning, I welcomed my mother's intervention.

We'd left Pittsburgh in the middle of the night. My father had assaulted a man at work. He'd found him seated at his desk, feet on an opened drawer, packing up my father's pictures and souvenirs. A younger man, brought in from the outside. He got his first three words in – 'You're out, Porter' – and then my father grabbed his ankles and spilled him backwards out of the chair. Then he picked him off the floor and shoved him only once, and the new manager found himself bursting through fresh drywall and skidding to a halt by the water cooler. And my father caught the first elevator to Canada, convinced that no one knew his secret name and true identity. Some time in the middle of that night, somewhere in the middle of upstate New York, my father Reg Porter reverted to Réjean Carrier, and I was allowed to retain my name of Phil, but Porter was taken from me forever. 'You weren't born in Cincinnati like we always said,' my mother explained. 'I'm sorry, but we had to tell you that. You were born in Montreal.'

We moved into the apartment of his older brother, Théophile. I bumped Dollard from his room, and my parents took the living-room sofa. Théophile's six daughters were married, or in the church. In a pantry-sized bedroom off the kitchen lived Aunt Louise who'd married an American in Woonsocket and seen all three of her sons go down with the *Dorchester* in 1942. She didn't speak, she only lit candles, and the smell of wax permeated the apartment. My mother would have the sheets and pillows stored away each morning by seven o'clock, and I don't think they went out during the day. I don't know what they and my aunt Béatrice, who spoke no English, did all day.

The first big fight had been over my schooling. School had been in session nearly a month when we arrived on Théophile's doorstep. I hadn't known a word of French, though I began collecting words from Dollard that first day. From him, everything began with '*maudit* ...' and ended with '... *de Christ sanglant.*' In a week I knew some nouns and adjectives; no verbs, no sentences. French neutralized my mother's education; she was like a silent actress. I learned to read her eyes, her lips, and to listen to her breathing, and her feelings came through like captions. She would nod her head and say, 'wee-wee', which made the simplest French words come out like baby-talk. She was one of those western Canadians of profound good will and solid background, educated and sophisticated and acutely alert to conditions in every part of the world, who could not utter a syllable of French without a painful contortion of head, neck, eyes and lips. She was convinced that the French language was a deliberate debauchery of logic, and that people who persisted in speaking it did so to cloak the particulars of a nefarious design, behind which could be detected the gnarled, bejewelled claws of the Papacy. She was, of course, too well-bred to breathe a word of this suspicion to anyone but me. All evening, then, as she stood next to Béatrice at the sink, peeling, washing, baking and frying our food, it was Béatrice's steady stream of incomprehensible opinions and my mother's head-jerking wee-wees, the smell of wax and Dollard's obscene mutterings that initiated me into a world that would be, for all I knew, mine forever.

My mother had wanted to send me to an English school, although the nearest one was at the end of two trolley rides. I was silent about it. English would obviously be easier, but not necessarily preferable. I wanted to belong, and no one I knew in Montreal spoke English, except my mother. Canadian schools, my mother said, were light-years ahead of American, and English was the only language for an intelligent boy who didn't want to become a priest. French school was so fundamentally *wrong*, it was alluring to contemplate. For the first time in my life no one could possibly expect anything from me. Théophile settled it. He was a member of the St-Jean-Baptiste Society. No one living under his roof would even study English, let alone go to school in it. Anyway, it wasn't safe. There was no way to get to an English school that didn't cut through the middle of the Jewish ghetto, where French boys were routinely butchered. He had this on good authority, though they didn't dare print it in the communist press. Dozens of French boys had disappeared – altar boys – they only used the purest blood. My mother retired to the bathroom. My father chimed in, 'They'd kill him on this street, for sure. They'd kill any kid on this street if he went to an English school.'

Tricks of the mind. Even in my memories of those three strange years, nuns and classmates seem to be speaking to me in English – a clear violation of the natural universe – and I seem to be writing papers and speaking up in class, always in English. This is clearly not so, for there's a band of three years in my life when I discovered nature where even now I'm still learning the English names. Fish, trees, flowers, weeds, food, drinks can all send me to the dictionary. And the discovery of myself as a sexual creature – slightly different from the discovery of sex itself – that too is a function of French.

For the first time in my life I felt that school was a punishment. Nuns were wardens, the cracking of the cane was arbitrary and malicious. We were prisoners serving time for a crime whose nature would presently be revealed. I assumed my guilt; it was my ignorance of the charge, not my innocence, that made the confusion so painful.

I was caned in the second week. The impossible had happened *to me*. I was made to mumble an act of contrition. I wasn't even Catholic. *'Pourquoi ça?'* I kept demanding as the cane kept whizzing down, day after day for a week. Even harder, for my question suggested arrogance. There would be no explanation. He was a Brother of the Order of Mary, who otherwise smiled at me when he passed me in the halls. In the second week, Soeur Timothée let it out: my cousin Dollard had been cutting classes and acting unrepentant to the brothers. *'Hôtage!'* she hissed at me, taking over the caning. *'Tu sais hôtage?'* I learned quickly enough. Finally my mother noticed the backs of my hands, the welts and bruises. She raged, with only my father and me to understand her.

'Discipline!' he exclaimed. 'That's what they give, and he has to learn to take it!' I hadn't told them about Dollard. I hadn't even told Dollard about the punishment I was taking on his behalf, but I hoped word would drift back to him before my fingers fell off. My father was defending them, in his way. Compared to *his* years with the brothers, when he'd been given to them at the age of five for eventual priesthood, my life had been one of silken pillows. If my hands hadn't been as soft as a girl's there wouldn't even be bruises. 'Look at Dollard's hands – they're like hockey gloves,' he shouted. My father wasn't defending the church – he hated it from the depths of his bowels – but he revered its implacable authority. Whatever they did to you, you should be grateful; it made you tough enough in later life to keep telling them to go to hell.

'Discipline!' my mother raged. 'You fools. You bloody fools – is that what discipline is to you? Treating children like animals? Beating them into submission? It's medieval, it's madness. You're crazy, can't you see? You're twisted, and I won't have you twisting your son the same way.' She grabbed my hands and clutched my fists to her chest. 'Discipline isn't just learning how to take pain. Discipline doesn't mean you have to be stupid. God, if the bloody church told you tomorrow the earth was flat, you'd start telling yourselves you knew it was flat all along, right? Wouldn't you? Wouldn't you?'

I felt guilty, terribly guilty, bringing on such an argument. There was injustice here, on every side. My father – that unemployed, wrecked shell of a man – was standing in for Théophile and Dollard, whose stupidities were unassailable, and for the brothers at school whose cruelties, given the system, were unremarkable and fairly even-handed. My father hadn't been inside a church in forty years, not since he'd fled the barbarities of a harsher time and place and taken those memories, that rage, into the streets of Montreal and beyond. But against my mother, his words and logic were pathetic.

Now his voice was weary. 'Okay,' he admitted. His fists were heavy in front of his face; he kept balling them up and flinging them open. 'You don't know how they think. How they work ... It's ...' and he shrugged his shoulders, empty of words. I wanted to complete it for him; I understood more about it than he ever would. What the brothers were doing to me to get to Dollard would have worked in any family in Papineau School – we were the freaks. I was suffering a complicated shame. Then my father came up with a new inspiration. 'You think the Sistine Chapel was painted without discipline?' There was a series of pictures taped to the dining-room wallpaper, cut from the pages of *Life* magazine, celebrating Vatican art. The Sistine Chapel won many arguments in the Hochelaga district of Montreal in the early fifties.

In memory, Pittsburgh came bursting through like a freak radio signal. In my junior-high classes, the sexes had mingled, the girls had steamed and giggled in a heavy-breasted, painted-up pool of pubescent sexuality. They wore whatever they could get away with. They stuffed lewd and graphic promises through the ventilation slats of our lockers and raced for the girls' rooms between classes to smoke like little hellions. They were utterly available, begging to be touched.

But in Papineau we entered and left by the '*Garçons*' and '*Filles*' sides of the building, as though joint entombment for eight hours a day was concession enough to sordid physiology; the nuns and brothers even positioned themselves like Holy Crossing Guards two and three blocks away, to prolong the segregation. Coeducation was a sad fact of life, but withering disapproval could safeguard our innocence at least till high school. The girls wore black jumpers and no make-up, and their hair was cut uniformly straight and short. Not a ponytail, not a bleach job in the lot. I'd been too young in Pittsburgh to act on my impulses, to inhale those lusty vapours rising from the breeding pens of an American junior high school. Now, I felt, I could. Just turn me loose, anywhere in America. I burned in hell, remembering it.

And then, miraculously, the nuns gave me a girl. At four o'clock after another gruelling day of faint comprehension, Soeur Timothée told me to stay after class – not for discipline – but to meet my own, private, ninth-grade tutor, Thérèse Aulérie. Tutor and general *ange gardien* in everything from penmanship (we were on the continental system, with crossed sevens, ones like giant carat marks; whenever I require assurance that indeed these things happened to me I have it still, in my hand-writing) to the foundations of all advanced knowledge: Latin, French and the Catholic religion. Thérèse was Papineau's outstanding student in classics, French, apologetics and even natural science.

Ninth-grade girls back in Pittsburgh simply had more going for them than Thérèse Aulérie, despite her brilliance. There was first of all the question of make-up, that bright impasto of sexual longing, so inno-vatively applied by American teenagers. They had Hollywood and tele-vision to guide them, not to mention the Terry Moore sweaters stretched over the mountain-building process we runty seventh- and eighth-graders could measure by the week, if not the hour (just as I scru-tinized my chin for each new black whisker, cherished each new fissure in my cracking vocal chords and checked every inch of my body for other rampant endocrinal signposts worth flaunting).

In Papineau, everything was hidden. Girls in jumpers, no make-up, no hair-styles; they took their cue from Soeur Timothée. But Thérèse Aulérie was a slight improvement. She had the palest skin and the greenest eyes I had ever seen (it was the first time I'd been forced to focus on such adult, literary features as fine skin and expressive eyes), and lips that were natural and pink to a sheen of edibility. She wore clear nail polish – a vanity, she later confessed – and the only other exposed acreage of flesh, her cheeks, was delicately flushed, and dimpled. Her

voice was low and throaty, a woman's voice coming from the face of
Margaret O'Brien. She looked so *nearly* familiar it seemed impossible
that she didn't speak a word of English and even regarded hearing it as a
low-grade, unclassifiable sin.

We began with apologetics. We had a small handbook of Nuns and
Monks and Teaching Orders, and my first job was to learn how to
identify the various orders by their special dress, their expertise, their
place and date of founding. I'd thought of them as exotic wildlife anyway: tracking them with an imprimatured bestiary seemed a natural
way of pinning them down. I started rattling off their dates and countries of origin with an ease that astonished her, leaving Thérèse to fill in
the substantive issues – for her at least: were they known best for their
piety or their charity? Their compassion or courage? Their humility or
brilliance? Most of our brothers were Marists, with a Sacred Heart in the
chapel. The nuns were mainly our local Greys and Ursulines, but a sharp
eye could spot a Blessed Virgin on special assignment. This part was
easy, like learning the makes and models of new cars. Thérèse, once she
dropped the ninth-grade condescension, was full of unofficial data
about every order. *Les laides, les bêtes, les gueules, les graisses.* Soeur
Timothée, I learned, was called Soeur La Morse. 'What's a *morse?*' I
asked, and Thérèse tapped imaginary tusks and made deep seal-like
grunts. 'Walrus!' I laughed, and she repeated, in a voice suddenly high
and girlish, 'wal-rus.' In fact, Thérèse Aulérie, for all her grades and piety
and possible calling as a Sister of Charity, was a sharp little cookie who
began confiding to me of her visits to the States, a Chinese restaurant
she'd been taken to in Manchester, New Hampshire, the weekends at
Old Orchard Beach and the television she'd stared at for a solid, slothful
weekend in a Burlington motel. She'd even gone to New York City when
she was six, and she still had all the postcards. In her America, everyone
spoke French except the people on television.

'Did you really go to school in America?' she asked in French. My
French wasn't good enough to answer more than an authentic, Dollardish *'ouai'.* No way to describe its wonders.

'Comme Hartchie?' she asked. *'Et Véronique?'*

It took me a few seconds to catch on. *'Et Juggie aussi,'* I laughed.

'Ah, Juggie,' she nodded gravely. *'Juggie j'aime beaucoup.'*

We sighed; I for the multiplicity of stories I couldn't build upon, the impossibility of representing myself in a language I didn't know, or to a girl who didn't know mine.

'*Et ton nom, était-il toujours Carrier là-bas?*'

It didn't seem strange to her that people changed names when they crossed the border. In America, I tried to explain, we'd sailed under a flag of translation. '*Porter,*' she tried, in her curious, high-pitched English. '*Non, c'est laid, ce nom-là. Carrier, c'est un bon nom canadien.*'

I answered, with sad conviction sealing the linguistic gaps, 'Anyway, names *ne fait rien.*'

She drew her desk closer. '*Épeles mon nom de famille. Divines.* Go ahead. Try!'

'A-U –' I began. And she giggled, shaking her head.

'*Mon vrai nom. Commences avec "o",* like dis, eh?' I loved it when she tried her English. It came out like Dollard's, but without the threat. '*C'est le vrai français, mon nom, de la France, pas d'ici.*' She wrote, 'O'L –'

'O'Leery?' I spelled.

'O'Leary,' she corrected. '*Ça c'est le nom de mon grandpère.*' She turned the paper as though admiring a work of art. 'Nice,' she said.

I felt I'd been handed a powerful interpretive tool, but I didn't yet know how to wield it. Here I was, a Carrier who spoke no French, and she was an O'Leary who read 'Archie' comic books but knew no English, and we were together in a darkening classroom in Montreal under a cross, flanked by the photos of the Cardinal of Montreal and the Holy Father. We were linked beyond simple assignments. My guardian angel, according to Sister Walrus, who would lead me from ignorance to power, just as the sisters and brothers would lead me from hellfire to righteousness.

Thérèse closed her book after the quiz on habits and orders and asked me, slowly and with grand gestures, can girls (she pointed to herself) in the ninth grade in America really wear lipstick (she ran her pinkie over her lips) and dress the way they want? She formed a gentle, wavy outline with her hands, passing over an imaginary female form just outside her square-cut jumper with all the lewdness (I fantasized) of a sailor describing his last night's conquest. Can they really go out on dates? She clawed my wrist at the word '*rendez-vous*'. Those new words burned themselves in my brain: *maquillage ... s'habiller comme l'on veut ... rendez-vous.* Do they all have cars? How late can they stay out? She was suddenly like a little girl, and somewhere in the late fall gloom, and then under the yellow globes of a four-thirty northern autumn night, I started imagining a Thérèse O'Leary in make-up, and I noticed how her jumper flared out modestly in front and filled out gently in the rear, and how a nice wide belt would have pinched it together, just right. And how her voice, that deep French purr, would have driven American boys wild.

It must have been in those weeks in our daily hour after school and in our walks away from school for two low, mean, icy, glorious unsupervised blocks to her trolley stop that the current in our little relationship shifted direction. By the end of our first month, her English improved to the level of fairly detailed conversation. I rummaged through my mother's suitcase and found a proper belt. Once on a Saturday I passed her with her parents at Dupuis Frères department store, and she was in a sweater and skirt, wearing lipstick and pearl earrings.

I came to think of my five hours a week with Thérèse as my parole from solitary. I came to understand my mother's use of the word 'drab' to describe the interiors and the streets, the minds and souls and conversations of east-end Montreal. One big icy puddle of frozen gutter water, devoid of joy, colour, laughter, pleasure, intellect or art. School and home and church and the narrow east-end streets that connect them are the same colour even now in my memory, linked in a language that I didn't understand except through its rhythms. Recitations in class took on a dirge-like quality, like the repeated Hail Marys on Sunday radio. Eventually even I, who knew neither Latin nor French nor the lists of martyrs to the Iroquois, could stand and repeat the proper syllables. The name of our school, Papineau, figured in Quebec history as a great patriot who had tried to rid the province of English and American influences, and his name was repeated on the street outside and on panel trucks and signboards of plumbers and plasterers and in the *épicerie* where Aunt Béatrice did her shopping. It seemed slightly blasphemous, like Latin ballplayers carrying the name of Jesus. The same few names popped up everywhere, with six Tremblays in my class and over half of us clustered alphabetically at 'La –' and nearly all of us ending in '– ier'. Our names were as predictable as Americans', as unmistakable as Chinese, and mine was one of the commonest. We were common, and we learned to feel comfortable only in the presence of other *bons noms canadiens*. 'Ignorance!' my mother had cried one night, fleeing the dinner table. She had bought red table napkins, something to brighten the winter gloom, and my uncle had slammed his to the floor, saying it would *'causer l'acide'*.

And so, my mother began meeting me after school, a block from where I parted from Thérèse. Sometimes we would ride the trolley downtown and go into Eaton's or Ogilvy's – places that felt off-limits to the rest of the family. And there I would glow in the mystical power of speaking English, a power that wasn't furtive or dirty, as it felt in the apartment. The power of not having to scratch for words and not biting back the urge to comment, or even attack.

On the furniture floor of Eaton's she said. 'I worked here, you know. I was even the head of this whole department.' We walked through the model home, the half-dozen bedrooms and dining rooms featuring different styles of decoration. 'Your father was one of the salesmen. Until I saw him, I never even bothered learning their names. I knew he was wrong for me. Knew from the beginning.' No one recognized her now, though it had been only thirteen years. She'd gone to the States, been lost to history. 'I was a very different woman in those days. I want you to understand that. It wasn't easy, back then, in this city. Women couldn't even vote. And they don't accept women here, not English women, not Protestant women. They'll never do that.' I could read her eyes and breath; I wanted to avoid the tears that I knew were coming. 'I deserve it all, don't I? Sleeping on a floor in Hochelaga. No wonder they don't want to remember me – I must look a sight.' She trailed her fingers in the dust of the dining-room tables and nightstands, then took me up to the cafeteria on the top floor. We would have our tea and scones, sometimes served with a little lemon curd. She perked up, over tea. 'I don't want you to despise them. They are what they are. Deep down, they're good people. They've taken us in when we could have ended up … I don't want to think how we could have ended up, and they've shared what they have. But I *do* resent them, I can't help it. I resent their tight little ways, not with money – darling, do you understand what I'm saying? Their fist-like little souls, always ready to fight you or slink away like a beaten dog – does that make sense? I don't want you growing up like them.'

It was always harder, going back to Hochelaga after scones and lemon curd and a few hours of uninterrupted English. The urge to speak our language seemed to die when the trolley crossed St. Lawrence. In a few weeks I would reach a linguistic equilibrium, and I probably could have been happy enough – given endless lemon curd or access to Thérèse O'Leary – existing like a child in either world. But I was being forced, subtly at first, every day, to make moral decisions. French or English were the terms, but they were merely covers for personalities inside and out that I wanted to keep hidden.

One Friday in early December my mother held me back from school. Quietly, she motioned me to put on my coat. We took the trolley downtown not quite to Eaton's, then walked up to Sherbrooke past the clean grey limestone and green copper roofs of McGill University, that Gibraltar of Englishness. 'Some day you'll go here,' she said. 'I don't care what it takes or if you graduate from French school or American schools – they'll have to let you in.' I welcomed her authority. We stood on Milton Street just outside the iron railings; I wanted to reach inside. I could understand the shouts of the students, their quiet conversations as young couples passed us on the sidewalk. 'Who are those men in black robes?' I asked. 'Judges?'

'Professors,' she said. 'This is the greatest university in the world.' She so rarely allowed herself the luxury of an uncontested assertion – 'too American' was her feeling about any claim to undisputed superiority – that I knew I'd been handed an indisputable fact. I trusted my mother more than any nun, even more than any Jesuit. 'Come,' she said, and we turned down Prince Arthur, through a maze of small half-streets that curled between Pine and St. Urbain. We stopped in front of a tall apartment block of dull cherry brick, where long icicles hung over the door. 'I want you to meet an important person in my life,' she said. 'And in yours, I hope.'

'Who?' And I swear, had she asked me, *Who do you think?* I would have answered, *My father. My real father.* There was something monumental inside, the clarity behind all the confusions. Her gloved finger ran down the row of buzzers. At 'Perleman, E.' she stopped.

We were buzzed inside. My mother's hands were shaking. 'Ella is a brilliant woman. A professor at McGill.' In the tiny elevator she whispered, 'I used to live right here, in this building. When I came back from England and got that job at Eaton's.'

'With her?'

'I called her last week. I haven't seen her in thirteen years. She sounded –' and her voice was stumbling now, 'grand. She's a grand girl.'

'You used to get letters from her,' I remembered. Back in Pittsburgh I saved the high-denomination Canadian stamps that came to us on those thick envelopes from Montreal.

'She's my dearest friend. The times we had! Oh, Lord, the times …'

Ella was standing by the elevator, a gnome-like woman of my mother's age, wrapped in a stiff green skirt and a man's sweater that smothered her body like a duffel bag. My mother had to stoop to hug her, and she was already losing control, while Ella merely patted her back and shoulders and murmured. 'There, there, Hennie,' in what seemed to be a lilting accent. Her dark brown eyes were wide and sad, and her skin was a fine, translucent pink. Her hair was entirely grey and nearly as short as mine. She looked, I thought, like Albert Einstein. She pulled us down the hall to her opened apartment door. I could easily see over her head into a living-room dingy with smoke and oppressive with apartment heat. It must have been eighty-five degrees inside, and I started clawing desperately at my scarf and *tuque,* as she picked up a lavender shawl and draped it over her shoulders.

'Dolly,' she called out, and a gaunt woman, slightly younger, shuffled out from the bedroom. 'This is Henny, whom I've spoken so much about. And her boy, Philip.' I nodded, regretting the day of school I was missing. 'This is Dolly. Dolly works in the accounts office at McGill. So.' Dolly took that as a sign to go to the kitchen and prepare some tea.

If McGill was the world's finest university and Ella one of its professors, I reasoned that she must be the smartest woman in the world. That went a long way to forgiving her appearance and her strange habits. She picked up a pipe from the nearest coffee table, and as she sucked on it, drawing in the flame, I could swear it *was* Einstein peering at me over the flame and bowl of the pipe. My mother was bearing up. She too was watching me, and I was behaving myself; nothing strange about a woman smoking a pipe. It was impossible to think of Ella ever crying, ever getting too personal and sentimental, and for that I was grateful.

'So. You must forgive two old women who haven't seen each other …'

26

Ella and my mother were seated across from me on the sofa, and Ella was patting my mother's hand. 'I must say you look well, Hennie, everything considered. Some of us got old rather quickly.'

'You look just the same, Ella.' My mother was staring down at her lap, at Ella's hand.

'Well, nothing ever happens in Montreal, so who can tell? The city hasn't changed one bit. The things we fought for have gradually come to pass – we can vote now, Hennie – isn't that grand? But the workers are still oppressed and the church still runs things and the police behave like Tartars and the corruption is still a public joke and our candidates still lose their deposits every election. Remember our election parties?' My mother smiled, and Ella let out a sharp bark of a laugh. 'We'd all come back here to this apartment' – she was looking at me again – 'the finest candidates who ever ran for public office in this country, and we'd sit around sipping sherry waiting for a call. And outside the police were waiting. If we'd actually won we'd have gone directly to jail. Oh, Lord, such innocent hopes! I might as well be just off the boat for all that's changed in twenty years!'

'Ella came from Austria, dear,' my mother explained. 'She studied with Freud.'

Ella was quick to jump in. 'No, no, dear. Never studied. *Was analysed* by one of his pupils. Which means only I *was discussed* over *kaffee* and *küchen*. The Perleman complex,' she giggled. 'No, I'm afraid I was too normal. I never made it into Freudian literature. You have heard perhaps of Freud, Philip?'

'Is it like a Freudian slip?'

'If you are not referring to a ladies' undergarment, yes, there is such a thing as a Freudian slip. You of course understand what this is – this Freudian slip as you call it?'

My mother was nodding fiercely, urging me on. What was it, a test? 'Usually when you're talking and something dirty slips out accidentally. Or something embarrassing, like those radio bloopers. There's a nun in school I keep being afraid I'm going to call a *morse*, because that's her nickname.'

'People always think Freud has to be dirty. Ah, well.'

'You never told me about this nun, darling.'

'What exactly is a *morse*, Philip?'

'You know, that big seal-like thing, with tusks.'

'You mean a walrus, dear?' My mother's face looked stricken with pain, and she turned to Ella. 'He's … you see?'

'Now, now. Mothers *worry*, don't they, Philip? It's perfectly all right to learn a second language. I've done it, many have done it.'

'You were forced to,' said my mother. 'It's not like having your mother tongue taken from you. They won't let him speak English. I'm the only person he can speak English with.'

Dolly came in from the kitchen, bearing a teapot on a silver tray, four fine china cups and a plate of biscuits around a jar of lemon curd. She lifted a lavender shawl off the teapot and Ella asked me, 'Do you know what this is called, Philip?'

'A cover?'

'A cosy. A tea-cosy. Very strange word, I always thought.'

'I like lemon curd,' I said, emphasizing those last two words. 'I don't see why it's called lemon curd. It's more like lemon pudding. I mean, milk gets curds. Curds and whey. Maybe because it's sour, but then why don't we have rhubarb curd and apple curd? Or do we? In French –' but I stopped myself.

'Dear,' said my mother, 'I'm sorry.'

'English is not an especially logical language, Philip. As you have discovered. But tell me – are you enjoying yourself in Montreal? At school?'

'It's all right.'

'Your mother tells me it's sometimes … a little primitive.'

'They *beat* you, darling.'

'They apologized. That's a big thing, getting them to apologize. La Morse herself, showed remorse.' They didn't appreciate my rhyme. 'It wasn't easy at the beginning even understanding things. Basic words, basic anything.'

'What do you study?'

'It seems all he studies is Catholicism,' said my mother.

The truth was, apologetics was the easiest subject, since it required no thought, just memorization. It was also the quickest way to get good grades. The math was easier than Pittsburgh math, once I learned the number system. In Latin, though the text was in French, I was starting from the same place as other students. Given an even chance, I would always excel. 'That's not true,' I said. The truth, I realized, was unspeakable. The truth was, I *liked* apologetics. I spooned deeply in the curd pot and smeared it over a biscuit.

'So. A difference of perception, maybe?'

My mother took this as a rebuke. Her head sank. I wanted to console her, but instead helped Dolly drag over a dining-room chair.

Ella looked at my mother; she looked at Dolly; I helped myself to more lemon curd. Finally Ella asked, in a softer voice, 'Do they make you go to Mass? Do they try to convert you?'

'I don't think so. I mean, everyone's Catholic, so they just assume I am too. I mean with a name like Carrier –' But I could see that, too, hurt my mother. 'I mumble the prayers, but I don't go to Mass.'

'You can go, dear. I don't want you to feel … different.'

'I don't feel different,' I said.

'Would you like to go to an English school?'

'I can't. My uncle –'

'Never mind about your uncle. Would you *like* to go to a good English school? The *best* English school? A private school?'

'I don't know.'

'Philip, your mother and I and Dolly have discussed a plan. If you say yes, your mother will discuss it with your father. Dolly and I, we have no children. Probably there's a limit to the amount of charitable contributions I can make. You can live with us, and we will send you. I know professors, I know musicians, writers, artists. We go out every night, or we have people here who are the leaders not just of this city, not just this country –'

'– the *world*, darling. Ella is known all over the world.'

'That's not the point. The point is, we want to share this – what should I call it? Power? Connection? Good fortune? You could stay here in your own room and go home on the week-ends, of course. You would be prepared for McGill. I don't know what else there is to say.'

'Say you will think about it, dear.'

'I don't think my mother really wants me to leave,' I said.

'She is the one who brought it up. She is deeply worried, what is happening to you.'

'Nothing is happening to me.'

'She wants what is best. French schools in this city are, well, substandard.'

Inwardly, I panicked. There seemed to be no way of saving myself from everyone's good intentions.

'Before it's *too late,* darling. Before you lose everything you've got. They'll take it from you, believe me,' and her voice suddenly cracked and her head fell to Ella's lap and I could hear the words torn from her chest. 'Like … they've … taken … it … from … me!'

Ella took little note of the distraction; she placed her hand in my mother's hair and said to me, coldly and evenly, 'Guess, please, Philip, how many products of classic French-Canadian education we have on the McGill faculty. Go ahead.'

I knew that any answer would be humiliating. 'Obviously,' she said, 'you've guessed correctly. How many French-Canadian *students* do you think I have?' She waited. 'Let me tell you a little parable about the power of education. On this continent at the present time there are approximately six million French Canadians – am I right?'

'Yes,' I admitted. It depended on how you counted our lost brothers and sisters in the West, New England and Louisiana. I'd just been reading about them, grieving for them, in my history class. My palms were sweating, my neck hairs rising.

'And there are approximately five million Jews on this continent,' she said. She smiled briefly. 'End of parable. Do you understand what I am saying about education? Do they teach you *that* in French school? Do you know how the minds of those people have been *wasted?* How they continue to be wasted? Have they taught you anything about Freud?'

'No,' I whispered.'

'Einstein?'

'Back in Pittsburgh.'

'Karl Marx?'

I felt a terrible pressure in my chest. It was the name that seemed to be hovering in the air all afternoon. All that talk of *the workers* and *the people* and the candidates who never got elected. There had been a cartoon circulated in school on the eve of the latest election: Karl Marx in a Santa suit, with 'Parti Libéral' stencilled on his sack of toys.

'No!' I retorted.

'They're doing a splendid job of educating you, aren't they? You should be spending your time learning about science, politics, history, literature –'

'– and how to get electrocuted for being Russian spies?' I demanded.

My mother raised her head, and Ella stared back at me, hard, for several seconds. 'Ella, I'm sorry –' my mother began, but Ella raised her hand, and my mother was silent. Dolly carried the tray back to the kitchen.

'I can't say I'm surprised,' said Ella.

'I'm going back to school,' I said. My mother reached out for me, imploring me to wait, we would all go to Murray's for lunch, but I thanked her, and the other women, for the lemon curd and tea, and wished them a pleasant lunch and a good afternoon.

There's a special light that strikes Montreal in April; a light so strong, so angled, that it bores through windows and the glass panels of apartment doors with the intensity of a projection beam. It acts like a magnifying lens, picking out cobwebs and dust motes, adding dimensions to the grain of wood, nubbiness to the sleekest fabric, seams and crannies to the tightest skin. The sidewalks resemble tidal basins with their residues of sand, and the snow is shrunk to black tongues of gritty ice, seeking shade. The walk home from school took a little longer, as I crushed little ice bridges over the swirling melt, and stood on rims of rounded ice till they snapped with a hollow thud and I could kick the chunks away. The days were longer, and even my tutorials with Thérèse ended in plenty of daylight. My grades were better than average, and the nuns' comments were even flattering. Nevertheless, Thérèse and I agreed that the tutoring should continue. Her English was far from perfect.

I think my mother found the courage, some time that winter, to keep calling Ella and to make their lunches a regular event. I was going downtown on my own, now that the weather had improved. Mick had come through with a job on St. Catherine Street, just as he'd promised. I took over an old stand of his just up from the train station, handing out mimeographed leaflets of naked girls behind strings of balloons, naked girls with one leg up in a bathtub, naked girls doing just about anything, plus the offer of a free drink or free admission. It was cold work and a little seedy; Mick, as a trusted long-time employee, had been promoted to inside work with the props, nearer the girls. My job next year, if I proved reliable.

'Where's this place at, kid?' and it was a pleasure to direct the tourists in their language, to hear them mutter to their buddies just off the train, 'Smart kid, you hear him?' and 'Ask him if he has a sister.' I learned to put on a touch of a Dollardish accent, to guarantee full credit for my linguistic accomplishment, and sometimes a little tip. I earned a quarter for every two hundred leaflets I passed, and a nickel for every one redeemed at the Club Lido.

Dollard had dropped out of school and gotten a job at Steinberg's, loading and delivering. Two of Théophile's sons-in-law got big jobs in the States, drywalling for a motel chain, and suddenly our little apartment was filled with new appliances. Béatrice stored an automatic washing machine on the back gallery so that the hot soapy water could gush over the cars below. We got a television set, the first anyone had seen, even though Canadian television was barely launched, rudimentary. That didn't stop me from buying the wires and rigging some rabbit-ears and tying them to our chimney in an attempt to coax something, anything, from the air. Burlington, Plattsburgh – those towns that provided night-time English radio in my room – where were you when it really counted? Even KDKA in Pittsburgh came in, most nights.

There was talk of our moving out. My mother's old teaching licence was approved by the Protestant school board, but she didn't dare mention it in Théophile's house. Béatrice crossed herself whenever the word 'Jew' entered the conversation, as it frequently did these days with Dollard's new employment; she might have thrown herself over the gallery at the mention of Protestants. My father looked for work, but he had to lie about previous employment – or find someone to lie for him. The future would always be insecure. I would hold up my hand against the glass of the front door, and April light passed through it like x-rays. The tangle over where to live and where to send me would flare again in the summer, and the fall could be another disaster. I studied my skeleton on the door while the grunts and curses and cleaning sounds passed in the air around me.

Everyone had a few hours to themselves on Sunday afternoon, after the Mass and big meal. We dressed for the meal, and even Dollard managed some pleasantness for the few hours it took. I kept him supplied with free-drink passes at the Club Lido. Thanks to Mick, I even got in a few hours' work backstage, drew close to undressed women, heard and understood all their complaints. I told my mother those nights I was at the Forum, standing for hockey.

Those warming Sunday afternoons Thérèse and I would meet at the trolley stop nearest her apartment, and if the weather was nice we'd walk to Parc LaFontaine. We had a bet: she'd read two English books for every French book I read. It wasn't fair; she'd discovered Nancy Drew and the Hardy Boys while I slogged through Claudel and St-Denys-Garneau. She was doing well, she had wonderful discipline. And on Sundays she wore her churchgoing, dinner-eating dress and earrings, and she was a marvellous sight. Once, a priest walked by; she stiffened, but he smiled down at us and chuckled, '*Ah, jeune Montréal!*' She made me ashamed of the money I earned working the train station; I spent all of it I could on her.

By May we could walk all the way downtown if we wanted. May in Montreal is like April in Paris; the light is more forgiving, the haze of green is everywhere and the schoolwork, despite nuns' warnings, starts to relent. I remember a Sunday in May as though it is borne to me now on the laser beams of April light, imprinted and never to be forgotten. Walking down St. Catherine Street with Thérèse O'Leary. We went to Murray's, and she'd taken my hand as we walked out. I'd ordered and paid in English, and she'd been terribly impressed. She'd promised me she'd do it, but had gotten too embarrassed at the last moment. We were walking behind a group of old ladies in white gloves and wide-brimmed hats, the tea-drinking ladies of Westmount, and Thérèse had been frightened of them, afraid of what they might be saying about her. Just gossip, I said, mindless things, and I translated some of it, to reassure her. She shook her head and acted ashamed. '*Sh' peux pas!*' she declared, pounding the side of her head with her fists, '*Idiote!*' then giggled. '*Mais tu peux, non?* You hunnerstan' every word, non? Smart guy!' She took my hand in both of hers and swung my arm like the clapper of the biggest bell in the world.

I'm Dreaming of Rocket Richard

We were never quite the poorest people on the block, simply because I was, inexplicably, an only child. So there was more to go around. It was a strange kind of poverty, streaked with gentility (the kind that chopped you down when you least expected it); my mother would spend too much for long-range goals – Christmas clubs, reference books, even a burial society – and my father would drink it up or gamble it away as soon as he got it. I grew up thinking that being an only child, like poverty, was a blight you talked about only in secret. 'Too long in the convent,' my father would shout – a charge that could explain my mother's way with money or her favours – 'there's ice up your cunt.' An only child was scarcer than twins, maybe triplets, in Montreal just after the war. And so because I was an only child, things happened to me more vividly, without those warnings that older brothers carry as scars. I always had the sense of being the first in my family – which was to say the first of my people – to think my thoughts, to explore the parts of Montreal that we called foreign, even to question in an innocent way the multitudes of unmovable people and things.

When I went to the Forum to watch the Canadiens play hockey, I wore a Boston Bruins sweatshirt. That was way back, when poor people could get into the Forum, and when Rocket Richard scored fifty goals in fifty games. Despite the letters on the sweatshirt, I loved the Rocket. I loved the Canadiens fiercely. It had to do with the intimacy of old-time hockey, how close you were to the gods on the ice; you could read their lips and hear them grunt as they slammed the boards. So there I stood in my Boston Bruins shirt loving the Rocket. There was always that spot of perversity in the things I loved. In school the nuns called me 'Curette' – 'Little Priest'.

I was always industrious. That's how it is with janitors' sons. I had to pull out the garbage sacks, put away tools, handle simple repairs, answer complaints about heat and water when my father was gone or too drunk to move. He used to sleep near the heating pipes on an inch-thick, rust-stained mattress under a Sally Ann blanket. He loved his tools; when he finally sold them I knew we'd hit the bottom.

Industriously, I built an ice surface, enclosed it with old doors from a demolished tenement. The goal mouth was a topless clothes-hamper I fished from the garbage. I battered it to splinters, playing. Luck of the only child: if I'd had an older brother, I'd have been put in goal. Luckily there was a younger kid on the third floor who knew his place and was given hockey pads one Christmas; his older brother and I would bruise him after school until darkness made it dangerous for him. I'd be in my Bruins jersey, dreaming of Rocket Richard.

Little priest that I was, I did more than build ice surfaces. In the mornings I would rise at a quarter to five and pick up a bundle of *Montréal Matins* on the corner of Van Horne and Querbes. Seventy papers I had, and I could run with the last thirty-five, firing them up on second- and third-floor balconies, stuffing them into convenient grilles, and marking with hate all those buildings where the Greeks were moving in or the Jews had already settled and my papers weren't good enough to wrap their garbage in. There was another kid who delivered the morning *Gazettes* to part of my street – ten or twelve places that had no use for me. We were the only people yet awake, crisscrossing each other's paths, still in the dark and way below zero, me with a *Matin* sack and him with his *Gazette*. Once, we even talked. We were waiting for our bundles under a street lamp in front of the closed tobacco store on the corner. It was about ten below and the sidewalks were uncleared from an all-night snow. He smoked one of my cigarettes and I smoked one of his and we found out we didn't have anything to say to each other except *merci*. After half an hour I said, 'Paper no come,' and he agreed, so we walked away.

Later on more and more Greeks moved in; every time a vacancy popped up, some Greek would take it – they even made sure by putting only Greek signs in the windows – and my route was shrinking all the time. *Montréal Matin* fixed me up with a route much further east, off Rachel near St-André, and so I became the only ten-year-old in Montreal who'd wait at four-thirty in the morning for the first bus out of the garage to take him to his paper route. After a few days I didn't have to pay a fare. I'd take coffee from the driver's thermos, his cigarettes, and we'd discuss hockey from the night before. In return I'd give him a paper when he let me off. They didn't call me Curette for nothing.

The hockey, the hockey! I like all the major sports, and the setting of each one has its special beauty – even old De Lorimier Downs had something of Yankee Stadium about it, and old Rocky Nelson banging out home runs from his rocking-chair stance made me think of Babe Ruth, and who could compare to Jackie Robinson and Roberto Clemente when they were playing for us? Sundays in August with the Red Wings in town, you could always get in free after a couple of innings and see two great games. But the ice of big-time hockey, the old Forum, that went beyond landscape! Something about the ghostly white of the ice under those powerful lights, something about the hiss of the skates if you were standing close enough, the solid *pock-pock* of the rubber on a stick, and the low menacing whiz of a Rocket wrist shot hugging the ice – there was nothing in any other sport to compare with the *spell* of hockey. Inside the Forum in the early fifties, those games against Boston (with the Rocket flying and a hated Boston goalie named Jack Gelineux in the nets) were evangelical, for truly we were *dans le cénacle* where everyone breathed as one.

The Bruins sweatshirt came from a cousin of mine in Manchester, New Hampshire, who brought it as a joke or maybe a present on one of his trips up to see us. I started wearing it in all my backyard practices and whenever I got standing room tickets at the Forum. Crazy, I think now; what was going on in me? Crying on those few nights each winter when the Canadiens lost, quite literally throwing whatever I was holding high in the air whenever the Rocket scored – yet always wearing that hornet-coloured jersey? Anyone could see I was a good local kid; maybe I wanted someone to think I'd come all the way from Boston just to see the game, maybe I liked the good-natured kidding from my fellow standees (''ey, you Boston,' they'd shout, 'oo's winning, eh?' and I'd snarl back after a period or two of silence, *'Mange la bâton, sac de marde ... ').* I even used to wear that jersey when I delivered papers and I remember the pain of watching it slowly unravel in the cuffs and shoulders, hoping the cousin would come again. They were Schmitzes, my mother's sister had met him just after the war. *Tante* Lise and Uncle Howie.

I started to pick up English by reading a *Gazette* on my paper route, and I remember vividly one spring morning – with the sun coming up – studying a name that I took to be typically English. It began *Sch,* an odd combination, like my uncle's; then I suddenly thought of my mother's name – not mine – Deschênes, and I wondered: could it be? Hidden in the middle of my mother's name were those same English letters, and I began to think that we (tempting horror) were English too, that I had a right, a *sch*, to that Bruins jersey, to the world in the *Gazette* and on the other side of Atwater from the Forum. How I fantasized!

Every now and then the Schmitzes would drive up in a new car (I think now they came up whenever they bought a new car; I don't remember ever sitting in one of their cars without noticing a shred of plastic around the window-cranks and a smell of newness), and I would marvel at my cousins who were younger than me and taller ('They don't smoke,' my mother would point out), and who whined a lot because they always wanted things (I never understood what) they couldn't get with us. My mother could carry on with them in English. I wanted to like them – an only child feels that way about his relatives, not having seen his genetic speculations exhausted, and tends to see himself refracted even into second and third cousins several times removed. Now I saw a devious link with that American world in the strange clot of letters common to my name and theirs, and that pleased me.

We even enjoyed a bout of prosperity at about that time. I was thirteen or so, and we had moved from Hutchison (where a Greek janitor was finally hired) to a place off St-Denis where my father took charge of a sixteen-apartment building; they paid him well and gave us a three-room place out of the basement damps. That was *bonheur* in my father's mind – moving up to the ground floor where the front door buzzer kept waking you up. It was reasonably new; he didn't start to have trouble with bugs and paint for almost a year. He even saved a little money.

At just about the same time, in the more spacious way of the Schmitzes, they packed up everything in Manchester (where Uncle Howie owned three dry-cleaning shops) and moved to North Hollywood, Florida. That's a fair proportion: Hutchison is to St-Denis what Manchester is to Florida. He started with one dry-cleaning shop and had three others within a year. If he'd really been one of us, we'd have been suspicious of his tactics and motives, we would have called him lucky and undeserving. But he was American, he had his *sch*, so whatever he did seemed blessed by a different branch of fate, and we wondered only how we could share.

It was the winter of 1952. It was a cold sunny time on St-Denis. I still delivered my papers (practically in the neighbourhood), my father wasn't drinking that much, and my mother was staying out of church except on Sunday – and we had just bought a car. It was a used Plymouth, the first car we'd ever owned. The idea was that we should visit the Schmitzes this time in their Florida home for Christmas. It was even their idea, arranged through the sisters. My father packed his tools in the rear ('You never know, Mance; I'd like to show him what I can do ...'). He moved his brother Réal and family into our place – Réal was handy enough, more affable, but an even bigger drinker. We left Montreal on December 18 and took a cheap and slow drive down, the pace imposed by my father, who underestimated the strain of driving, and by my mother, who'd read of speedtraps and tourists languishing twenty years in Southern dungeons for running a stop sign. The drive was cheap because we were dependent on my mother for expense money as soon as we entered the States, since she was the one who could go into the motel office and find out the prices. It would be three or four in the afternoon and my father would be a nervous wreck; just as we were unloading the trunk and my father was checking the level of whisky in the glove compartment bottle, she'd come out announcing it was highway robbery, we couldn't stay here. My father would groan, curse and slam the trunk. Things would be dark by the time we found a vacancy in one of those rows of one-room cabins, arranged like stepping stones or in a semicircle (the kind you still see nowadays out on the Gaspésie with boards on the windows and a faded billboard out front advertising 'investment property'). My mother put a limit of three dollars a night on accommodations; we shopped in supermarkets for cold meat, bread, mustard and Pepsis. My father rejoiced in the cheaper gas; my mother reminded him it was a smaller gallon. Quietly, I calculated the difference. Remember, no drinking after Savannah, my mother said. It was clear: he expected to become the manager of a Schmitz Dry Kleenery.

The Schmitzes had rented a spacious cottage about a mile from the beach in North Hollywood. The outside stucco was green, the roof tiles orange, and the flowers violently pink and purple. The shrubs looked decorated with little red Christmas bulbs; I picked one – gift of my cousin – bit, and screamed in surprise. Red chilies. The front windows were sprayed with Santa's sleigh and a snowy 'Merry Christmas'. Only in

English, no *'Joyeux Noël'* like our greeting back home. That was what I'd noticed most all the way down, the incompleteness of all the signs, the satisfaction that their version said it all. I'd kept looking on the other side of things – my side – and I'd kept twirling the radio dial, for an equivalence that never came.

It was Christmas week and the Schmitzes were wearing Bermuda shorts and T-shirts with sailfish on the front. *Tante* Lise wore coral earrings and a red halter, and all her pale flesh had freckled. The night we arrived, my father got up on a stepladder, anxious to impress, and strung coloured lights along the gutter while my uncle shouted directions and watered the lawn. Christmas – and drinking Kool-Aid in the yard! We picked chili peppers and sold them to every West Indian cook who answered the back doorbell. At night I licked my fingers and hummed with the air-conditioning. My tongue burned for hours. That was the extraordinary part for me: that things as hot as chilies could grow in your yard, that I could bake in December heat, and that other natural laws remained the same. My father was still shorter than my mother, and his face turned red and blotchy here too (just as it did in August back home) instead of an even schmitzean brown, and when he took off his shirt, only a tattoo, scars and angry red welts were revealed. Small and sickly he seemed; worse, mutilated. My cousins rode their chrome-plated bicycles to the beach, but I'd never owned a two-wheeler and this didn't seem the time to reveal another weakness. Give me ice, I thought, my stick and a puck and an open net. Some men were never meant for vacations in shirtless countries: small hairy men with dirty winter boils and red swellings that never became anything lanceable, and tattoos of celebrities in their brief season of fame, now forgotten. My father's tattoo was as long as my twelve-year-old hand, done in a waterfront parlour in Montreal the day he'd thought of enlisting. My mother had been horrified, more at the tattoo than the thought of his shipping out. The tattoo pictured a front-faced Rocket, staring at an imaginary goalie and slapping a rising shot through a cloud of ice chips. Even though I loved the Canadiens and the Rocket mightily, I would have preferred my father to walk shirtless down the middle of the street with a naked woman on his back than for him to strip for the Schmitzes and my enormous cousins, who pointed and laughed, while I could almost understand what they were laughing about. They thought his tattoo was a kind of tribal marking, like kinky hair, thin moustaches, and slanty eyes – that if I took off my shirt I'd have one too, only smaller. *Lacroix,* I said to myself: how could he and I have the same name? It was foreign. I was a Deschênes, a Schmitz in the making.

On Christmas Eve we trimmed a silvered little tree and my uncle played Bing Crosby records on the console hi-fi-short-wave-bookcase (the biggest thing going in Manchester, New Hampshire, before the days of television). It would have been longer than our living room in Montreal; even here it filled one wall. They tried to teach me to imitate Crosby's 'White Christmas', but my English was hopeless. My mother and aunt sang in harmony; my father kept spilling his iced tea while trying to clap. It was painful. I waited impatiently to get to bed in order to cut the night as short as possible.

The murkiness of those memories! How intense, how foreign; it all happened like a dream in which everything follows logically from some incredible premise – that we should go to Florida, that it should be so hot in December, that my father should be on his best behaviour for nearly a month ... that we could hope that a little initiative and optimism would carry us anywhere but deeper into debt and darkest despair ...

I see myself as in a dream, walking the beach alone, watching the coarse brown sand fall over my soft white feet. I hear my mother and *Tante* Lise whispering together, yet they're five hundred feet ahead ('Yes,' my mother is saying, 'what life is there for him back there? You can see how this would suit him. To a T! To a T!' I'm wondering is it me, or my father, who has no future back there, and *Tante* Lise begins, 'Of course, I'm only a wife. I don't know what his thinking is –'), but worse is the silent image of my father in his winter trousers rolled up to his skinny knees and gathered in folds by a borrowed belt (at home he'd always worn braces), shirtless, shrunken, almost running to keep up with my uncle who walks closer to the water, in Bermuda shorts. I can tell from the beaten smile on my father's lips and from the way Uncle Howie is talking (while looking over my father's head at the ships on the horizon), that what the women have arranged ('It would be good to have you close, Mance ... I get these moods sometimes, you know? And five shops are too much for Howie ...') the men have made impossible. I know that when my father was smiling and his head was bobbing in agreement and he was running to keep up with someone, he was being told off, turned down, laughed at. And the next stage was for him to go off alone, then come back to us with a story that embarrassed us all by its transparency, and that would be the last of him, sober, for three, four or five days ... I can see all this and hear it, though I am utterly alone near the crashing surf and it seems to be night and a forgotten short-wave receiver still blasts forth on a beach blanket somewhere; I go to it hoping to catch something I can understand, a hockey game, the scores, but all I get wrenching the dial until it snaps is Bing Crosby dreaming of a white Christmas and Cuban music and indecipherable commentary from Havana, the dog races from Miami, *jai alai*.

That drive back to Montreal lasted almost a month. Our money ran out in Georgia and we had to wait two weeks in a shack in the Negro part of Savannah, where a family like ours – with a mother who liked to talk, and a father who drank and showed up only to collect our rent, and a kid my age who spent his time caddying and getting up before the sun to hunt golf balls – found space for us in a large room behind the kitchen, recently vacated by a dead grandparent. There were irregularities, the used-car dealer kept saying, various legal expenses involved with international commerce between Canadian Plymouths and innocent Georgia dealers, and we knew not to act too anxious (or even give our address) for fear of losing whatever bit of money we stood to gain. Finally he gave us $75, and that was when my father took his tools out of the back and sold them at a gas station for $50. We went down to the bus station, bought three tickets to Montreal, and my father swept the change into my mother's pocketbook. We were dressed for the January weather we'd be having when we got off, and the boy from the house we'd been staying in, shaking his head as he watched us board, muttered, 'Man, you sure is crazy.' It became a phrase of my mother's for all the next hard years. 'Man, you sure is crazy.' I mastered it and wore it like a Bruins sweater, till it too wore out. I remember those nights on the bus, my mother counting the bills and coins in her purse, like beads on a rosary, the numbers a silent prayer.

Back on St-Denis we found Réal and family very happily installed. The same egregiously gregarious streak that sputtered in my father flowed broadly in his brother. He'd all but brought fresh fruit baskets to the sixteen residents, carried newspapers to their doors, repaired buzzers that had never worked, shovelled insanely wide swaths down the front steps, replaced lights in the basement lockers, oiled, painted, polished ... even laid off the booze for the whole month we were gone (which to my father was the unforgivable treachery); in short, while we'd sunk all our savings and hocked all our valuables to launch ourselves in the dry-cleaning business, Réal had simply moved his family three blocks into lifelong comfort and security. My father took it all very quietly; we thought he'd blow sky-high. But he was finished. He'd put up the best, and the longest, show of his life and he'd seen himself squashed like a worm underfoot. Maybe he'd had one of those hellish moments when he'd seen himself in his brother-in-law's sunglasses, running at his side, knowing that those sunglasses were turned to the horizon and not to him.

Eyes

You jump into this business of a new country cautiously. First you choose a place where English is spoken, with doctors and bus lines at hand, and a supermarket in a *centre d'achats* not too far away. You ease yourself into the city, approaching by car or bus down a single artery, aiming yourself along the boulevard that begins small and tree-lined in your suburb but broadens into the canyoned aorta of the city five miles beyond. And by that first winter when you know the routes and bridges, the standard congestions reported from the helicopter on your favourite radio station, you start to think of moving. What's the good of a place like this when two of your neighbours have come from Texas and the French paper you've dutifully subscribed to arrives by mail two days late? These French are all around you, behind the counters at the shopping centre, in a house or two on your block; why isn't your little boy learning French at least? Where's the nearest *maternelle?* Four miles away.

In the spring you move. You find an apartment on a small side street where dogs outnumber children and the row houses resemble London's, divided equally between the rundown and remodelled. Your neighbours are the young personalities of French television who live on delivered chicken, or the old pensioners who shuffle down the summer sidewalks in pyjamas and slippers in a state of endless recuperation. Your neighbours pay sixty a month for rent, or three hundred; you pay two-fifty for a two-bedroom flat where the walls have been replastered and new fixtures hung. The bugs *d'antan* remain, as well as the hulks of cars abandoned in the fire alley behind, where downtown drunks sleep in the summer night.

Then comes the night in early October when your child is coughing badly, and you sit with him in the darkened nursery, calm in the bubbling of a cold-steam vaporizer while your wife mends a dress in the room next door. And from the dark, silently, as you peer into the ill-lit fire alley, he comes. You cannot believe it at first, that a rheumy, pasty-faced Irishman in slate-grey jacket and rubber-soled shoes has come purposely to *your* small parking space, that he has been here before and he is not drunk (not now, at least, but you know him as a panhandler on the main boulevard a block away), that he brings with him a crate that he sets on end under your bedroom window and raises himself to your window ledge and hangs there nose-high at a pencil of light from the ill-fitting blinds. And there you are, straining with him from the uncurtained nursery, watching the man watching your wife, praying silently that she is sleeping under the blanket. The man is almost smiling, a leprechaun's face that sees what you cannot. You are about to lift the window and shout, but your wheezing child lies just under you; and what of your wife in the room next door? You could, perhaps, throw open the window and leap to the ground, tackle the man before he runs and smash his face into the bricks, beat him senseless then call the cops … Or better, find the camera, affix the flash, rap once at the window and shoot when he turns. Do nothing and let him suffer. *He is at your mercy,* no one will ever again be so helpless – but what can you do? You know, somehow, he'll escape. If you hurt him, he can hurt you worse, later, viciously. He's been a regular at your window, he's watched the two of you when you prided yourselves on being young and alone and masters of the city. He knows your child and the park he plays in, your wife and where she shops. He's a native of the place, a man who knows the city and maybe a dozen such windows, who knows the fire escapes and alleys and roofs, knows the habits of the city's heedless young.

And briefly you remember yourself, an adolescent in another country slithering through the mosquito-ridden grassy fields behind a housing development, peering into those houses where newlyweds had not yet put up drapes, how you could spend five hours in a motionless crouch for a myopic glimpse of a slender arm reaching from the dark to douse a light. Then you hear what the man cannot; the creaking of your bed in the far bedroom, the steps of your wife on her way to the bathroom, and you see her as you never have before: blond and tall and rangily built, a north-Europe princess from a constitutional monarchy, sensuous mouth and prominent teeth, pale, tennis-ball breasts cupped in her hands as she stands in the bathroom's light.

'How's Kit?' she asks. 'I'd give him a kiss except that there's no blind in there,' and she dashes back to bed, nude, and the man bounces twice on the window ledge.

'You coming?'

You find yourself creeping from the nursery, turning left at the hall and then running to the kitchen telephone; you dial the police, then hang up. How will you prepare your wife, not for what is happening, but for what has already taken place?

'It's stuffy in here,' you shout back. 'I think I'll open the window a bit.' You take your time, you stand before the blind blocking his view if he's still looking, then bravely you part the curtains. He is gone, the crate remains upright. 'Do we have any masking tape?' you ask, lifting the window a crack.

And now you know the city a little better. A place where millions come each summer to take pictures and walk around must have its voyeurs too. And that place in all great cities where rich and poor co-exist is especially hard on the people in-between. It's health you've been seeking, not just beauty; a tough urban health that will save you money in the bargain, and when you hear of a place twice as large at half the rent, in a part of town free of Texans, English and French, free of young actors and stewardesses who deposit their garbage in pizza boxes, you move again.

It is, for you, a city of Greeks. In the summer you move you attend a movie at the corner cinema. The posters advertise a war movie, in Greek, but the uniforms are unfamiliar. Both sides wear moustaches, both sides handle machine guns, both leave older women behind dressed in black. From the posters outside there is a promise of sex; blond women in slips, dark-eyed peasant girls. There will be rubble, executions against a wall. You can follow the story from the stills alone: moustached boy goes to war, embraces dark-eyed village girl. Black-draped mother and admiring young brother stand behind. Young soldier, moustache fuller, embraces blond prostitute on a tangled bed. Enter soldiers, boy hides under sheets. Final shot, back in village. Mother in black; dark-eyed village girl in black. Young brother marching to the front.

You go in, pay your ninety cents, pay a nickel in the lobby for a wedge of *halvah*-like sweets. You understand nothing, you resent their laughter and you even resent the picture they're running. Now you know the

47

Greek for 'Coming Attractions', for this is a gangster movie at least thirty years old. The eternal Mediterranean gangster movie set in Athens instead of Naples or Marseilles, with smaller cars and narrower roads, uglier women and more sinister killers. After an hour the movie flatters you. No one knows you're not a Greek, that you don't belong in this theatre, or even this city. That, like the Greeks, you're hanging on.

Outside the theatre the evening is warm and the wide sidewalks are clogged with Greeks who nod as you come out. Like the Ramblas in Barcelona, with children out past midnight and families walking back and forth for a long city block, the men filling the coffeehouses, the women left outside, chatting. Not a blond head on the sidewalk, not a blond head for miles. Greek music pours from the coffeehouses, flies stumble on the pastry, whole families munch their *torsades molles* as they walk. Dry goods are sold at midnight from the sidewalk, like New York fifty years ago. You're wandering happily, glad that you moved, you've rediscovered the innocence of starting over.

Then you come upon a scene directly from Spain. A slim blond girl in a floral top and white pleated skirt, tinted glasses, smoking, with bad skin, ignores a persistent young Greek in a shiny Salonika suit. 'Whatsamatta?' he demands, slapping a ten-dollar bill on his open palm. And without looking back at him she drifts closer to the curb and a car makes a sudden squealing turn and lurches to a stop on the cross street. Three men are inside, the back door opens and not a word is exchanged as she steps inside. How? What refinement of gesture did we immigrants miss? You turn to the Greek boy in sympathy, you know just how he feels, but he's already heading across the street, shouting something to his friends outside a barbecue stand. You have a pocketful of bills and a Mediterranean soul, and money this evening means a woman, and blond means whore and you would spend it all on another blond with open pores; all this a block from your wife and tenement. And you hurry home.

Months later you know the place. You trust the Greeks in their stores, you fear their tempers at home. Eight bathrooms adjoin a central shaft, you hear the beatings of your son's friends, the thud of fist on bone after the slaps. Your child knows no French, but he plays cricket with Greeks and Jamaicans out in the alley behind Pascal's hardware. He brings home the oily tires from the Esso station, plays in the boxes behind the appliance store. You watch from a greasy back window, at last satisfied. None of his friends is like him, like you. He is becoming Greek, becoming Jamaican, becoming a part of this strange new land. His hair is nearly white; you can spot him a block away.

On Wednesday the butcher quarters his meat. Calves arrive by refrigerator truck, still intact but for their split-open bellies and sawed-off hooves. The older of the three brothers skins the carcass with a small thin knife that seems all blade. A knife he could shave with. The hide rolls back in a continuous flap, the knife never pops the membrane over the fat.

Another brother serves. Like yours, his French is adequate. *'Twa lif d'hamburger,'* you request, still watching the operation on the rickety sawhorse. Who could resist? It's a Levantine treat, the calf's stumpy legs high in the air, the hide draped over the edge and now in the sawdust, growing longer by the second.

The store is filling. The ladies shop on Wednesday, especially the old widows in black overcoats and scarves, shoes and stockings. Yellow, mangled fingernails. Wednesdays attract them with boxes in the window, and they call to the butcher as they enter, the brother answers, and the women dip their fingers in the boxes. The radio is loud overhead, music from the Greek station.

'Une et soixante, m'sieur. Du bacon, jambon?'

And you think, taking a few lamb chops but not their saltless bacon, how pleased you are to manage so well. It is a Byzantine moment with blood and widows and sides of dripping beef, contentment in a snowy slum at five below.

The older brother, having finished the skinning, straightens, curses, and puts away the tiny knife. A brother comes forward to pull the hide away, a perfect beginning for a gameroom rug. Then, bending low at the rear of the glistening carcass, the legs spread high and stubby, the butcher digs in his hands, ripping hard where the scrotum is, and pulls on what seems to be a strand of rubber, until it snaps. He puts a single glistening prize in his mouth, pulls again and offers the other to his brother, and they suck.

The butcher is singing now, drying his lips and wiping his chin, and still he's chewing. The old black-draped widows with the parchment faces are also chewing. On leaving, you check the boxes in the window.

Staring out are the heads of pigs and lambs, some with the eyes lifted out and a red socket exposed. A few are loose and the box is slowly dissolving from the blood, and the ice beneath.

The women have gathered around the body; little pieces are offered to them from the head and entrails. The pigs' heads are pink, perhaps they've been boiled, and hairless. The eyes are strangely blue. You remove your gloves and touch the skin, you brush against the grainy ear. How the eye attracts you! How you would like to lift one out, press its smoothness against your tongue, then crush it in your mouth. And you cannot. Already your finger is numb and the head, it seems, has shifted under you. And the eye, in panic, grows white as your finger approaches. You would take that last half inch but for the certainty, in this world you have made for yourself, that the eye would blink and your neighbours would turn upon you.

A Class of New Canadians

Norman Dyer hurried down Sherbrooke Street, collar turned against the snow. 'Superb!' he muttered, passing a basement gallery next to a French bookstore. Bleached and tanned women in furs dashed from hotel lobbies into waiting cabs. Even the neon clutter of the side streets and the honks of slithering taxis seemed remote tonight through the peaceful snow. *Superb,* he thought again, waiting for a light and backing from a slushy curb: a word reserved for wines, cigars and delicate sauces; he was feeling superb this evening. After eighteen months in Montreal, he still found himself freshly impressed by everything he saw. He was proud of himself for having steered his life north, even for jobs that were menial by standards he could have demanded. Great just being here no matter what they paid, looking at these buildings, these faces, and hearing all the languages. He was learning to be insulted by simple bad taste, wherever he encountered it.

Since leaving graduate school and coming to Montreal, he had sampled every ethnic restaurant downtown and in the Old City, plus a few Levantine places out in Outremont. He had worked on conversational French and mastered much of the local dialect, done reviews for local papers, translated French-Canadian poets for Toronto quarterlies, and tweaked his colleagues for not sympathizing enough with Quebec separatism. He attended French performances of plays he had ignored in English, and kept a small but elegant apartment near a colony of *émigré* Russians just off Park Avenue. Since coming to Montreal he'd witnessed a hold-up, watched a murder and seen several riots. When stopped on the street for directions, he would answer in French or accented English. To live this well and travel each long academic summer, he held two jobs. He had no intention of returning to the States. In fact, he had begun to think of himself as a semi-permanent, semi-political exile.

Now, stopped again a few blocks farther, he studied the window of Holt Renfrew's exclusive men's shop. Incredible, he thought, the authority of simple good taste. Double-breasted chalk-striped suits he would never dare to buy. Knitted sweaters, and fifty-dollar shoes. One tanned mannequin was decked out in a brash chequered sportscoat with a burgundy vest and dashing ascot. Not a price tag under three hundred dollars. Unlike food, drink, cinema and literature, clothing had never really involved him. Someday, he now realized, it would. Dyer's clothes, thus far, had all been bought in a chain department store. He was a walking violation of American law, clad shoes to scarf in Egyptian cottons, Polish leathers, and woollens from the People's Republic of China.

He had no time for dinner tonight; this was Wednesday, a day of lectures at one university, and then an evening course in English as a Second Language at McGill, beginning at six. He would eat afterwards.

Besides the money, he had kept this second job because it flattered him. There was to Dyer something fiercely elemental, almost existential, about teaching both his language and his literature in a foreign country – like Joyce in Trieste, Isherwood and Nabokov in Berlin, Beckett in Paris. Also it was necessary for his students. It was the first time in his life that he had done something socially useful. What difference did it make that the job was beneath him, a recent Ph.D., while most of his colleagues in the evening school at McGill were idle housewives and bachelor civil servants? It didn't matter, even, that this job was a perversion of all the sentiments he held as a progressive young teacher. He was a god two evenings a week, sometimes suffering and fatigued, but nevertheless an omniscient, benevolent god. His students were silent, ignorant and dedicated to learning English. No discussions, no demonstrations, no dialogue.

I love them, he thought. They need me.

He entered the room, pocketed his cap and earmuffs, and dropped his briefcase on the podium. Two girls smiled good evening.

They love me, he thought, taking off his boots and hanging up his coat; I'm not their English-speaking bosses.

I love myself, he thought with amazement even while conducting a drill on word order. I love myself for tramping down Sherbrooke Street in zero weather just to help them with noun clauses. I love myself standing behind this podium and showing Gilles Carrier and Claude Veilleux the difference between the past continuous and the simple past; or the sultry Armenian girl with the bewitching half-glasses that 'put on' is not the same as 'take on'; or telling the dashing Mr Miguel Mayor, late of

Madrid, that simple futurity can be expressed in four different ways, at least.

This is what mastery is like, he thought. Being superb in one's chosen field, not merely in one's mother tongue. A respected performer in the lecture halls of the major universities, equipped by twenty years' research in the remotest libraries, and slowly giving it back to those who must have it. Dishing it out suavely, even wittily. Being a legend. Being loved and a little feared.

'Yes, Mrs David?'

A *sabra:* freckled, reddish hair, looking like a British model, speaks with a nifty British accent, and loves me.

'No,' he said, smiling. '*I were* is not correct except in the present subjunctive, which you haven't studied yet.'

The first hour's bell rang. The students closed their books for the intermission. Dyer put his away, then noticed a page of his Faulkner lecture from the afternoon class. *Absalom, Absalom!* his favourite.

'Can anyone here tell me what the *impregnable citadel of his passive rectitude* means?'

'What, sir?' asked Mr Vassilopoulos, ready to copy.

'What about *the presbyterian and lugubrious effluvium of his passive vindictiveness?*' A few girls giggled. 'OK,' said Dyer, 'take your break.'

In the halls of McGill they broke into the usual groups. French Canadians and South Americans into two large circles, then the Greeks, Germans, Spanish and French into smaller groups. The patterns interested Dyer. Madrid Spaniards and Parisian French always spoke English with their New World co-linguals. The Middle Europeans spoke German together, not Russian, preferring one occupier to the other. Two Israeli men went off alone. Dyer decided to join them for the break.

Not *sabras,* Dyer decided, not like Mrs David. The shorter one, dark and wavy-haired, held his cigarette like a violin bow. The other, Mr Weinrot, was tall and pot-bellied, with a ruddy face and thick stubby fingers. Something about him suggested truck-driving, perhaps of beer, maybe in Germany. Neither one, he decided, could supply the name of a good Israeli restaurant.

'This is really hard, you know?' said Weinrot.

'Why?'

'I think it's because I'm not speaking much of English at my job.'

'French?' asked Dyer.

'French? Pah! All the time Hebrew, sometimes German, sometimes little Polish. Crazy thing, eh? How long you think they let me speak Hebrew if I'm working in America?'

'Depends on where you're working,' he said.

'Hell, I'm working for the Canadian government, what you think? Plant I work in – I'm engineer, see – makes boilers for the turbines going up North. Look. When I'm leaving Israel I go first to Italy. Right away-bamm I'm working in Italy I'm speaking Italian like a native. Passing for a native.'

'A native Jew,' said his dark-haired friend.

'Listen to him. So in Rome they think I'm from Tyrol – that's still native, eh? So I speak Russian and German and Italian like a Jew. My Hebrew is bad, I admit it, but it's a lousy language anyway. Nobody likes it. French I understand but English I'm talking like a bum. Arabic I know five dialects. Danish fluent. So what's the matter I can't learn English?'

'It'll come, don't worry.' Dyer smiled. *Don't worry, my son;* he wanted to pat him on the arm. 'Anyway, that's what makes Canada so appealing. Here they don't force you.'

'What's this *appealing?* Means nice? Look, my friend, keep it, eh? Two years in a country I don't learn the language means it isn't a country.'

'Come on,' said Dyer. 'Neither does forcing you.'

'Let me tell you a story why I come to Canada. Then you tell me if I was wrong, OK?'

'Certainly,' said Dyer, flattered.

In Italy, Weinrot told him, he had lost his job to a Communist union. He left Italy for Denmark and opened up an Israeli restaurant with five other friends. Then the six Israelis decided to rent a bigger apartment downtown near the restaurant. They found a perfect nine-room place for two thousand kroner a month, not bad shared six ways. Next day the landlord told them the deal was off. 'You tell me why,' Weinrot demanded.

No Jews? Dyer wondered. 'He wanted more rent,' he finally said.

'More – you kidding? More we expected. *Less* we didn't expect. A couple with eight kids is showing up after we're gone and the law in

Denmark says a man has a right to a room for each kid plus a hundred kroner knocked off the rent for each kid. What you think of that? So a guy who comes in *after* us gets a nine-room place for a thousand kroner *less*. Law says no way a bachelor can get a place ahead of a family, and bachelors pay twice as much.'

Dyer waited, then asked, 'So?'

'So, I make up my mind the world is full of communismus, just like Israel. So I take out applications next day for Australia, South Africa, USA, and Canada. Canada says come right away, so I go. Should have waited for South Africa.'

'How could you?' Dyer cried. 'What's wrong with you anyway? South Africa is fascist. Australia is racist.'

The bell rang, and the Israelis, with Dyer, began walking to the room.

'What I was wondering, then,' said Mr Weinrot, ignoring Dyer's outburst, 'was if my English is good enough to be working in the United States. You're American, aren't you?'

It was a question Dyer had often avoided in Europe, but had rarely been asked in Montreal. 'Yes,' he admitted, 'your English is probably good enough for the States or South Africa, whichever one wants you first.'

He hurried ahead to the room, feeling that he had let Montreal down. He wanted to turn and shout to Weinrot and to all the others that Montreal was the greatest city on the continent, if only they knew it as well as he did. If they'd just break out of their little ghettos.

At the door, the Armenian girl with the half-glasses caught his arm. She was standing with Mrs David and Miss Parizeau, a jolly French-Canadian girl that Dyer had been thinking of asking out.

'Please, sir,' she said, looking at him over the tops of her tiny glasses, 'what I was asking earlier – *put on* – I heard on the television. A man said *You are putting me on* and everybody laughed. I think it was supposed to be funny but *put on* we learned means get dressed, no?'

'Ah – *don't put me on*,' Dyer laughed.

'I yaven't 'erd it neither,' said Miss Parizeau.

'To put some*body* on means to make a fool of him. To put some*thing* on is to wear it. Okay?' He gave examples.

'Ah, now I know,' said Miss Parizeau. 'Like bullshitting somebody. Is it the same?'

'Ah, yes,' he said, smiling. French Canadians were like children learning the language. 'Your example isn't considered polite. "Put on" is very common now in the States.'

'Then maybe,' said Miss Parizeau, 'we'll 'ave it 'ere in twenty years.' The Armenian giggled.

'No – I've heard it here just as often,' Dyer protested, but the girls had already entered the room.

He began the second hour with a smile that slowly soured as he thought of the Israelis. America's anti-communism was bad enough, but it was worse hearing it echoed by immigrants, by Jews, here in Montreal. Wasn't there a psychological type who chose Canada over South Africa? Or was it just a matter of visas and slow adjustment? Did Johannesburg lose its Greeks, and Melbourne its Italians, the way Dyer's students were always leaving Montreal?

And after class when Dyer was again feeling content and thinking of approaching one of the Israelis for a restaurant tip, there came the flood of small requests: should Mrs Papadopoulos go into a more advanced course; could Mr Perez miss a week for an interview in Toronto; could Mr Giguère, who spoke English perfectly, have a harder book; Mr Côté an easier one?

Then as Dyer packed his briefcase in the empty room, Miguel Mayor, the vain and impeccable Spaniard, came forward from the hallway.

'Sir,' he began, walking stiffly, ready to bow or salute. He wore a loud grey chequered sportscoat this evening, blue shirt and matching ascot-handkerchief, slightly mauve. He must have shaved just before class, Dyer noticed, for two fresh daubs of antiseptic cream stood out on his jaw, just under his earlobe.

'I have been waiting to ask *you* something, as a matter of fact,' said Dyer. 'Do you know any good Spanish restaurants I might try tonight?'

'There are not any good Spanish restaurants in Montreal,' he said. He stepped closer. 'Sir?'

'What's on your mind, then?'

'Please – have you the time to look on a letter for me?'

He laid the letter on the podium.

'Look *over* a letter,' said Dyer. 'What is it for?'

'I have applied,' he began, stopping to emphasize the present perfect construction, 'for a job in Cleveland, Ohio, and I want to know if my letter will be good. Will an American, I mean –'

'Why are you going there?'

'It is a good job.'

'But Cleveland –'

'They have a blackman mayor, I have read. But the job is not in Cleveland.'

Most honourable Sir: I humbly beg consideration for a position in your grand company …

'Who are you writing this to?'

'The president,' said Miguel Mayor.

I am once a student of Dr Ramiro Gutierrez of the Hydraulic Institute of Sevilla, Spain …

'Does the president know this Ramiro Gutierrez?'

'Oh, everybody is knowing him,' Miguel Mayor assured. 'He is the most famous expert in all Spain.'

'Did he recommend this company to you?'

'No – I have said in my letter, if you look –'

An ancient student of Dr Gutierrez, Salvador del Este, is actually a boiler expert who is being employed like supervisor is formerly a friend of mine …

'Is he still your friend?'

Whenever you say come to my city Miguel Mayor for talking I will be coming. I am working in Montreal since two years and am now wanting more money than I am getting here now …

'Well …' Dyer sighed.

'Sir – what I want from you is knowing in good English how to interview me by this man. The letters in Spanish are not the same to English ones, you know?'

I remain humbly at your orders …

'Why do you want to leave Montreal?'

'It's time for a change.'

'Have you ever been to Cleveland?'

'I am one summer in California. Very beautiful there and hot like my country. Montreal is big port like Barcelona. Everybody mixed together and having no money. It is just a place to land, no?'

'Montreal? Don't be silly.'

'I thought I come here and learn good English but where I work I get by in Spanish and French. It's hard, you know?' he smiled. Then he took a few steps back and gave his cuffs a gentle tug, exposing a set of jade cufflinks.

Dyer looked at the letter again and calculated how long he would be correcting it, then up at his student. How old is he? My age? Thirty? Is he married? Where do the Spanish live in Montreal? He looks so prosperous, so confident, like a male model off a page of *Playboy*. For an instant Dyer felt that his student was mocking him, somehow pitting his astounding confidence and wardrobe, sharp chin and matador's bearing against Dyer's command of English and mastery of the side streets, bistros and ethnic restaurants. Mayor's letter was painful, yet he remained somehow competent. He would pass his interview, if he got one. What would he care about America, and the odiousness he'd soon be supporting? It was as though a superstructure of exploitation had been revealed, and Dyer felt himself abused by the very people he wanted so much to help. It had to end someplace.

He scratched out the second 'humbly' from the letter, then folded the sheet of foolscap. 'Get it typed right away,' he said. 'Good luck.'

'Thank you, sir,' said his student, with a bow. Dyer watched the letter disappear in the inner pocket of the chequered sportscoat. Then the folding of the cashmere scarf, the draping of the camel's hair coat about the shoulders, the easing of the fur hat down to the rims of his ears. The meticulous filling of the pigskin gloves. Mayor's patent leather galoshes glistened.

'Good evening, sir,' he said.

'*Buenas noches,*' Dyer replied.

He hurried now, back down Sherbrooke Street to his daytime office where he could deposit his books. Montreal on a winter night was still mysterious, still magical. Snow blurred the arc lights. The wind was dying. Every second car was now a taxi, crowned with an orange crescent. Slushy curbs had hardened. The window of Holt Renfrew was still attractive. The legless dummies invited a final stare. He stood longer than he had earlier, in front of the sporty mannequin with a burgundy waistcoat, the mauve and blue ensemble, the jade cufflinks.

Good evening, sir, he could almost hear. The ascot, the shirt, the complete outfit, had leaped off the back of Miguel Mayor. He pictured how he must have entered the store with three hundred dollars and a prepared speech, and walked out again with everything off the torso's back.

I want that.

What, sir?

That.

The coat, sir?

Yes.

Very well, sir.

And *that.*

Which, sir?

All that.

'Absurd man!' Dyer whispered. There had been a moment of fear, as though the naked body would leap from the window, and legless, chase him down Sherbrooke Street. But the moment was passing. Dyer realized now that it was comic, even touching. Miguel Mayor had simply tried too hard, too fast, and it would be good for him to stay in Montreal until he deserved those clothes, that touching vanity and confidence. With one last look at the window, he turned sharply, before the clothes could speak again.

Extractions and Contractions

Student Power

Leaving my office on the twelfth floor and boarding the elevator with ten students, I have this winter's first seizure of claustrophobia. Eleven of us in heavy overcoats, crammed shoulder to shoulder in an overlit stainless steel box, burning up. The elevator opens on eleven and two students turn away, seeing that it's full. We stop on ten but no one is waiting. We are trapped by the buttons other people press before they take the stairs. We will stop on every floor, it is one of those days, though we can take no one in and all of us, obviously, are dressed for the street. On eight as the doors open and no one presses 'c' to close them quickly, I have a sense of how we must appear to any onlooker – like a squad of Gothic statuary, eyes averted upward, silent, prayerful. On seven I sense there will be a student waiting as the door opens. He looks in, smiles, and we smile back. The doors do not close and we wait. He opens his briefcase and assembles a machine gun. We cannot move; we are somehow humiliated by overcrowding. No one presses 'c'. A burst of fire catches us all, economically gunned down by a grinning student. The doors close and do not open again until we tumble out in the main lobby.

The Street

Early November is colder this year than last. Twelve floors up, without windows, I forget about the cold. I have been reading Faulkner for five hours and haven't thought once of winter. I have been thinking, in fact, that with my citizenship papers I can now apply for government support in the summer. I could have before, but it didn't seem right.

It is cruel to confront the streets now: snowless but windy and in the lower twenties. Such mildness will not return until late March. November and March, deadly months. Depressing to think the dentist, like winter, is waiting. The cold wind on a bad tooth anticipates so much. I try to remember these streets as they were in June; a sidewalk café, the devastating girls in the briefest skirts and bra-less sweaters. These streets had so many tourists in the summer, forever asking directions and making me feel at home. At the end of the block parked in a taxi space, I spot a modest car with snow on the trunk and Maryland plates. On the left edge of the back bumper is a tattered *McCarthy for President* sticker and on the right, as I kick off a little snow, is the red-framed bilingual testament: *I'm Proud to Be a Canadian / Je suis fier d'être canadien.*

The Dentist

My teeth, my body, my child, my wife and the baby she is carrying are all in the hands of immigrants. All Jews. I do not know how this develops; because I am an immigrant too, perhaps. Our friends warned us against the indigenous dentists. Between hockey pucks and Pepsi caps, they said, Quebec teeth are only replaced, never filled.

This dentist's office is in a large, formerly brick office building that was stripped to its girders over the summer and then refaced with concrete panels and oblong windows. Inside, however, not a change. The corridors are still reminiscent of older high schools, missing only the rows of olive-drab lockers. The doors are still darkly varnished and gummy from handling. The doctors and accountants still have their names in black on stippled glass. All this, according to Dr Abramovitch, pains a dentist, whose restorative work is from the inside out. 'Rotten inside,' he snorts, poking my tooth but meaning the building. He is a man of inner peace, rumoured to be a socialist. The rest of our doctors are socialists. His degrees are in Hebrew but for one that puzzles me more, in Latin. I am in the chair waiting for the freeze to take effect before I realize that *Monte Regis* means Montreal. I then remember a novel I have just read, a French-Canadian one, in which the narrator, a vendor of hot dogs, must decide on a name for his hot dog stand. The purists suggest *Au roi du chien chaud*. He chooses *Au roi du hot dog*. The author, I am told, is a separatist. I wonder if he cares that at least one outsider had read him. Poor Montreal, I now think, puts up with so much.

There is a battle this afternoon to save a tooth. The pulp is lost but the enamel is good. It is cheaper, he explains, to pull the tooth. But after pulling there must be a bridge and years later, another one. But pulling only the nerve (his brow smooths out) and packing the canal, though the work is tedious and expensive, is lavishly recommended. 'I get forty-five for a nerve job, ten for a straight extraction,' he says. *Pulling a nerve* is a sinister phrase, smacking of an advanced, experimental technique. But he is appealing, I can see, to all that is aesthetic in dentistry. No McTeague, this man, though his wrists bulge with competence. His extractions have been praised. I debate denying him any nerve, for with a numb jaw I can play the hero. *Lace the boot tighter, Doc. I gotta lead my men ...* finally, though, no John Wayne stuff for me. I consent, and he rams a platinum wire up the holes he has drilled, plunges it up and down then pulls it out, yellow with nerve scum. This is not how I pictured my nerve, though I had never hoped to look at a nerve, surely not my own, surely not this afternoon when I left my office. Brain surgery, too, I am told, is painless after the skull is cut through. I can hear the platinum probe grinding in my cheekbone nearly under my eye and I think of those pharmaceutical ads that used to appear in the *National Geographic* of Incas performing brain surgery, spitting cocaine juice into the open skull as they cut.

'Success,' he pronounces. He is happy, the tooth will drain, in a week he'll pack it. Leaving, I have my doubts. No John Wayne, certainly, I'm beginning to feel like Norman Mailer. A nerve ripped from my body at thirty. I am a young man, haven't deteriorated much since twenty-one, expect to remain the same at least till thirty-five. But somehow, some day, some *minute,* the next long decline begins to set in. At forty I will be middle-aged. At forty-five, twenty-five years from my grave. When does it start – with a chipped tooth? A broken nose? A broken leg even? Oh, no. It begins in choices. The road downhill is slick with fat and fallen hair and little pills. Bad styles and bad convictions. Painkillers, contraceptives, tranquillizers and weak erections. Pulled nerves.

St. Catherine Street

From the dentist's, east on St. Catherine is an urban paradise. No finer street exists in my experience, even in November. St. Catherine should be filmed without dialogue or actors, just by letting the crowds swarm around a mounted camera and allowing a random sound track to pick up the talk, Dopplering in and fading out, from every language in the world.

But west on St. Catherine, especially in November, is something else. Blocks of low buildings after Guy Street, loan offices on top and business failures down below. Auto salesrooms forever changing franchises, drugstores offering two-hour pregnancy tests, news and tobacco stands, basement restaurants changing nationalities. But if it can be afforded, or if one lives only with a wife, a convenient location. Someday Montreal will have its Greenwich Village and these short streets between St. Catherine and Dorchester will be the centre.

I stop at an unlighted tobacconist's for the papers. One window bin is full of pipes and tins of tobacco, the other of dusty sex magazines from every corner of the Western World. The owner stands all day at the door and opens it only if you show an interest. Otherwise, it's locked, without lights. I stop in daily for my *Star* and *Devoir*. I always have two dimes because he keeps no observable change. He always responds, '*Merci.*' His face implies that he has suffered; also that he survives now in his darkened store by selling far more than the *Star*, *La Presse* and all the Greek and German stag magazines. I have seen men enter the store and say things I couldn't understand and the owner present them with Hungarian, with Yiddish, with Ukrainian, with Latvian papers. Then they chat. Perhaps he speaks no English and just a word or two of French. Like my dentist, a man, ultimately, of mystery.

My Wife

Is it most significant that I say first she is a Ph.D. teaching at McGill and making more than I; or that she is the mother of our five-year-old boy, and is now eight months pregnant and still teaching? Or that she is Indian and is one of those small radiant women one sees on larger campuses, their red or purple *sari*-ends billowing under Western overcoats? I'm home early to let the frozen jaw thaw and to see if the nerveless tooth will keep me from lecturing tonight. My wife should be in her office and our son at the sitter's.

The apartment seems emptier than usual; there's been some attempt at tidying, the lights are off and the afternoon gloom through the fibreglass curtains is doubly desolate. I drop the briefcase, turn on the lights in the front room, then put coffee water on to boil in the dark narrow kitchen. Roaches scurry as I hit the light. I realize, on touching the cups, that the heat is low – maybe off. We have only five rooms but a very long hall; it curves twice and divides the apartment sharply. It costs us a great deal.

There is nothing distinctive about our place: given our double income, our alleged good taste, our backgrounds, this becomes distinctive. Other Indian, or semi-Indian, couples we know keep a virtual bazaar of silks and brasses and hempen rugs and eat off the floor at least once a week. Burn fresh incense every day. And though I do not like them, I sometimes envy them. There are days in November even without aching teeth that I realize how little I've done to improve our lives, how thwarted my sense of style has become.

I am sipping coffee when I hear the toilet flush in the rear of the apartment. I hurry back and find my wife rearranging the covers over her belly. She smiles and tells me to sit and keep time while she rests.

Contractions

Starting three hours earlier she's been having regular contractions of a mild variety; so mild that she hasn't bothered to call me. The cycle is steady but speeding up. 'I'm sorry I haven't done the shopping,' she says, smiling like a Hemingway heroine whose pain would crush a man. She assures me the contractions are light – almost delicious. Indians like massages, have special names for pressures and positions; it is something I have learned, something I can administer. 'It's a false alarm,' she insists. Nevertheless I decide to call Dr Lapp. He seems ignorant of the case until I remind him that my wife is the Indian lady. 'Ah, yes,' he says, 'don't panic.' I am to take her in only if they get severe and come every two minutes.

'This is silly,' she protests when they begin coming every two minutes. 'I'm actually looking forward to them.' She wants me to leave her at home and go back to school to eat and prepare my lecture. But I stand by my duty: pack her bag, call the sitters and tell them I'll pick up our boy around ten-thirty. They offer to have him spend the night, but I refuse. I want him with me.

The Hospital

We live just off St. Catherine, just where we want to be, but the hospital is suburban, in the deadly western sections, because all of Dr Lapp's patients live there. We do not have a French doctor because, I suppose, of the rumoured Catholic position on the primacy of the fetus. Dr Lapp is from Boston but interned at McGill and for some reason, stayed. One doesn't trust a people until one trusts their doctors. This suburban hospital is reached by a three-dollar taxi ride. It fits into the neighbourhood like a new church or modern school; low, long, red-brick, like every duplex on every street in the far western sections of Montreal. This is where my colleagues live; this is all they know of Montreal if, like me, they came here late: a bus line, a transfer point, the Metro stops, and school. Some shopping, some bookstore browsing, a downtown bank, a movie or two a month. None of them speaks a dozen words of French.

The doors of this hospital are marked: TIREZ / PULL, POUSSEZ / PUSH, and beyond the CAISSE / RECEPTIONIST, I see a sign: ASCENSEUR / ELEVATOR. For some reason I am thinking of a little test I once administered to some friends of mine in the English department, and not of my wife, who is being admitted. It was a recognition test. All of the men had either been born or had lived at least five years in Montreal. I supplied some everyday words and asked if they could give equivalents in English, and some of the words, I recall, were *tirez*, *poussez* and *défense de stationner*, and *arrêtez*. A man who owned a car identified both *arrêtez* and *sortie*. The others felt embarrassed and a little defensive. They told me that I should give such a test to some of the others, those who were harder to know and not quite so friendly, who lived in converted stables and in lofts down in the Old City, whose second wives were French-Canadian and whose children went to rugged little *lycées* in Outremont. Those men were, admittedly, a little frightening. Also a little foolish. Is there nothing in between? I wonder now what I was trying to prove my first year here with my evening courses in conversational French, my subscriptions to French magazines, my pride in reserving English for school and home, no place else. The depth of my commitment – to trivia.

Mongolism

Secretly I have been worrying that this second child will be mongoloid. It seems that the papers and all the polite journals that flood our house have recently featured technical articles for the common reader on mongolism. I know the statistics and I know what to look for even in a newborn infant. Position of the ears, size of tongue, bridge of nose, shape of feet, length of fingers. Blood, heart, lungs. The options: to commit him on sight to a home that will clean him, feed him, and let him die from the simplest illness; or to take him home and try to make him comfortable, all the time hoping that his weakened organs will overcome our love, our guilt, and fail him. Strangely, I do not fear anything physical. Because I am a professor and tend to minimize the physical? Because I seek punishment for the way we live, what we're doing to our boy who deserves better, with too many sitters and too much unlicensed television while we read and prepare? I support, in a bloodless and abstract way, euthanasia. Youth in Asia. I fear for the child because I refuse to doubt myself? I fear for the child because I fear even more my intentions toward him?

I remember the night he must have been conceived. My wife had been off her pills, for they make her sick too many mornings. She would vomit and teach, vomit and teach. I was sick with migraine. We had been quiet in bed. I gave her a kiss and turned away. A few minutes later, as I turned back in the dark, my lips brushed her nose. She had turned toward me, not away, and suddenly it was like discovering a beautiful stranger in my bed; there was nothing tender that night, nothing to become this child like his begetting. The only good sign. As for the rest, no health can come from something so unplanned, from parents so slovenly, an apartment so pest-infested and uninviting.

Evening Lecture

Another three-dollar ride home, quick change from possible paternity clothes, no supper or preparations, heat definitely gone, then a brisk walk down St. Catherine to school. Even in winter, when the weather can be the most unpleasant on the continent, I've found myself surfacing from the Metro and gawking at the buildings and people rather than moving on, out of the cold. Tonight, maybe a father for the second time, I walk slowly, smiling. I'll never be quite at home here, though now even a citizen; I'm as much a stranger in my way as the others that I know. Colleagues in the suburbs, legendary swingers down in the stables near the docks – this city makes fools of us all.

Then I think that living here is perhaps a low-grade art experience. I feel the life of the sidewalk, feel content for inexplicable reasons, simply for being here. Where else in the world is *Englais* spoken? I read in the paper of a French-Canadian student leader explaining in English why he demonstrated: *We are not complotting,* he said. *We are manifesting for more subventions.* And I understood every word. I shouldn't complain of those western suburbs and of the isolation of the housewives that I teach, nor should I worry about my tolerant, scholarly friends who see so little around them. Perhaps they see beyond the obvious, beyond the neutralizing bilingualism that surrounds them. Perhaps I'm only stuck on the obvious.

There are hundreds, thousands of evening students milling along the boulevard and side streets in front the school. The boulevard is five lanes wide but pinched to a trickle while parents, boyfriends, and taxis drop off students. I am caught in a crowd moving slowly toward the revolving doors, and I am thinking now only of the lecture, wondering how I'll pick up my boy after the lecture and get him fed and dressed for school in the morning and finally – Lord – what we'll do if this is the real baby, tonight, six weeks before the Christmas holidays when he was providentially due. Must everything we do be so tightly budgeted? In *Buddenbrooks* the hero dies prematurely after a dental visit, without a nerve even being discussed. I could die tonight of a dozen things, all deserved.

An Indian

From the hundreds in front of the school, I am grabbed by an Indian man in high Tashkent fur cap and lamb's-wool coat. He seizes an elbow as though in anger, his gloved fingers press painfully through my coat and sports jacket.

'This is not the Krishna Temple?'

I give him directions.

He frowns, presses me harder, for this does not please him. Crowds of students swirl around us. Why seize me, I want to cry, the scent of a martyred wife is that strong? He can tell? But his grip is serene, impersonal, and painful.

'Nevertheless, I will enter,' he says, 'this place.'

'Fine.'

'I must present documents.' Again, he is asking. I tell him he mustn't.

'What this place is?'

'A university.' I know this will confuse him. This is the largest academic building in the Commonwealth, I am told, but it looks nothing like a school. He presses harder.

'It is very late.'

The lobby is packed like a department store, which it already resembles with its escalators and high ceilings. We push through a door, two by two, and his grip loosens until I begin to pull away.

'You are not a student,' he says, or asks, 'you are,' and he strains as though making a difficult judgement, 'another thing.'

And then suddenly he drops my arm and takes off through the crowd. No chance to catch him, *shake him* and demand how he found me, of all people, tonight of all nights. A brown angel, not of death but perhaps of impairment? My wife in pain? Dying? The baby? Me? I push to the escalator then turn quickly in order to find him in the lobby and it is not difficult; he cuts through the crowd as though somehow charmed, just as I had feared. Students part to let him pass, even those who do not see him.

I call my wife during the intermission. The contractions have stopped, she's had a pill and will spend the night. Home after breakfast. A little fatigued, they said. She is preparing her Wednesday lecture.

The Night

From school I take a taxi to the baby-sitter's – two dollars – and gather my son in his blanket and carry him back to the waiting cab. Another two-fifty. I get home to find it much colder, the first heat failure of the winter. What does this mean? I put him in our bed, look for extra blankets but can't find them, call the landlord's answering service, then crawl in with my boy, fully dressed in the clothes I lectured in.

Sometime deep and cold in the night he pulls the cover from me and tugs my hand until I waken. He is crying, standing on the rug with his pyjama bottoms down and pointing toward the bathroom. I follow his hand and see – in several peaks – the movement he'd run to the bathroom to prevent. The largest mounds are on the rug; several more, including what he's stepped on and carried far down the hall and all over the bathroom floor, is on the hardwood overlap around the rug.

It is three in the morning. The time of the crack-up. I stoop, shivering, over piles of gelatinous shit on our only decent possession, an Irish wool rug. My boy, guilty and frightened, steps up his crying. *Back to bed,* I snap, weary but forgiving, and he counters, 'Where's Mommy?' but there is not time to explain. 'You're bad!' he cries, and hits me, screams louder, and I'm close to tears. Can I just leave it, I wonder, not so much wanting to as not knowing where to start. Then I carry him to the bathroom, clean his feet, his bottom, and return him to bed. I have never been so awake; I can see perfectly with no lights on. I mop the hall and bathroom floor. In the half-dark kitchen I grab a knife and cereal bowl, then the rug shampoo and brush from an undisturbed plastic tub under the sink. I scrape the rug with the knife, try to pick up everything I can see with the help of the bathroom light, then dip the brush in hot soapy water and begin to scrub.

For a minute or two it goes well, then I notice glistening shapes staggering from the milky foam; the harder I press, the more appear. *My child has roaches,* his belly is teeming, full of bugs, a plague of long brown roaches is living inside him, thriving on our neglect. The roaches creep and dart in every direction, I whack them with the wooden brush but more are boiling from the foam and now they appear on my hand and arm. I see two on the shoulder of my white shirt. I shout but my throat is closed after an evening lecture – I sputter phlegm. These are not my son's; they are the rug's. The other side of this fine Irish rug that we bought for a house in the suburbs that we later decided against, this rug that we haven't turned in months and haven't sent out to be cleaned, is a sea of roaches. I drop the brush and look underneath. Hairpins and tufts of tissue: an angry wave of roaches walking the top of the brush and glistening in the fibres like wet leaves beginning to stir. *My brush,* I want to cry: the brush was my friend. I pick it up and run with it down the hall, the filthiest thing I've ever held. I hear the roaches dropping to safety on the floor. It occurs to me as I open the apartment door and then the double doors of the foyer, and as I fling the brush over one curb of parked cars, that a drop of soapy water anywhere in this apartment would anger the roaches: the drawers, the mattresses, the good china, the silverware at night. First brushes, then rugs, and anything fine we might possibly buy or try to preserve; everything will yield to roaches. All those golden children of our joint income, infested.

Morning Dawns

After the rug I do the floors again, even the kitchen and hall and living room. I rewash every dish, spray ammonia where I can't reach. Then I throw away the mops and sponges, as the pharaohs killed their slaves, then killed the slaves that had dug the graves, killed the slaves that killed the slaves ... not a sponge, a rag, a bucket, a mop, a scrap of newspaper or length of paper-towelling left. At six o'clock in a freezing apartment, with an aching former nerve, I open the windows and clean the outside, wiping with my handkerchief, then throwing it away. By six o'clock near-light, by street and alley lamp, the place looks clean and ready for people. Ready for more than our basic used Danish. *Ready for youth,* I let myself think: for sitars in the corner, fishnets on the wall, posters, teakwood chests. In with pillows and garish cottons, out with sofas, tables and doors. Sitting on the Danish sofa, wrapped in my overcoat, I can almost hear the guests arriving, smell the incense, sway to Ravi Shankar records ...

But I'm not young, any more.

I part the fibreglass curtains. It is snowing heavily now, with tiny flakes. The cars will be stuck – thank God we walk. The brush I threw is white, straddled by the tracks of an early car. After such roaches, what improvement? A loft, a farmhouse, a duplex five miles out? Five years in this very place living for the city, the city our prize. For what we've caught, stopped, saved, we could have camped along St. Catherine Street. Holding on to nothing, because we were young and didn't need it. Always thinking: there is nowhere else we'd rather be. Nowhere else we can be, now. Old passports, pulled nerves, resting in offices. I think of my friends, the records they cry over, silly poems set to music, and I could cry as well. For them, for us. At the window I watch the men brush off their windshields, hear the engines trying to start. My son will soon be waking. I drop the curtains and go to put on water.

At the Lake

All those lakes up north with unsavoury names – Lac Têtard, Lac Bibitte, Lac Sangsue (who would buy a cabin to share with tadpoles, biting flies and leeches?) – take their names from a surveyor's map and not from their pests. Long ribbony Sangsue stretches out at the flanks of two steep ridges six miles long and a quarter-mile wide. When I bought the property on Lac Bibitte, Serge explained to me, 'Sure, *bibitte* means bug. But look at the lake, round like a ball on top and shaped like an egg down here. It's not Lac des Bibittes, you know ...' Têtard, on the other side of Mont Tremblant, has a triangular head and a broad branching river that drains its tail like larval legs. Anyway, the names might discourage some people. Closer to the city the developers have been at work and the homely names have gone through their initial manorial transformations: Lac des Mulets, Lac Quenouille and Lac des Castors into Lac Gagnon, Lac Ouellette and Lac Sauvé; thence into their death agonies as 'Lac Paradis: 45-minutes-on-4-lane-open-all-year fully winterized landscaped-in-your-choice-of trees-ranchettes-from $10,000.' I have the diminishing satisfaction that a place is worth twice as much after three years of unimprovement and decided deterioration.

There are families on the lake who've blasted crannies into the soaring granite cliffs a hundred feet above the water: Germans who thread their way like mountain goats balancing a weekend's beer on their heads, who dive like Acapulco professionals from a board on their porch into its unsounded depth below. I have watched them in summers past from the wide porch of our cabin on the low, marshy shore across the way – fat men of fifty in bikini briefs walking to the board, their laughter and joking clear, if foreign, from a mile away. Beer can in hand, laughter clapping over the water, he raises his arms in a diving motion but releases his empty can instead and sends it spiralling to the water. Then he crumples from the board – it's serious and competent he is – straightening in time and cutting the water like a missile.

We used to go up for the middle of every week from early July when the black flies died until the end of September when autumn was well advanced. I'm an academic and like the blessed commuter who lives in the city and drives to a suburban job, I found myself always moving against the crowds. We abandoned the lake on weekends to the waterskiers and speedboaters, when gasoline generators and long horn blasts waked us from the dream of a northern retreat. I preferred Wednesdays on the lake. August Wednesdays when it might be eighty-five degrees in the city and bone-warming seventy at the lake after a swim, when the sun burned with a rare intensity through the clear, polished air. Erika and I would lie on towels on the dock, dangling our fingers for bluegills to nibble, peering down the pilings to the sandy bottom where the sluggish mountain carp sifted through the mosses clinging to the wood.

I spent those summers envying the Europeans and a few Canadians who've blasted the granite and erected the A-frame bunkers on girders sunk in into the bare rockface (their twin flag-standards flying down at dock level, Red, Black, and Gold of the *Bundesrepublik,* and the adopted Maple Leaf), and I envied Serge, who hadn't missed a weekend at the cabin in fifteen years. Every weekend he has added cubits to his lands, his sewage, his dockery, his cabin, his soul; whereas I – a younger man more aware a thousand times of ravages, impurity and decay – have found the battle, or challenge, overwhelming. I ask myself what did I really want: electric blankets, pavement, a stove and fridge? And I say no, of course not; I wanted my son to grow up with nature. Skier, swimmer, fisherman, even hunter; I wanted him to grow up unflawed. I wanted the lake accessible yet remote, I wanted my cabin rustic but livable, I wanted a granite resolve to do on my marshy shore what old Germans had done on their cliffs; yet I wanted never to lose my immemorial torpor, my hours of dozing on a creaky dock peering at carp through the widening cracks. I wanted the end of black flies but no spraying, no lancing the swamps fed by fifteen feet of winter snows – relief from modest unfulfilments, exemption from levies I couldn't pay.

I was suckered into buying the place. Serge had advertised it in an English paper, and I'd called him at his hardware store in Lachute, gotten complicated directions, and then headed off one Sunday morning for the Laurentians, up past St-Jovite into Mont Tremblant

Park. It was high summer, cool in the mountains (I drove with the window halfway up), the air was clear and the colours pure, as though I'd just awakened from a nap. The leaves were waxen, not yet dusty. The gravel road branched twice, snaked its way around the rim of Lac Sangsue, then sent off a single trail that rose steeply through an uncleared forest, like a logging road. I peered about for *gros gibier* prancing by the ravine at the edge of the trail. In the first mile there were two cabins, both of tarpaper studded with tin foil. I climbed one last long grade then came suddenly on the lake. There was an extensive marina and dozens of cars were parked over a sandy clearing. Most were foreign and expensive: Mercedes-Benzes, Renault 3000s, Volvos. I drove a VW van and had been feeling, until that moment, properly rustic and prepared. By prearrangement, I sent out three long *ooo-gahs* on the VW horn, and from far across the basin of the egg-shaped lake, a tall bearded man in tan shorts swung his arms over his head then got into his boat and speeded my way.

I said I was suckered. In the keel of the aluminum boat lay two large trout, and propped in the bow were two trolling rods with Daredevil spoons. Serge was about forty-five with stiff black hair and a well-trimmed beard, mostly grey over the chin. 'Just caught them twenty minutes ago – c'mon, you like to fish?'

We sped to his cabin and had a beer. There were two large rooms, one for cooking and eating with floor-to-ceiling windows looking out on the lake, and an elevated unwindowed room with a high-beamed ceiling containing a wood-burning fireplace, bunk beds covered with animal skins, a guncase and some mounted trophies. On the dining table I saw a freshly cut loaf of the round white bread they sell by the roadsides up north, a pot of still warm coffee, and Henri Troyat's *Tolstoi* in Livre de Poche. I'd always wanted to believe that somewhere not too far from where I would settle, *quincailliers* read the classics and fished (and academics worked with their hands and fell asleep sore and exhausted), that nature preserved as well as provided. That there was, in a part of the world I aspired to buy, a different heartbeat from the one that was dwarfing my manhood. Serge gutted the trout, fried the *filets* in garlic and butter, and I swabbed my plate with dabs of fresh bread, as I would after snails in a good French restaurant. We discussed manly things: dressing venison, tracking deer, baking corn and potatoes. I felt like a

Boy Scout. We got back in the boat and Serge hauled up the minnow trap he kept at the end of his dock. He dumped a few minnows into a coffee can, threw out a tadpole that had slithered in and had already sucked the flesh from two minnows' bones, and then extracted a small-ish fish that was three or four times longer than a minnow, and sleeker than a sunfish. *Trout,* I thought: *trout already! Lousy with trout! I'll buy!*

'Ah, just what we need.'

'A trout,' I said knowingly. Cannibalistic brutes.

'No, it's what you say in English?' He snapped its neck and laid it out in his hand. His hand was long, thick, pink-palmed, with old cuts etched in grease. 'Carp, no?'

I almost laughed. Carp, *here?* In this lovely lake? We were circling out beyond his dock, heading at high speed down the middle of a blue mountain lake. Water gurgled under my feet. *Carp are garbage fish.* Where I grew up we used to hunt carp with bows and arrows where the sewer pipes emptied into the river. If the water was clear enough, and the smell not too bad, we could see them below the surface. And where it was really bad we used to shoot at their fat black humps above the water line. Twenty-pound garbage bags. Suckers, we called them. Sewer carp. If we caught one, no torture was undeserved. We cut them, burned them, stuck them, kicked them. Then we nailed them head-down to a tree. Sometimes they'd still be flopping the next morning. I wanted to save my son from that kind of nature.

'Mountain carp,' he said. 'Keeps the lake clean. In Bibitte you got only carp, bluegill and trout. You get your perch in here on your *doré,* and – pfft – there goes your trout. They eat the little trout – see? And trout most of all goes for *this.*' He took my line, the heavy spoon and striped spinner, and then cut it off. He threaded catgut through the dead carp, through the mouth and out the anus, then reattached the cluster of hooks so they nestled at his tail.

'Lethal,' I said.

He winked. On his own spinner he simply attached a longish plastic ribbon, white on one side, with spots. We were under the high bluffs where Germans waved down. 'Your place is just across,' he said. 'That little cabin with the yellow door.' That was the first time I saw it. 'We'll go ashore after we catch your supper.' I was hooked.

There was still time that first summer, it being early July when we bought it, for a lot of indoor camping in the cabin. There was, by communal agreement, no electricity. The cabin had been a fishing camp with a wood-burning stove, an icebox, a pair of iron bunk-frames and rusty springs with giant sodden mattresses that wouldn't burn, and a two-drawered dresser with a blistered top. We brought new things with us on every visit; a two-burner Coleman stove and a cold chest with twenty-five pounds of ice inside. We learned to live on cans of soft drinks, steak and fruit, cereal and powdered milk, and at night after the baby fell asleep, cups of instant coffee on the porch. We bought sleeping bags, a card table, a chemical toilet, lawn chairs and a pump. I threw away the springs and iron frames. I bought hoes, shovels, trowels, scythes and rakes; fishing rods, snorkels, grass seed and paint. Drapes, incinerator and asphalt tiles. An aluminum boat like Serge's, decidedly no motor. I liked to hear the water bubbling under me as I rowed. Each small repair revealed the bigger ones I couldn't yet handle. But that's why I bought the cabin, to gain skills, to become more competent. One summer I would devote to the dock; another to indoor plumbing. Eventually we would build on higher ground, where Serge had already sunk a foundation. That first August I scythed half an acre of virgin grass, picked a dozen quarts of delicious wild raspberries, dug out the little marshes, and lined the cutoffs with rock. Built a retaining wall. I dug out a substantial base for the incinerator, then built a fence around it from the iron poles and rusty springs of the old bunk beds, to keep the raccoons away at night.

After a month it was possible to sit under the naphtha lamp reading Painter's *Proust* at ten in the evening and step out onto the porch with a hot cup of coffee into a blackness primevally bright, stars spread like grains of sugar on a deep purple velvet. If I'd ever felt pride in something I'd done, and in a decision I'd made, it was this. Erika would come out too, sensing I'd left the cabin. If the mosquitoes had not been out, we could have shed our clothes and picked our way cautiously to the dock; we could have sat on the granite boulders and dangled our feet in black water in the dead of night when it seems less cold than daytime. I moved the baby out, bundled up safely, to let him sleep as we talked. But we stood instead on the porch wrapped only in the sounds of water slapping the aluminum boat, wind disturbing the trees, the sharp mosquito whines, and miles away, tunnelled over water and through the mountain ridges, the logging trucks changing gears just outside St-Jovite. That was the peak of my satisfaction.

On the first and last visits, in a summer, I would go alone. Too much work to do, no time for swimming and guarding a two-year-old from the rickety dock and water. I had come to see myself mirrored in my property; each summer I would try frantically to keep pace with nature, even to gain a little. We could live three days comfortably without help or supplies, and we could come and go with little more than a full, or empty, ice chest. We were still years away from Serge's standard, and more years away from my private dream of a hand-assembled cedar chalet (FOB Vancouver, $5,600), but at least we'd never lust for such German comforts as battery-powered television, twin 25-horsepower outboards, and kennels full of yapping lapdogs. I could see how sensible summers could stabilize a winter's excess and suggest humbler ambitions than the manipulation of knowledge.

I went up alone on a Sunday in late September. Few cars were there: Serge's Renault of course, and the Germans' Mercedes. Serge and the Europeans got along, especially in the winter when they staged snowmobile races on the lake. I rowed to the cabin, proud of my summer calluses, the tan, the rightness of owning something and trying to keep it the way it had always been. I beached the boat and pulled it under the porch, turned it over, then chained the prow to one of the pilings. First thing next summer, I told myself, clear out the scrap wood. Reinforce the steps. Paint the porch. I leaned the oars against the cabin, and unlocked the front door. At first I didn't believe what I saw. I sagged against the door and covered my eyes.

A large rock lay in the middle of the sleeping-room floor. The back-window drapes fluttered. Glass crunched and scraped underfoot. The sheets and blankets were chewed to fluffiness. Maybe some dishes were missing, I couldn't tell. My fishing rod still hung above the bed. Thank God, we'd taken home the sleeping bags the week before. The boxes of sugar and cereals were chewed open and littered everywhere. Raccoons, mice; the whole north woods had tramped through the cabin, except that 'coons don't throw rocks. I sat at my card table where the naphtha lamp lay leaking on its side. Hoping almost to hurt myself, I pounded the table. I'd never been invaded, never been stolen from before.

Later, of course, I swept up. After a long time I threw away the rock. The back window had always been shutterless. I had no yardstick to measure the frame; replacing glass would require a *vitrier* paid by the hour, driven in from St-Jovite and rowed to the cabin, sometime next spring in the middle of an academic week. I had only an ax and the old blistered dresser, antique or not. I knocked it down into planks in half a dozen blows. I nailed the drawer-bottoms to the sidings; they covered the hole but it looked like hell. Then I went on with my chores, letting water out of the pump, sealing the chimney flues, storing the oars, latching the other shutters, stripping down the beds, and burning the remains of sheets and blankets and rodent dung with all the splintered wood and cereal boxes. Erika would not have to know.

In the winter I have to think of other things: I dare not believe that Serge still drives to St-Jovite and parks his car for the weekend, then snowmobiles the rest of the way over back trails (chasing wolves, he told me once, finding a deer carcass steaming in a snowbank and circling out from it till he finds the pack); that the snow on the lake is as hard as concrete from the Ski-Doo rallies and the racket must be louder than a dozen sawmills at peak production. Our winter life doesn't allow for dreaming like that.

Spring is always an ugly season in the north; the snows melt slowly and with maximum inconvenience. Ours is not a landscape for unassertiveness; subtleties are easily lost. The stabbing summer green, the blood-red autumn, the pure white death of winter – but not the timid buds, the mud, the half-snow and week-long icy rains of spring. I begin in April to think of the damage up north, the puddles that must have formed under the tons of snow, the ravenous stirring-about of whatever animal spent the winter in my sleeping bag. Ice will float on the lake till the middle of May. Serge will take his ritual swim on the fifteenth of April. I will be marking final papers, delaying till the last possible Sunday the computing of my taxes. On my side of the lake the black flies are thick till the end of June. Erika can't take the flies, her face swells out, her eyes seal shut. Old bites will bleed for weeks. I go up alone on the first of July.

This time, I bring a yardstick. Window putty. All my sharpened tools. My swimming trunks and snorkel. I turn the boat over and haul it into the sun. Cautiously, I open the cabin. It is precisely as I left it: no famished bears, wolverines, caches of dynamite, mutilated corpses, no terrorists playing cards. Just the trapped coolness of winter inside a gloomy little camp with the shutters sealed, on a bright summer Monday with the temperature in the mid-seventies. I wanted to call out to Erika, as though she were with me – as though I had confided all my fears – '*It's safe. We made it through another winter. I'll go out and catch our lunch!*' And I'll say it next week, after I fix the window.

As the vision of liquor lures the drunkard off the wagon, so the lake called me on a hot summer day. I measured the window frame and lifted out the shards of glass, primed the pump, and repaired the broken lamp. I pumped up the Coleman stove and I put water on for coffee. The cabin had warmed up; I changed into my swimming trunks and dug out my snorkel.

As always the water stunned for a moment, one of those expanded moments I'd embraced as the essence of all I wanted from a place in the woods. Pain, astonishment and a swoon of well-being.

I paddled about for a timeless afternoon, snorkelling halfway across the lake, where only hands flashed white and puckered in my vision, then back along the shore near the dock, watching the bottom with its placid carp and bluegills rising to nibble my fingers. The deep exaggerated breathing through the snorkel was the sound of summers on Lac Bibitte. I was my own breath universalized; it was my collective body that drifted over the underwater swarms of tadpoles that rose from the mossy branches. *Cities of tadpoles!* I knew only that my back was burning, that the coffee water had boiled, and that I was ready for coffee on the dock and sun on my face and belly before locking up and heading back home.

What finally happened to me that day is still happening. I remember pulling myself out of the water, drying myself with the towel I'd left on the dock. I felt myself restored. I was going to fish a bit, then maybe measure the loose planks on the dock. I went back inside where the valiant Coleman had boiled a large pan of water, and I stood barefoot on the asphalt tile aware of slivers of glass still about, but feeling too strong too care. Feeling reckless, swimsuit dripping heavily – *plop, plop* – almost thickly, on the floor. I spooned in the coffee, poured the water, snapped off the burner. My back was already registering the heat.

I must have turned about then, coffee in hand, taken a step or two toward the door. Barefoot, I felt something in the puddle of water at my feet. Water was still rolling down my legs. Thinking only of broken glass, I then glanced down at my feet.

In the puddle that had formed as I was making my coffee, three long brown leeches were rolling and twisting, one attached to the side of my foot and the other ones half on the tiles, slithering away. Another *plop* and a fourth dropped from my trunks, onto my foot, and into the wetness. I dropped the coffee, perhaps I deliberately poured it over my feet – I don't remember. I don't remember much of the next few minutes except that I screamed, ran, clawed at my trunks and pulled them off. And I could see the leeches, though I tried not to look, hanging from my waist like a cartridge belt. I swatted and they dropped in various corners of the cabin. I heard them dropping and I heard myself screaming, and I was also somewhere outside the man with leeches, screaming; I watched, I pitied, I screamed and cried.

Even later, when I was dressed and searching the cabin for the dark, shrivelled worms, scooping them up with a coffee spoon and dropping them in the flames of a roaring fire in the stove, my body was shaking with rage and disillusionment. I watched the man with the blistered back sit in his wretched little cabin, burning leeches. After an hour, losing interest, I turned away. I haven't been back since.

Among the Dead

In a certain season (the late winter) and in certain areas (those fringes between the city, and the river that makes it an island) Montreal is the ugliest city in the world. Despite its reputation, its tourist bureaus, most of the island of Montreal will break your heart. Most of us live with broken hearts, thumping little fists constricting our throats. In this, Montreal is truly the Paris of North America. The same bleakness, the same *bidonvilles* stretching for miles beyond the city walls. Our dream had always been salvation and *bonheur*, even knowing that we'd ingested the worst of both worlds: the suspicions and ignorance of the *petit commerçant*, with the arrogant sprawl of America. Therefore, the Québec compromise, cropping up everywhere as *le bongoûtisme québécois*. Drive up the *grands boulevards* of Montreal: Viau, Pie-Neuf, Lajeunesse, Décarie – it's like a walk through those Parisian jungles filled with stalls, rat-faced children and orange-haired women in hagglers' smocks. The difference is space: in Montreal you're in your car and you can drive for miles and the *bongoûtisme* is unrelenting. In the easy targets like Monsieur Muffler and Poulet Frit à la Kentucky, in all those self-appointed *rois des bas prix*, the Gaz, the Chars Usagées, the famous Chien-Chaud Steamé, to the beauty shops where greying heads get the standard Pontiac-Laurentian maroon rinse. Once you climb the containing mountain, or drive east around its flank, you've left the old and beautiful Montreal for good. Following Viau or Pie-Neuf north, you come inevitably to the river, and those vain rows of summer cabins perched over water thicker than most canned soups. You pass miles of flat-roofed duplexes, even where land is cheap and space no problem, a style forgivable only if it were public housing. It is not. Crossing the waters you leave Montreal, arriving on another island – Ile Jésus, consolidated now as the City of Laval – and if you turn directly east off the new Pont-Viau, you come to an old village called St-Vincent-de-Paul (a few abandoned stone houses whose padlocked doors stand five feet off the highway's edge), the true village now a *cantonnement* of gas stations, laundromats, show-rooms and loan offices. And then on the fringes of the village the road suddenly widens, the cheap buildings disappear (federal funds leave immediate traces), and a giant billboard stands off to the left, near the high stone walls and turrets:

1. Pénitencier St. Vincent de Paul
2. Annexe Industrielle
3. Ferme Annexe
4. Unité Spéciale de Correction
5. Institution Leclerc

And there, I turn in.

Because I am a journalist and I want to reach people directly, I volunteered to lead discussions at the prison. Because I work on a liberal paper and I supposedly know more than I can print, and because the prisoners read all the papers but lack the background, my weekly presence was thought to be rehabilitating. Down the road from the village, well beyond the main prison and the two annexes, the Unité Spéciale stands behind a remote tower, in a field of bulldozed snow. Monsieur Paré, the cultural co-ordinator, escorts me through three walls of sliding bars. The thirteen men in bleached blue shirts and brown chino pants pass through a metal-detector and into the classroom. They lock us in. The roof of the classroom is wire mesh; a guard with a shotgun paces the catwalk overhead. This is maximum security. It is a form of perpetual solitary confinement.

Only in the classroom is there relief from *bongoûtisme.* Suave muttonchops and collar-length hair grace the guards' dull broken faces. A subwarden sits resplendent in his pumpkin shirt, silver tie and bottle-green suit. The suit of the cultural co-ordinator shimmers like a garbage sack, over a shrimp-pink tie and Merthiolate shirt. Yet their faces are tight, and grey with distraction.

Three months ago, when I started coming out, I asked for the dossiers of the men in my class. A reporter's prerogative, to hope that facts will match suspicion. They do not. The men have killed for money and sport, in anger and fear, by accident and design. Two Indians killed a fisherman, then cut him up for bait. Others specialized in executions:

lightning raids on east-end taverns in front of witnesses who turned away. One child-rapist, kept here for his own protection. Others made the front pages: FATHER OF SIX KILLED IN ROBBERY HOLD-UP AT ROYAL BANK: GUARD SHOT. All but the child-rapist would have admitted as much. It's the only thing they're proud of.

We are locked in the room for three hours; the guard stands over us, his rifle's shadow, like a cold draft from an unheated cellar, lies flat across the wall. We are each other's hostage, despite the guard and the row of buttons on the wall behind me, despite the rotunda just outside the door where another guard keeps us covered. This is a new society: the ultimate in authority, but recognizable in convention and etiquette, nuance and taboo, madness and waste. It is a society based totally in the present – the future has been legislated out and the past is irrelevant. 'We're the most dangerous men in Canada – DO WE LOOK IT?' 'That button's in case we rush you – DO YOU THINK WE WILL?' No – you don't look like criminals, only like prisoners. Lining them up, who could pick the rapist from the hit-man? Or the journalist? No – they don't act like killers, they're courteous and respectful. Sometimes lucid, sometimes mad with theory and self-instruction. Yet they *could* rush me. They can kill. They don't feel guilt. In some profound way, they cannot be reached. It is a society based on a single premise satisfactory to all: that from nine months before they were born until three days after they die, they will have passed an abbreviated life without ever having been wanted by a single soul. They never had a childhood, nor did they ever grow up.

We are talking today of strikes, or trying to. Not wholly a Montreal phenomenon, but raised here to a kind of perfection. In the past two years we've been struck by nearly everybody, from policemen to garbage collectors, prison guards to air controllers. The prevalence of strikes and the militancy of unions, along with the total absence of control and theory, is a striking example of political *bongoûtisme,* a kind of rampant self-expressionism that quickly becomes a caricature. The prisoners, in one sense, are revolutionaries. WHAT REVOLUTION EVER GOT STARTED THAT DIDN'T FIRST EMPTY THE PRISONS? Who has a greater stake in social change? On the other hand, they've never had much use for working men. They never were on the labour market, they always had buyers for the services they offered; for a man willing to make the effort, Montreal is an embarrassment of riches. Working men are the incarnations of hated fathers, brothers and prison guards. They were always too smart to follow their fathers into a pension of eighty a month, a beer on the gallery when you're too old and sick to enjoy it. Too smart for that Yvon Deschamps world of *'un bon bosse et un jobbe stedy.'* The dreams of the prisoners are more transcendent: a new planet, a new liberated man. These men, who pride themselves on their realism, their shrewdness, their nihilism, bloom like flower-children at the mention of Ouspensky, Gurdjieff, Transcendental Meditation – any form of mysticism that teaches the world is illusion and the imprisoned self can be known, developed and set free. Half the time, even if the guard above us were listening, he wouldn't understand a word. The rest of the time, he might be tempted to start blasting away.

I know their dreams. I too was raised in those flat duplexes. My night light was a ten-watt bulb in the lower ventricle of a plastic *sacrecoeur.* Even as I speak to them of minimum wages and equitable distribution, I see myself a Jesuit instructing the Iroquois. I dream my immolation. For too long our mandate to survive on this continent was derived from what the Iroquois had done to our fathers' confessors. Here we are, the favoured and educated sons of *bongoûtisme,* free of so many old tyrannies – Confederation, America, France, God, the bad old politics, the ignorance – yet the struggle still burns within us. Within me. Socialism appeals to my conservative instincts. Independence, because my heart is broken like everyone else's.

Monsieur Paré escorts me back through the three sliding gates, praising my patience and good-citizenship. Just think, an important man like me, doing it free. The men, they don't appreciate it enough. On the bench in the lobby sits a wife waiting to enter the visiting room. She's in ski-slacks and a fuzzy pink sweater she nervously pulls as she waits. Her hair is chopped straight, tinted the requisite maroon; she looks like a stray from a women's wrestling team, or perhaps the roller derby. Paré nods to her and asks, 'How's Reggie?' then draws me aside. 'You know Reggie? Held up a bank and shot a teller? A year ago? Yesterday he tells the warden he's a political prisoner. Says he did it under orders from the F, L, you know? Now – look what he's got in there. Look –' and he jerks his thumb in the door's direction. 'How do you like that? Keeps his wife waiting while he talks to *them.*'

Them: two emissaries from a volunteer group to aid political prisoners. Two fiery, vital, Gauloise-smoking idealists from the university.
Two staggeringly beautiful, slim, animated girls dressed in proletarian
sweaters and jeans, in oversized tinted glasses, glistening boots, nodding
vigorously at everything Reggie says, laughing with him, believing him
as he's never been believed in his life. Two twenty-year-old students
from homes in Outremont where *bongoûtisme* is nipped at the borders,
while Reggie's wife, the same age and looking twenty years older, sits
sucking a cigarette, tapping her toes to a tune in her head.

'I tell you, my friend, if that was me deciding who was political and
who wasn't in this damn prison, I'd stick him in solitary so fast he
couldn't even say F ... L ... you know?'

That vacant, sullen lump on the bench, shaped by a valiant brassière
and forceful stitching, drops her cigarette and reaches for another. She
was as young and slender as those girls inside, three years ago.

'It's his right, my friend,' I say to Paré. That Créditiste face, those
swirling sideburns. 'Who's to say, any more?'

I know those girls. I have been the husband of Madeleine Lacroix, and if
those girls knew that, they'd drop poor Reggie before any of them could
mouth those three sacred, forbidden initials. Back in university, she was
Midou Tremblay, taking a certificate in physical therapy. I was in political science, even then leaning to journalism. We married and she
worked five years in a hospital where she got her second education, in
politics, and it was more than her background had prepared her for.

'I'm only treating symptoms!' she cried out one night. She'd been
tossing about, breathing loudly, in a way to attract sympathy but repel
attention.

'Of course. You're a therapist,' I said, which was just the answer she
was waiting for.

'No! All of us are treating symptoms. I'm interested in the causes.
The real causes. The colonial causes.'

She was then twenty-six, sitting up nude in bed. She'd determined
suddenly to become a leader, to make herself charismatic. She dressed,
then announced, 'Your paper disgusts me.' She never came back.

It's not a bad paper. It does know more than it dares to print; feels more than it cares to make public. It also has a Paris bureau, and I took it. Three years I stayed in Paris, thinking that what I wrote home some-how mattered, when all that it made me was an easy ironist. I was in Paris while Montreal burned. When I came back, a woman named Madeleine Lacroix was the head of a hospital-worker's local, still as slim as any student, her glasses as wide and tinted, her sweaters just as flat-tering. If, as a therapist, she commanded the lame to walk, they would have no choice. On every level she is the complete radical, living a dream of liberation that no prisoner could envision. Only a husband could.

It is always terrifying to meet a truly hard woman – not hard in the old sense of crude, and not in the new sense of competent and commit-ted – hard as a cinder is hard, as though the fires of transfiguration had already passed through her and what we are seeing is not a person but the brilliant, essential residue. It is a political quality; the politician's cunning likeness to a human being is the most striking thing about him. It torments me that I once loved her, knew her so deeply, watched her slow maturing with pride instead of wonder. As I drive these streets of the North End, she is still beside me and I am still filling her full of startling insider's facts, and she is still stammering, 'But isn't that against the law? Won't they get in trouble?' Even now, driving back down Viau in the pale winter twilight, I want to reach for her hand (how well I know the pattern of veins on her delicate hands: they were always truck-driver thick under the Outremont flesh); I want to catch glimpses of her profile and assure myself that only a sensitive eye – mine – could perceive the beauty that would slowly emerge. It has. It torments me that I was taken in, that I failed to see, that she could change, that *anything* could change so drastically. Not even prisoners change so utterly. Watching her on television with the other political leaders, I wonder if she still behaves the same after sex, if her fingers still bleed in the winter, if she still worries about her thighs. Do her parents still not talk to each other?

Everywhere on the streets I see Madeleine Lacroixs. By the hundreds. Except, perhaps, here on Viau between the river and the Métropolitaine, still the heart of *sacrecoeur* country. Here between the worlds of my dead mother and my ex-wife, where it's almost comic if you can keep your balance. The snow removers have been on strike, and the ploughed-up banks are ten feet high on the shoulders of the road. Narrow chasms have been cut through the snow in front of stores; tiny depressions gnawed through the banks where buses let off reluctant passengers. From some remote perspective, in the depth of winter, the whole city must seem a maze of constricted ruts, like the trails worn through tall grass by herds of buffalo on their way to water. You see, Midou? We're a resistant race, when not transfiguring.

Waiting at the red light with me is a snow-removal truck, one of the fleet of rusting hulks with an unreadable name scrawled on the door and an extra six feet of planking attached to the driver's side above the bed, to break the force of the thrown snow, when the crews are working. The young driver stares down at me, forcing a nod. His smashed-in door is wired shut. Long before the light changes, he roars from the intersection, forcing me to cut back in behind him.

What possible cargo is he carrying? From what, to whom? Window frames with shattered panes, slabs of asphalt sheeting, splintered boards and broken cinder blocks, rusted rolls of wire mesh, and tons of bundled paper, tearing away in a spume of dust. It is as though he is carting the remnants of a dozen chicken-coops. The truck seems a low, brute force of nature, bearing its debris down a potholed boulevard as I helplessly follow, working the windshield washer to keep it all in sight.

I know suddenly that I'm in danger. As though I'd been speeding up steadily, unconsciously, on a sheet of ice, simply because it was smooth and the tires were quiet. I have faith enough in omens to know too late that the truck is a pirate on the streets, out purely to cut and damage. I'm already pulling back, looking for a break in the walls of snow to turn off, when half a cinder block bursts loose from the mounds above me and I helplessly slide in position to receive it. It burrows across the hood like a meteorite, bounces once indecisively, hanging in front of the windshield as I swerve, then skids harmlessly off the fender into the gutter snow. By the time I straighten out, the truck's red lights have already receded. Other cars have taken my place, in cautious pursuit, rushing to embrace the city.

He Raises Me Up

The lone satisfaction is recognizing the comedy. Not that it is funny, being stranded at two in the morning on a deserted cloverleaf in the dead of winter. It is the situation. New car, three hundred miles over the warranty, of course. Two in the morning on a night I'd not worn boots or cap or even gloves. Erika in her party coat and unlined gloves. The cloverleaf desolate as only cold concrete under mercury lamps can be. Merciless quiet. And a car that even I know to be ruined, though freshly waxed that afternoon. First speck of rust, proudly Brillo-ed out. Even with the hood down I can smell the inner damage, the ozone, the thermal clatter, the fusion of once-moving parts.

Comic because of the way I'm dressed, the five dollars (babysitting money) in my pocket, the faith I'd placed in advertising, the simplicity of my dream of merely getting home in a well-groomed car after a *paella* dinner with Haitian friends; like the great comic heroes of the silent films, a simple man oddly dressed with a modest aim of, say, crossing the street. Wind blows his bowler, his skimmer, into what – a woman's purse? Fresh concrete? A baby carriage? Guileless but guilty, before he crosses that street a city will learn to cringe. Some enormous frailty will be exposed: technology, wealth, politics, marriage, whatever organizing idiocy that binds us all together will come flying apart, for the moment. Not funny for the clown, of course; his features remain deadpan, as grim as mine wondering if I should try to start the engine one last time, for heat.

A mile or two down the road a yellow light, the oil indicator, had flashed on. I'd thought it was odd, being low on oil so suddenly. No reason for it, I'd had it changed a thousand miles before, checked at least twice a week. All very proper. Nevertheless, a twenty-four-hour garage had loomed ahead and I drove in to add the oil. It took two quarts and the engine even then was smoking. But I know nothing of motors; neither did the boy who added the oil and checked the stick. I'd driven off, the yellow light didn't object. Two miles later we climbed a bridge and the light went on again. No shoulders, no turning back. I drove on and we landed here at the foot of the bridge, just off a cloverleaf where no one turns.

Cars are an apt measurement of the inner man. Blessed are the carless. Like dwellers in high-rises, their every need at hand, never required to answer an unmonitored door, to touch a shovel, to call a heating company. Never to mow, to paint, to polish, never to fret over plumbing and roof. Radiantly helpless. Fortunate too are the tinkerers, grown men driving around with tool chests in their trunks, those grease-stained knuckles, those teen-age tattoos under the business suits. Rapturously self-reliant. And for the rest of us there comes a moment when we prowl the vacant city in a cashmere coat, doubling back over a deserted bridge where any witness would take you for a potential suicide. Flagging at cars that spray your shoes with a grey pasty slime. *Clown,* you tell yourself. If necessary there's still that garage where you added oil. But your wife is in the car and the garage is still out of sight. Somehow, you feel, the night is all but empty. *All but.* One car, one driver, had seen you. Saw your motor smoking. Saw you leave. Saw your wife in her cocktail dress, bundling the expensive coat tighter around the throat. As you crest on the bridge and start down the far side, he turns on his lights and cruises silently to her, off the cloverleaf where no one turns. By the time you panic and run the half-mile back, red lights recede in the distance. Your wife, unmurdered, lies asleep across the seat. She asks you to stay, now that you're back.

This is the car I had looked after the best. Little noises, little inconveniences, immediately repaired. This is my second car. The first one got us through our student days, my first two jobs, over two kids, our moves across country. It picked up dents that we didn't fix, it ran for weeks low on oil, the floors in the back where I'd never sat or put my feet in seven years had never been cleaned. Grocery slips, trading stamps, newspapers and candy wrappings, shreds of paper diapers, bottom thirds of ice cream cones and the meatless stubs of hot dog buns. When I scraped it clean and hosed it out the day before trading it in (it was a van with eighty thousand miles) I even found some student papers from my first teaching job. It was an indictment of the way we were living, of what we'd become, and I vowed I'd never let it happen again. And since that day seven months ago, I have been meticulous.

Perhaps when your time has come, all the care is superficial. That old indestructible graduate school Volkswagen was my youth, belonging to the years when they paid for my promise, when I carried no insurance, and the government returned more to me than I ever paid in. When teachers said 'Read this' and 'Write that' and the freshmen I taught so indifferently thought I was a god.

Speaking of God, He sends a tow truck off the bridge. I can sense the throbbing yellow light and hear the far-off clunk of chains from a good mile away, and he turns off the bridge a hundred yards from us. I flag him down from the middle of the road, and though he has another couple in the cab (far older than us, a stunned woman of fifty and her embarrassed husband) and a sleek new domestic sedan on his tow (I've lost the knack of identifying the American cars, even the low-priced three are huge these days), he promises to return to me in about an hour. 'Can you start it?' he asks and I tell him I'm afraid to. 'How's the oil?' And I admit that the oil is gone.

'Your motor's jammed.'

'Serious?'

'Finished.'

Seven blissful months I have maintained my posture. Posture in the universe. An oiled, greased, rustless, spotless, vacuumed, silent car. Some exercises for the muscle tone, a diet to bring down my weight. A visit to the dentist for the first time in years, and a settling of the old dental scores that I knew were mounting against me. I'd been aware for over a year that my mouth was botched and those pulpy bitches were all but doomed. And the dentist, like a priest, had confirmed it all.

'What did he say?'

'He said the motor's jammed.'

'Is that serious?'

'He said it's finished.'

This satisfies her. She still trusts.

'Wake me when he comes back,' she says.

Even on that first day when I came in for the professional brushing and X-rays, he'd poked around a bit with a pick, lifting out food, chipping at holes, testing the pavement over the nerves. He's a whistler, my dentist, soft aimless tunes as he drills, as he packs, as he strangles the urge to lecture me, burrowing deeper to pull a nerve. 'You were dying, you know,' he says. Tiny reservoirs of abscess have been draining through the pulp and out the gums, rivulets of poison inching up the nerve canal into the sinus cavity. 'Ah, yes,' he says, turning his back, whistling a bit, 'thinking about your mouth has ruined my day.' A day of special urgency last week, when two canals had to be packed and all my fillings removed. 'It's not just your hygiene, which is bad enough … it's your bite.

'How old are you?'

'Thirty-one.'

He whistles. 'Unless I change your bite, you won't have a tooth in your head five years from today. I'll change the biting surface of every tooth. We'll immobilize your jaw for a day or two, till it loses muscle-memory. You'll need to learn to bite again. Like a child …'

Like the victim of some terrible brain damage.

Stroke.

His car, his teeth. Inescapable indices of the inner man. Not his wife, not his children, not his work – I used to think these things before I was thirty-one. How can she sleep in this burned-out car? How can she be so trusting? How do my children call me daddy – seven years old and he hasn't seen through me yet. The dentist will cost me a thousand dollars – I gambled and lost. Five dollars is all I have for a tow, a taxi and seven hours of baby-sitting. I acknowledge my own defects; no thirty-year warranties yet on the market. And that is the lesson of thirty-one years.

But *this*, this smoking engine, this jammed motor, I will fight. Though I'm three hundred miles over the warranty, my heart is pure and ready to fight. In a cold seizure I see the world composed of symbol, an underlying metaphysics concretely manifest. There is maintenance, for which we are responsible; and the yellow lights, for which we are not. This car has suffered a stroke, a heart attack, in the prime of life, the blowing of a cerebral gasket. Cut down while jogging, aneurysm in the organic garden.

I sense the return of the amber lights, long before they cross the bridge. He pulls off in front, jockeys back at full speed, and skids to a stop inches from my bumper. Erika wakes, clutches my arm before realizing where she is. The bad dream is only starting.

He hooks us up, a grim little Lou Costello, coatless, in overalls. I go out to talk. Penetrating moisture of 4 a.m.; I'd been dry but frozen inside the car, and now I'm shivering. 'Okay, where to?'

'Can you fix it at your place?'

'Buddy – it's jammed. Nobody can fix it.'

'Then dump it at the dealer's.'

'Twenty-five dollars.'

'Take a cheque?'

'Nope.'

'Shell? Gulf?'

'Nope.'

He takes his hand off the winch. Whistles a little tune, bends down to loosen the hooks.

'Look – I don't have twenty-five on me. When I went out tonight I didn't *expect* –'

'Look, buddy. I just turned down three other guys out on the expressway. I don't *need* to take no cheques.'

'But I've got identification. All you need. Look, I could fly to Europe. Tonight. I can stay in a hotel. I can get anywhere. All I need is a tow –'

'You got one of those bank cards?'

'Yes!' I nearly cry out with gratitude. 'Yes, yes.'

He takes it, stamps it in the cab of his truck, 'MAX'S SPORTING GOODS,' and writes in underneath, 'Camping equipment, twenty-five dollars.' No winks, no significant gestures, no more whistling. He hits the switch to tighten the chains. Somewhere deep in the exchange, lies an issue. An important one on a summer night perhaps, about the rights of a victim and consumer. About the arrogance of providers, the frailty of identity. The man is a freelancer, his truck bears no names. A gypsy? Max moonlighting? How many gypsy tow trucks ply the city streets, the bridges and deserted cloverleafs, night after night making hundreds of dollars between midnight and dawn, when, like bats, they disappear?

'That your wife?'

He stops the winch and the chains give an eerie shudder. 'Better get her out.'

'What if we stay in the car?'

He shrugs. 'Not safe.'

'What else?'

'Illegal.'

'We'll stay with the car.'

Erika wakes as I slip in beside her. Through the windshield we see the icy rods of arc lamp, the diffuse brown urban night. The chain rumbles taut, gathered like a spire at the pulley wheel, taller even than the saurian light-standards. The steering wheel jerks sharply as we follow the curve of the cloverleaf, back to the city. How peaceful is this surrender, stretched out on the front seat, feet up, head against the cool, moist window, holding Erika in both arms, swaying in the metal sling of my broken car.

Words for the Winter

September, month of the winding down. For a month we've lived the charade of ruddy good health up in the mountains north of Montreal. Swimming, rowing, tramping up the mountain just behind our cabin, baking trout over the coals at night. Drinking from the last pure-water lake in the Laurentians, reading by sunlight on the dock, sleeping in the cool mountain air from dark till the sunrise at 5 a.m. This is how I dreamed it would be: water, trout and mountains. And in this small way, I have succeeded.

Serge rows over around seven o'clock with two large trout, cleans them in our sink, and Erika spices them for baking. It was Serge who built our cabin and half the others on the lake after his family opened it up for exploitation. He's a Peugeot dealer in St-Jovite with a beard and a sordid past, and in the compulsive way of people who have painfully come through, he tells us about his failures, his vices, his present contentment. Like most reformed sinners and drinkers I've met, he is a mystic. 'This lake, you know,' he tells us in English, for emphasis, 'he save my life. Every weekend now for ten year I am coming to him by myself. Without him, I am a dead man. Three time already, I am a dead man.'

I have seen the scars. A knifing from his *voyou* days in Montreal. A cancerous lung. His heart. But he's a fit man now. He makes me feel that I'm only a teacher too young to have suffered and deserved the lake, but too old to ever learn the proper physical skills. To buy this cabin I simply answered a newspaper ad, got into his boat and saw those trout he'd caught that morning. As we talk, he cuts little wedges of pine to shore up our cabin and make the door fit tighter. He cuts cardboard to make the pump airtight. Unobtrusive skills I'll never master. Lurid stories I can only hope to copy, of gamblers in Acapulco, jail terms, a bankruptcy, an oath in an oxygen tent to be reborn.

The city lies an hour and a half to the south. We drop six hundred feet

97

and gain two weeks of summer. A stagnant dome of dust and fumes squats over the city. September is still hot, street smells penetrate closed windows. It is a street of tenement, some of greystone, some of dark brick, some with porches, and some with the traditional winding outside staircases of old Montreal. The neighbourhood has been French, then Jewish, then Italian and now Greek, with Chinese and West Indians waiting their turn. A Ukrainian Church, a *yeshiva,* an Esso station, and a Greek grocery store bracket the street. We rent a nine-room flat in the three-story tenement. The flat across the hall has been subdivided; a large and violent family of Greeks in the back four rooms, two students and a Jamaican night watchman in the front three rooms, with one kept as a dining room, equipped with a stove and fridge. Above us a commune of hippies; above them, a nameless horde of student-age workers, French-Canadian, who often fight. In the single basement flat lives an extended family of Jamaicans with uncountable children all roughly the same age. Our four-year-old son plays with two of theirs; rugged, gentle boys of five and seven.

The winters are an agony. In January our broad summer street narrows to a one-lane rut, an icy *piste de luge* banked by walls of unmovable cars. I stand with the Greeks and West Indians at the bus stop, wrapped in double gloves, double socks, and a scarf under my stocking cap, stamping my feet under a fog of human warmth. We stand like cattle in a blizzard, edging closer than we would in summer, smoke and vapour rising through the wool, each of us dreaming of heat and coffee. The Greeks and West Indians must want to die.

You survive by subtraction. Pick a date: March 15, say. The coldest days bring wind and an arctic sun, much suffering, but one day less. Warmer days, those above zero, inevitably bring snow – and one day less. Some time in January we enter the trough, two weeks of winter torpor when pipes burst and cars give out and the wind cuts viciously through the flat, rattling under the doors and around the windows – your tongue could stick to those icy windows – and water could boil on the ancient radiators. The sky is a pitiless, cloudless blue, and tons of sulphur are pushed into the shrunken air. The day is reached when the city voluntarily closes down. You cancel classes like everyone else, you eat whatever you find in the fridge, your child has a nosebleed every few minutes. It's then you think of your landlord in Florida, of your own days before coming here, when winter was short and bracing, a good time for steady work. Your students hobble to classes on their *après-ski* plaster casts – proud souvenirs of the climate they love. You think of the rings of winter that surround Montreal: caribou foraging north of the mountains, men in the mining camps, timber wolves riding the flatcars into the city, holing up in the cemeteries and living on suburban strays. We are in the dentist's chair for another forty days. Even Erika sleeps late, turns in early, and admits to constant headaches. Christopher suffers his nosebleeds and hasn't been out in twenty days. The mice have left us alone. The Jamaican children come up to play, riding tricycles through our endless flat.

Only the mailman still makes it through. By the time one of us dresses warmly enough to step out to the mail-slots, our letters have already been fished out of the mutilated slot – years of theft have left the brass doors buckled – and have been ripped into tiny pieces and dropped like an offering outside our door. Letters from Germany, computerized cheques and bills. I know who does this: the Greek girl across the hall. She will go to stores for you. She will play with your boy when she finds him alone. And she will steal his toys and kick the smaller Jamaican girls when she finds them alone. Last summer her father beat her in the hall, in front of me and the Laflamme kids who live next door; a slim scar-faced tyrant whose wife stood behind him, looking at her fingers. Laflamme's kids howled with pleasure, *'Ooo, Irène va pleurer!'* but she didn't, not for the moments that I could bear to watch. I wanted to protect her, for whatever she'd done, that bruised furtive little thing with the Anne Frank face. That cheat, that thief, that cunning wretched child.

I buy the traps six at a time and throw the whole thing out, when successful, in a single grand gesture, wasting a garbage sack but feeling cleaner. Laflamme's kids pick up all the sacks on garbage nights, and I've watched them, in their curiosity, untie the empty ones and dump out the mouse and trap, lift spring and kick the mouse aside; thus saving a trap and garbage sack to take back home.

There are worse things than mice. The lake has taught us to live with black flies and leeches. Now the mice have lost their power to offend. Kit is fascinated, leaves peanuts for them in old jar lids. At night we hear the dragging of the lids, the busy tapping of tiny claws on the ancient linoleum. One got trapped with a peanut half-expelled. Their fur bloodless, eyes unclotted, they seem merely frozen in gesture. I'm almost afraid to lift that clamp from their neck, for fear if I did they'd rise to bite me, or slide unconscious up my sleeve.

This evening I was reading in the living room, the large front double room that looks out over the street. There came a tapping so low and rhythmic that I absorbed it into my reading. I hadn't wanted to leave the chair. But the tapping persisted and I knew it came from closer than I wanted to admit, from the parlour behind the sliding doors, where we keep the summer tires and suitcases. I could see the leather lid of Erika's suitcase panting from inside, as though it had an embolism. It was her old belted bag from Germany, the one she kept her secrets in, everything portable and priceless from her first twenty years. I could picture the inside of that bag as though I had x-ray vision, the mouse-nests of shredded paper. For a moment I allowed myself to think exactly what it meant about us, about me. I have stained her with the froth of mice, their birth and death, in all my dreams and failures.

I bent to touch the suitcase and a single mouse leaped out, squeezing between the lid and clasp where she'd forgotten to re-cinch the belts. A small black one. Without opening the lid, expecting to hear the chirping of a dozen more inside, I cradled the suitcase like a baby in my arms and carried it down the hall past Erika who was reading in the bedroom. I placed it flat in the dry bathtub. She followed me in, standing at the door.

'Did you kill it?'

'There may be more inside,' I said.

The flat is long and cheap and full of pests. Four usable bedrooms and a dining room, a double living room, kitchen, and two studies. It costs us ninety dollars a month, plus heat. We took it at my insistence, after Erika decided to quit her job and return to school. I wanted to sink into the city, to challenge it like any other immigrant and go straight to its core. We painted everything when we moved, put down rugs and tried to grow plants. At night, by muted lamp, with our leather chairs, white tables, colourful paintings, the front room looks beautiful. But the rest of the flat has defeated us.

I return to the parlour. No squeals from the closet, but I open it anyway, knocking the old shoes with a tube of Christmas wrapping paper, and the black little thing scurries out, under the door to the hall and down the hall past the bathroom, with me in pursuit. 'Mouse in the hall,'

Erika calls out in an even voice, still on her knees and lifting papers out of the tub to give them a shake and a repacking. The mouse darts into the dining room, under the radiator where the linoleum has lifted and there must be a hole. I've spoken to Laflamme about it – he refused to act without the landlord's directive, and gave me a box of steel wool instead. 'Stuff it under there,' he said, 'it's mouseproof.' And the landlord stays in Florida until the first of April.

I can hear the mouse under the radiator. I can see the old lids they've dragged underneath.

'No mice,' she announces from the bathroom. 'But *do* something.'

She snaps the locks, tightens the belts. I poke twice with the cardboard tube, but it's too thick to reach all the way.

'If there'd been mice in there I would have left you.'

I'll have to force him out. The pipes are scalding hot.

'There are some things that would kill me,' she says.

We have D D T in the back, an old aerosol can for roaches, and I fetch it. She wouldn't leave, not literally. But she would retreat a little further, which is worse. Some things would kill me, too. There are old droppings on the pantry shelves where we store only hardware. Cold drafts along the wood – there's a hole somewhere, Monsieur Laflamme. *Il y a un trou dans la … dans le … pantry?* Moving here was going to perfect my French, which remains what it always was: a nicely polished vintage car poking along a new expressway. A danger to myself and others. A tall can of Raid, cold to the touch, might do the trick. I lay down a cover of spray, until my eyes smart and the coughing begins.

'What are you spraying?' she calls.

'Guess.'

'Is that you coughing – or it?'

Best not to speak. Better indeed to kill, with my shoe if necessary. First come the roaches, staggering up the walls and falling back. I hear activity under the coils, I see a shadow slinking along the moulding, around the clumps of steel wool, in the shadow of the drapes and television. A slow shadow I prod once with the cardboard to knock into the open. He can barely walk, his front paws splay, his back legs drag. I douse him again from six inches out till his black coat glistens and he stops for good. His eyes are shining, his motion arrested, and he could kill a city of bugs by walking among them. I spray again, idly, and he doesn't move. I get a garbage sack and spread its top; then, the other tube of wrapping paper and chopstick the mouse into the sack. There is a puddle of Raid beneath him, reflecting light like a lake of gasoline. If I had the man's Florida address, I'd send him this. I will move Erika's bag, then wash.

In the spring of this year, a tragedy. Nikos, a quiet boy of six who often played with the Jamaicans in our building, fell to his death from the second-floor balcony next door. I'd seen him sitting on the rail eating his lunch, and I'd waved. A second later he flashed silently across my vision, a white shirt striking the muddy yard with a whip-sharp crack. I was the only witness. I was afraid to touch him; his body heaved in agonies that seemed adult, one leg kicking in and out. I was screaming on the silent street, 'Ambulance! Police! *Au secours!*' and the street slowly bristled to life. Women who never came out opened their doors and ran toward me, those squat Greek women with their hands flat on their cheeks as they ran, and I was still over the body screaming, 'Did you call for help? Did you call the police?' but they fought to get to the boy. A single word was passed, *Nikos, Nikos,* and wailing began from the steps to the sidewalk as I pushed an older woman back. 'Are you the mama? *Nikos's mama?*' but I didn't think she was and I pushed her till she fell. 'Listen to me. Understand. His neck is broken. He cannot be touched –' But they were like the insane, their faces twisted around their open mouths and accusing eyes. *Oh, God, I had dreamed of loving the Greeks,* and now I wished to annihilate them. One of theirs lay injured and I stood accused – a man, a foreigner, tall and blond – and they attacked. From below my shoulders they leaped to hurl their spittle, to scratch my face, to rip my shirt and trenchcoat. I was consumed with hatred for them all, a desire to use my size and innocence, my strength and good intentions, to trample them, to will them back to Greece and their piggish lives in the dark. They pecked like a flock of avenging sparrows, and one finally broke through to throw herself on the child and roll his body over.

Her scream was the purest cry of agony and sorrow I have ever heard. In the distance, a siren. The women let me go; all they had wanted was to scream. I gained the sidewalk and started walking. I felt a pity for us all that I had never felt before. Next to me stood Irene, the mail thief from across the hall.

'Who was it that fell – Nickie?' she asked.

She kept up with me. I was almost running.

'He was a dumb kid anyway,' she said.

'Try to think better of him now, Irene.'

'He's my cousin. You should see the toys he's got up there. And he's a crybaby.'

'He didn't cry this time, Irene, so cut it out.'

'Those old women – wow, they really gave it to you, eh? I heard them talking and they thought you did it. They thought you're the devil or something – really crazy, eh?'

We were walking up the steps to our building, a father and daughter to anyone passing. 'Irene – who's going to tell his mother?'

'I don't know. My ma is her sister. His pa went back to Greece a long time ago. That was pretty stupid of him playing up on the balcony like that, eh?'

For a moment, in my hatred, I thought she'd done it; shades of *The Bad Seed*, she'd been up there all along taking his toys and making his morning miserable. But no one had left the building. Accidents were still possible, even here. We were standing by the mail-slots. Our letters, as usual, lay shredded on the steps.

'Irene – tell me one thing. Why do you tear up our mail?'

'Who says I do that? It was Nikos did it.'

'Don't lie. I'm not going to hit you. I want to know *why*.'

Her voice was a woman's; her face, Anne Frank's. 'Okay. I'll tell you. But I won't say it again. Nikos said we should do it. I told him about the way you waited for the mail all the time. So he thought that would really get you mad. It was him that did it. See if it happens again.'

'Listen: Nikos was an innocent little kid. You're the one that knows how to hurt. And you know I wouldn't go to your father because of what he'd do to you. You know I disapprove of that even more than stealing.'

'Boy, you sure must think I know a lot,' she said. 'I don't even know what you're talking about.' And with that she extracted a key from her purse and disappeared, singing softly, behind the outer door of her apartment.

Late April rain, the snow is down on the west-facing slopes. Our mail has been left alone. I am learning to appreciate small favours: mail, mouselessness, the stirrings of spring. I enter the apartment carrying two bags of groceries, and walk directly to the kitchen to begin unloading. I'd kicked the door shut, but left the key ring dangling outside. Then I went out again to fetch Kit from downstairs and drive down to McGill to pick up Erika from the library – and I discovered that the keys were gone. Stolen. No car keys, no way now of getting back inside. Even Laflamme was useless since we'd never trusted him with a spare key. I went downstairs and found Kit drawing on cardboard boxes that he and his friends had hauled in from the alley. The basement apartment is the worst I've seen, with a ceiling that drips, broken plaster, linoleum worn through to the mossy boards and children everywhere, holding sandwiches as they play. They have no furniture, only beds and a table to eat from. I ask the mother and the eldest daughter if I can leave him there while I take a bus to find my wife, to get a key.

'Daddy – I want to go with you,' he calls, running to the door and dropping his peanut butter sandwich.

'You can't, dear. It's still cold and you don't have a coat.'

'Get my coat.'

'That is something I cannot do. You'll have to stay. Now let me go.' He's clutching my trenchcoat, suddenly aware that I'm leaving him behind and not just letting him play.

'Kit – let go.'

He gives a jerk just as I try to break free; I feel the seam of my trenchcoat opening up, tearing like a zipper as Kit and his friends giggle. 'Goddammit!' I scream and before I know it I've freed my coat and seized him by the shoulders and begun to shake him violently. 'I told you to let go, I told you twice. Why can't you listen! What do I have to do to make you listen?' His face is inches from mine and white with terror. In his eyes I can read his hope that I'm only playing, and I want to stamp that out too. '*Understand?*' I give him a final shake. Limp in my arms he belches, and part of his sandwich comes heaving out.

I run from the basement, from Kit's screaming, the twin halves of my trenchcoat flapping on my back like the pattern for an immensely fat man's pair of pants. *My keys, my keys.* Car, house, office and cabin. The locker in the basement, the trunks in the locker. The cabin is elaborately locked; I will have to smash a window. The car is locked, rolled up tight.

Again a window. The front of my shirt is stained, the Greeks at the bus stop are staring at me.

At this moment, Irene must be in the flat. There is much to steal that we will never miss. Something infinitely small but infinitely complicated has happened to our lives, and I don't know how to present it – in its smallness, in its complication – without breaking down. I who live in dreams have suffered something real, and reality hurts like nothing in this world.

Going to India

A month before we left I read a horror story in the papers. A boy had stepped on a raft, the raft had drifted into the river. The river was the Niagara. Screaming, with rescuers not daring to follow, pursued only by an amateur photographer on shore, he was carried over the falls.

It isn't death, I thought, it's watching it arrive, this terrible omniscience that makes it not just death, but an execution. The next day, as they must, they carried the photos. Six panels of a boy waving ashore, the waters eddying, then boiling, around his raft. The boy wore a T-shirt and cut-off khakis. He fell off several feet before the falls. Who would leave a raft, what kind of madman builds a raft in Niagara country? Children in Niagara country must have nightmares of the falls, must feel the earth rumbling beneath them, their pillows turning to water.

I was raised in Florida. Tidal waves frightened me as a child. So did 'Silver Springs', those underground rivers that converge to feed it. Blind white catfish. I could hear them as a child, giant turtles snorting and grinding under my pillow.

My son is three years old, almost four. He will be four in India. Born in Indiana, raised in Montreal – what possible fears could he have? He finds the paper, the six pictures of the boy on a raft. He inspects the pictures and I grieve for him. I am death-driven. I feel compassion, grief, regret, only in the face of death. I was slow, fat and asthmatic, prone to sunburn, hookworms and chronic nosebleeds. My son is lean and handsome, a tennis star of the future, and I've tried to keep things from him.

'What is that boy doing, Daddy?'

'I think he's riding a raft.'

'But how come he's waving like that?'

'He's frightened, I think.'

'Look – he felled off it, Daddy.'

'I know, darling.'

'And there's a water hill there, Daddy. Everything went over the hill.'

'Yes, dear. The boy went over the water hill.'

'And now he knows one thing, doesn't he, Daddy?'

'What does he know?'

'Now he knows what being dead is like.'

2.

A month from now we'll be in India. I've begun to feel it, I've been float-ing for a week now, afraid to start anything new. Friends say to me, 'You still here?' not just in disappointment, more in amazement. They've already discarded the Old Me. 'Weren't you going to India? What hap-pened – chicken out?' They expect transmutation. 'I *said* June,' I tell them, but they'd heard April. 'I'd be afraid to go,' one friend, an artist, tells me. 'There are some things a man can't take. Some changes are too great.' I tell him I *am* afraid, but that I have to go.

I never cared for India. My only interest in the woman I married was sexual; that she was Indian did not excite me, nor was I frightened. Convent-trained, Brahmanical, well-to-do, Orthodox and Westernized at once, Calcutta-born, speaker of eight languages, she had simply overwhelmed me. We met in graduate school at Indiana. Both of us were in comparative literature, and she was returning to Calcutta to marry a forty-year-old research chemist selected by her father. Will you marry him? I asked. Yes, she said. Will you be happy? Who can say, she said. Probably not. Can you refuse? I asked. It would be bad for my father, she said. Will you marry me? I asked, and she said, 'Yes, of course.'

It was Europe that drove me mad.

Five years ago I threw myself at Europe. For two summers I did things I'll never do again, living without money enough for trolley fare, waking beside new women, wondering where I'd be spending the next night, with whom, how I'd get there, who would take me, and finally not caring. Coming close, those short Swedish nights, those fetid Roman nights, those long Paris nights when the *auberge* closed before I got back and I would walk through the rain dodging the Arabs and queers and drunken soldiers who would take me for an Arab, coming close to say-ing that life was passionate and palpable and worth the pain and effort and whoever I was and whatever I was destined to be didn't matter. Only living for the moment mattered and even the hunger and the insults and the occasional jab in the kidneys didn't matter. It all reminded me that I was young and alive, a hitchhiker over borders, heedless of languages, speaking just enough of everything to cover my needs, and feeling responsible to no one but myself for any jam I got into.

I would have given anything to stay and I planned my life so that I could come back.

Not once did I think of India. Missionary ladies from Wichita, Kansas, went to India. Retired buyers for Montgomery Ward took around-the-world flights and got heart attacks in Delhi bazaars. I was only interested in Europe.

At graduate school in Indiana I was doing well, a Fulbright was in the works, my languages were improving, and a lifetime in Europe was drawing closer. Then I met the most lushly sexual woman I had ever seen. Reserved and intelligent, she confirmed in all ways my belief that perfection could not be found in anything American.

But even then India failed to interest me. I married Anjali Chatterjee, not a culture, not a subcontinent.

3.

When we married, the Indian community of Indiana disowned her. Indian girls were considered too innocent to meet or marry Western boys although hip Indian boys always married American girls. Anjali was dropped from the Indian Society, and only one Indian, a Christian dietician from Goa, attended our wedding. So the break was clean, my obligations minimal. I had her to myself.

Her parents were hesitant, but cordial. Also helpless. They had my horoscope cast after the marriage, but never told us the result. They asked about my family, and we lied. To say the least, I come from uncertain stock. My parents had been twice divorced before divorcing each other. Four of the five languages I speak are rooted in my family, each grandparent speaking something different, and the fifth, Russian, reflects a secret sympathy that would destroy her parents if they knew. I have scores of half brothers and sisters, cousins-in-law, aunts and uncles known by the cars they drive, or by the rackets they operate. My family is broad and fluid and, though corrupt, fabulously unsuccessful. Like gypsies they cover the continent, elevating a son or two into law (a sensible precaution), some into the civil service, others into the army and only one into the university. My instructions for this trip are simple: do not mention divorce. My parents are retired, somewhat infirm, and comfortably off. After a while we can let one die (when we need the sympathy), and a few months later the second can die of grief. They will leave their fortune to charity.

4.

E. M. Forster, you ruined everything. Why must every visitor to India, every well-read tourist, expect a sudden transformation? I, too, feel that if nothing amazing happens, the trip will be a waste. I've done nothing these past two months. I'm afraid to start anything new in case I'll be a different person when I return. And what if this lassitude continues? Two fallow months before the flight, three months of visiting, then what? What the hell is India like anyway?

I remember my Florida childhood and the trips to Nassau and Havana, the bugs and heat and the quiver of joy in a simple cold Coca-Cola, and the pastel, rusted, rotting concrete, the stench of purple muck too rank to grow a thing, too well to ever be charmed by the posters of palms and white sand beaches. Jellyfish, sting rays, sand sharks and tidal waves. Roaches as long as my finger, scorpions in my shoe, worms in my feet. Still, it wasn't India. Country of my wife, heredity of my son.

Will *his* children speak of their lone white grandfather as they settle back to brownness, or will it be their legendary Hindu grandmother, as staggering to them as Pushkin's grandfather must have been to him? Appalling, that I, a comparatist who needs five languages, should be mute and illiterate in my wife's own tongue! And worse, not to care, not for Bengali or Hindi or even Sanskrit.

I thought you were going to India –

I am, I am.

But –

Next week. Next week.

And don't forget those pills, man. Take those little pills.

5.

We are going by charter, which still sets us back two thousand dollars. Two thousand dollars just on kerosene! Another two thousand for a three-month stay; hundreds more in preparation, in drip-dry shirts, in bras and lipsticks for the flocks of cousins; bottles of aftershave and Samsonite briefcases for their husbands. A complete set of the novels of William Faulkner for a cousin writing her dissertation. Oh, weird, weird, what kind of country am I visiting? To prepare myself I read. *Nothing could prepare me for Calcutta,* writes a well-travelled Indian on his return. City of squalor, city of dreadful night, of riots and stabbings, bombings added to pestilence and corruption. Somewhere in Calcutta, squatting or dying, two aged grandmothers are waiting to see my wife, to meet her *mlechha* husband, to peer and poke at her outcaste child. In Calcutta I can meet my death quite by accident, swept into a corridor of history for which I have no feeling. I can believe that for being white and American and somewhat pudgy I deserve to die – somewhere, at least – but not in Calcutta. Receptacle of the world's grief, Calcutta. *Indians, even the richest, are corrupted by poverty;* Americans, even the poorest (I add), are corrupted by wealth. How will I react to beggars? To servants? Worse: how will my wife?

6.

I know from experience that when Anjali dabs the red *teep* on her forehead, when the gold earrings are brought out, when the miniskirts are put away and the gold necklace and bracelets are fastened to her neck and arms (how beautiful, how inevitable, gold against Indian skin), when the good silk saris with the golden threads are unfolded from the suitcases, that I have lost my wife to India. Usually it's just for an evening, in the homes of McGill colleagues in hydraulics or genetics, or visitors to our home from Calcutta, who stay with us for a night or two. And I fade away those evenings, along with English and other familiar references. Nothing to tell me that the beautiful woman in the pink sari is my wife except the odd wink during the evening, a gratuitous reference to my few accomplishments. The familiar mixture of shame and gratitude; that she was born and nurtured for someone better than

I, richer, at least, who would wrap her in servants, a house of her own, a life of privilege that only an impoverished country can provide. One evening I can take. But three months?

7.

Our plane will leave from New York. We go down two days early to visit our friends, the Gangulis. To spend some money, buy the last-minute gifts, another suitcase, enjoy the air-conditioning, and eat our last rare steaks. I've just turned twenty-seven; at that age, one can say of one's friends that none are accidental, they all fulfil a need. In New York three circles of friends almost coincide; the writers I know, the friends I've taught with or gone to various schools with, and the third, the special ones, the Indo-Americans, the American girls and their Indian husbands.

Deepak is an architect; Susan was a nurse. Deepak, years before in India, was matched to marry my wife. She was still in Calcutta, he was at Yale, and he approved of her picture sent by his father. One formality remained – the matching of their horoscopes. And they clashed. Marriage would invite disaster, deformed children most likely. He didn't meet her until his next trip to India when he'd gone to look over some new selections. Alas, none were beautiful enough and he returned to New York to marry the American girl he'd been living with all along.

Deepak's life is ruled by his profound good taste, his perfect, daring taste. Like a prodigy in chess or music he is disciplined by a Platonic conception of a yet-higher order, one that he alone can bring into existence. Their apartment in the East Seventies was once used as a movie set. It is subtly Indian, yet nothing specifically Indian strikes the eye. One must sit a moment, sipping a gin, before the underlying Eastern-ness erupts from the steel and glass and leather. The rug is Kashmiri, the tables teak, the walls are hung with Saurashtrian tapestries – what's so Western about it? The lamps are stone-based, chromium-necked, arching halfway across the room, the chairs are stainless steel and white leather, adorned with Indian pillows. It is a room in perfect balance, like Deepak; like his marriage, perhaps. So unlike ours, so unlike us. Our apartment in Montreal is furnished in Universal Academic, with Danish sofas and farm antiques, everything sacrificed to hold more books. The Who's-Afraid-of-Virginia-Woolf style.

But he didn't marry Anjali. I did. He married Susan, and Susan, though uncomplaining and competent, is also plain and somewhat stupid. Very pale, a near-natural blonde, but prone to varicosed chubbiness. An Indian's dream of the American girl. And so lacking in Deepak's exquisite taste that I can walk into their place and in thirty seconds *feel* where she had been sitting, where she'd walked from, everything she'd rearranged or brushed against. Where she's messed up the Platonic harmony even while keeping it clean. Still, Deepak doesn't mind. He cooks the fancy meals, does the gourmet shopping: knows where to find mangoes in the dead of winter, where the firmest cauliflower, the freshest *al dente* shrimp, the rarest spices, are sold. When Deepak shops he returns with twenty small packages individually wrapped and nothing frozen. When Susan returns it's with an A & P bag, wet at the bottom.

When the four of us are dining out, the spectators (for we are always on view) try to rearrange us: Deepak and Anjali, Susan and me. Deepak is tall for a Bengali – six-two perhaps – and impressively bearded now that it's the style. He could be an actor. A friend once described him as the perfect extra for a Monte Carlo scene, the Indian prince throwing away his millions, missing only a turban with a jewel in the centre.

How could he and Anjali have a deformed child?

I'm being unfair. He is rich and generous, and there is another Deepak behind the man of perfect taste. He told me once, when our wives were out shopping, that he'd tried to commit suicide, back in India. The Central Bank had refused him foreign exchange, even after he'd been accepted at Yale. He'd had to wait a year while an uncle arranged the necessary bribes, spending the time working on the uncle's tea estate in Assam. The uncle tried to keep him on a second year, claiming he had to wait until a certain bureaucrat retired; Deepak threw himself into a river. A villager lost his life in saving him, the uncle relented, a larger bribe was successful and Deepak the architect was sprung on the West. He despises India, even while sending fifty dollars a month to the family of his rescuer.

But his natural gift, so resonant in itself, extends exactly nowhere. He rarely reads, and when he does he confines himself to English murder mysteries. He is a man trapped in certain talents, incapable of growth, yet I envy him. They eat well, live well, and save thousands every year. They have no children, despite Susan's pleading, and they will have none until the child's full tuition from kindergarten through university is in the bank. While we empty our savings to make this trip to India. We'll hunt through bazaars and come up with nothing for our house. There is malevolence in our friendship; he enjoys showing me his New York, making the city bend to his wishes, extracting from it its most delicate juices. We discuss India this last night in America; aside from the trips to land a wife, he's never been back. And he won't go back, despite more pleading from Susan, until his parents die.

8.

None of Deepak's restaurants tonight: it is steak, broiled at home. Thick steaks, bought and cut and aged especially, but revered mainly for wet red beefiness. 'Your meat *chagla*,' he calls out from the kitchen, spearing it on his fork and holding it in the doorway, while Anjali, Susan and I drink our gin and our son sips his Coke. A *chagla* is a side of beef. 'Normally I use an onion, mushroom and wine sauce, but don't worry – not tonight. Onions you will be having – bloody American steak you won't.'

The time is near; two hours to lift-off. Then Deepak drives us to the airport because he says he enjoys the International Lounge, especially the Air-India lounge where any time, any season, he can find a friend or two whose names he's forgotten, either going back or seeing off, and he, Deepak, can have a drink and reflect on his own good fortune, namely not having to fly twenty-four hours in a plane full of squalling infants, to arrive in Bombay at four in the morning.

And so now we are sitting upstairs sipping more gin with Susan and Deepak, and of course two young men run over to shake his hand and to be introduced, leaving their wives, who are chatting and who don't look up....

'Summer ritual,' he explains. 'Packing the wife and kids off to India. That way they can get a vacation and the parents are satisfied and the wives can boss the servants around. No wonder they're smiling....' Looking around the waiting room he squints with disgust. 'You'll have a full plane.'

No Americans tonight, the lounge is dark with Indians. We're still in New York, but we've already left. 'At least be glad of one thing,' Deepak says. 'What's that?' I ask. He looks around the lounge and winks at us. 'No cows,' he says.

No, please, I want to say, don't laugh at India. This trip is serious, for me at least. 'Don't ruin it for me, Deepak,' I finally say. 'I may never go over again.' 'You might never come back either,' he says. We are filing out of the lounge, down a corridor, and up a flight of stairs. Anjali and Deepak are in good spirits. Susan is holding our son, who wants another Coke.

'... and the beggars,' Deepak is saying. '*Memsahib,* take my fans, my toys, my flowers, my youngest daughter –'

'– then suddenly a leprous stump, stuck in the middle of the flowers and fans,' says Anjali.

'Maybe that's India,' I say, 'in an image, I mean.'

Deepak and Anjali both smile, as if to say, *yes, perhaps it is. Then again, perhaps it isn't. Maybe you should keep your eyes open and your mouth shut.* And then we are saying goodbye, *namaste*-ing to the hostess, and taking our three adjoining seats. India is still a day away.

9.

'Listen for the captain's name,' says Anjali. Need I ask why? Anjali's erstwhile intendeds staff the banks, the hospitals, the courts, the airlines, the tea estates of Assam and West Bengal. They are all well-placed, middle-aged, fair-completed, and well-educated Brahmins.

'D'Souza,' we hear. An Anglo-Indian, not a chance.

'I heard that Captain Mukherjee is flying for Air-India now,' she tells me. 'He was very dashing at Darjeeling in '58, flying for the air force.' Another ruptured arrangement.

There are times when I look at her and think: She, who had no men before me will have many, and I, who had those girls here and there and everywhere even up to the day I married but none after, will have no more, ever. All of this is somehow ordained, our orbits are conflicting, hers ever wider, mine ever tighter.

This will be a short night, the shortest night of my life. Leaving New York at nine o'clock, to arrive six hours later in London's bright morning light, the sunrise will catch us east of Newfoundland around midnight New York time. During the brief, east-running night two businessmen behind me debate the coming British elections. Both, as Indians, feel sentimental toward Labour. As businessmen, they feel compromised. They've never been treated badly. Both, in fact, agree that too many bloody Muslims have been admitted, and that parts of England are stinking worse than the slums of Karachi or Bombay. Both will be voting Tory.

In the absurd morning light of 3 a.m. while the plane sleeps and the four surly sari-clad hostesses smoke their cigarettes in the rear, I think of my writing. Flights are a time of summary, an occasion for sweating palms. If I should die, what would I make of my life? Was it whole, or just beginning? I used to write miniature novels, vividly imagined, set anywhere my imagination moved me. Then something slipped. I started writing only of myself and these vivid moments in a confusing flux. That visionary gleam: India may restore it, or destroy it completely. We will set down an hour in London, in Paris, in Frankfurt and even Kuwait – what does this do to the old perspectives? Europe is just a stop-over, Cokes in a transit room on the way to something bigger and darker than I'd ever imagined. Paris, where I survived two months without a job; Frankfurt where six years ago I learned my first German – *wo kann man hier pissen?* How will I ever return to Europe and feel that I've even left home? India has already ruined Europe for me.

10.

From London we have a new crew and a new captain: His name is Mukherjee. Anjali scribbles a note to a steward who carries it forward. Minutes later he returns, inviting Anjali to follow him through the tiny door and down the gangway to the cockpit. Jealous Indians stare at her, then at me. And I, a jealous American, try to picture our dashing little captain, moustached and heavy-lidded, courting my wife when he should be attending to other things.

She stays up front until we land in Paris. My son and I file into the transit room of Orly, and there in a corner I spot Anjali and the captain, a small, dark, sleepy-looking fellow with chevroned sleeves a mite too long for his delicate hands.

'Hello, sir,' he says, not reaching for my hand. He holds a Coke in one, a cigarette in the other. 'Your wife's note was a very pleasant distraction.'

'Nice landing,' I say, not knowing the etiquette.

'Considering I couldn't find the bloody runway, I thought it was. They switched numbers on us.'

'So,' I say. 'You're the fam –'

'No, no – I was just telling your wife: you think that I am Captain *Govind* Mukherjee formerly Group Captain Mukherjee of the IAF. But I am Sujit Mukherjee – regrettably a distant cousin – or else I would have met this charming lady years ago. I was just telling your wife that Govind is married now with three children and he flies out of Calcutta to Tokyo. I *knew* she was not referring to me in the chit she sent forward and I confess to a small deception, sir – I hope I am forgiven –'

'Of course, of course. It must have been exciting for her –'

'Oh, exciting I do not know. But disappointing, *yes,* decidedly. You should have seen the face she pulled spotting Sujit Mukherjee and not Govind –' Then suddenly he breaks into loud, heavy-lidded laughter, joined by Anjali and a grey-haired crew member standing to one side.

'This is my navigator, Mr Misra,' says the captain. 'Blame him if we go astray.'

'And this is our son, Ananda,' I say.

'*Very* nice name, Ananda. Ananda means happiness.'

'Are you the driver?' Ananda asks.

'Yes, yes, I am the *driver,*' the captain bursts into laughter, 'and Misra here is my wiper,' and Misra breaks into high-pitched giggles. 'Tell me, Ananda, would you like to sit with us up front and help drive the plane?'

'Would I have to go through that little door?'

'Yes,'

'No,' he says decisively. He holds my hand tightly, the captain and navigator bow and depart, and then we go for a Coke.

Somewhere out there, I remind myself, is Paris.

11.

Back in the plane the purser invites me forward; Captain Mukherjee points to the seat behind him, the rest of the crew introduce themselves, a steward brings me lemonade, and the plane is cleared for leaving the terminal. Then an Indian woman clutching a baby bursts from the building, dashes across the runway waving frantically.

'Air-India 112 – you have a passenger –'

'Stupid bloody woman,' the captain says under his breath. 'Air-India 112 returning for boarding,' he says, then turns to me: 'Can you imagine when we're flying the jumbo? Indians weren't meant for the jumbo jets.'

Then the steward comes forward, explaining that the woman doesn't speak Hindi, English or Tamil and that she doesn't have a ticket and refuses to take a seat. The only word they can understand is 'husband'. The captain nods, heavy-lidded, smiling faintly. 'I think I should like a glass of cold water,' he says, 'and one for our passenger.' He takes off his headphone, lights a cigarette. Turning fully around he says to me: 'We have dietary problems. We have religious problems and we have linguistic problems. All of these things we prepare for. But these village women, they marry and their husband goes off to Europe and a few years later he sends for them. But they can't read their tickets and they won't eat what we give them and they sit strapped in their seats, terrified, for the whole trip. Then they fall asleep and we can't wake them. When they wake up themselves they think they're on a tram and they've missed their stop, so they tell us to turn around. London, Paris, Rome – these are just words to them. The husband says he will meet her in Paris – how is she to know she must go through customs? She can't even read her own language let alone *douane*. So she goes to the transit room and sits down and the husband she's probably forgotten except for one old photograph is tapping madly on the glass and when the flight reboards she dutifully follows all the people –'

'Captain, someone is talking to her.'

'Fine, fine.'

'She is to meet her husband in Paris.'

'Did you tell her this is Paris?'

'She won't believe *me*, Captain. She wants you to tell her.'

'Misra – take my coat and go back and tell her.' To me he adds, 'She wouldn't believe I'm the captain. Misra makes a very good captain with his grey hair. Where is my bloody ice water?'

'Yes, Captain. Right away, Captain.'

Moments later we are taxiing down the runway, gathering speed and lifting steeply over Paris. The Seine, Eiffel Tower, Notre Dame, all clear from the wraparound windows. And, for the first time, my palms aren't sweating. Competence in the cockpit, the delicate fingers of Captain Mukherjee, the mathematical genius of Navigator Misra, the radar below, the gauges above. I settle back and relax. Below, the radar stations check in: Metz, Luxembourg, Rüdesheim, Mainz. I recognize the Rhine, see the towns I once hitchhiked through, and bask in the strangeness of it all, the orbits of India and my early manhood intersecting.

We descend, we slow, and Frankfurt appears. We turn, we drop still lower, slower, 200 miles per hour as we touch down. Everything perfect, my palms are dry again. It's been years since I felt such confidence in another person. The silence in the cockpit is almost worshipful.

The ground-crew chief, a grey-bearded Sikh, comes aboard and gives the captain his instructions for take-off, which the captain already knows. The weather conditions in Kuwait: 120° with sandstorms. Mukherjee nods, smiles. I ease out silently; *namaste*-ing to the captain and crew, thanking them all as they go about their chores.

12.

Within an hour we are farther East than I've ever been. Down the coast of Yugoslavia, then over the Greek islands, across the Holy Land. What if the Israelis open fire? Those SAM missile sites, Iraqi MIGs scrambling to bring us down. Trials in Baghdad, hanging of the Jewish passengers. India is officially pro-Arab, an embarrassment which might prove useful.

This was the shortest day of my life. The east is darkening, though it's only noon by New York time. An hour later the stars are out; we eat our second lunch, or is it dinner? Wiener schnitzel or lamb curry. Ananda sleeps; Anjali eats her curry, I my Wiener schnitzel.

'After Kuwait things will deteriorate,' she says. 'The food, the service, the girls – they always do.'

We've been descending and suddenly the seat-belt sign is on. Kuwait: richest country in the world. City lights in the middle of the desert, and an airfield marked by permanent fires. Corridors of flames flapping in a sandstorm and Captain Mukherjee eases his way between them. Sand stings the window, pings off the wings like Montreal ice.

'The ground temperature is forty-five degrees centigrade' the hostess announces, and I busily translate: 113° F.

'The local time is 10:00 p.m.'

I whisper to Anjali, '"I will show you fear in a handful of dust…"'

'Through passengers ticketed on Air-India to Bombay and New Delhi will kindly remain in the aircraft. We shall be on the ground for approximately forty-five minutes.'

I can feel the heat through the plastic windows. Such heat, such inhuman heat and dryness. I turn to Anjali and quote again:

> 'Here is no water but only rock
> Rock and no water and the sandy road…'

A ground crew comes aboard. Arab faces, one-eyed, hunched, followed by a proud lieutenant in the Kuwaiti uniform. These are my first Muslims, first Arabs. They vacuum around our feet, pick up the chocolate wrappers, clear the tattered London papers from the seats. It's all too fast, this 'voyage out', as they used to call it. We need a month on a steamer, shopping in Italy, in Cairo, bargaining in the bazaars, passing serenely from the Catholic south to the Muslim heartland, thence to holy, Hindu India. The way they did it in the old novels. In Forster, where friendship and tolerance were still possible. No impressions of the Wasteland in a Forster novel. No one-eyed, menacing Arabs. But Forster is almost ninety, and wisely, he remains silent. The price we pay for the convenience of a single day's flight is the simple diminishment of all that's human. Just as Europe is changed because of India, so India is lessened because of the charter flight. I'm bringing a hard heart to India, dread and fear and suspicion.

13.

We are in the final hours over the Persian Gulf and the Arabian Sea, skimming the coast of Iran then aiming south and east to Bombay. Kuwait gave us children who play games in the aisles, who spill their Cokes on my sleeve. Captain Mukherjee, Misra and the crack London crew ride with us as passengers; the new stewardess is older, heavier, and a recent blonde. No one sleeps, though we've set our watches on Bombay time and it is suddenly three o'clock in the morning.

'Daddy will be leaving for the airport now,' says Anjali.

I've never met her parents. They've flown 1,500 miles to meet us tonight, to see us rest a day or two before joining us in the flight back to Calcutta.

'The airport will be a shock,' she says. 'It always is.'

'Anything to get off this plane.'

Three-thirty.

Ananda has taken the window seat; he sits on his knees with his face cupped to the glass. He's been to India before, three summers before. He's forgotten his illness, remembers only an elephant ride and a trip to the mountains where he chased butterflies up the slopes.

Twenty minutes to India. I can feel the descent. Businessmen behind me agree on the merits of military rule.

'*Ladies and gentlemen –*'

The lights go on, a hundred seat belts buckle on cue. Lights suddenly appear beneath us. There are streets, street lamps, cars, bungalows, palm trees. My first palms since Florida – maybe I'll like it here – and we glide to a landing, our fifth perfect landing of the day.

Everyone is standing, pulling down their coats and baggage. I'd forgotten how much we carried aboard (three days ago, by the calendar): a flight bag of clothes for Ananda, camera equipment, liquor and cigars for my father-in-law, my rain hat and jacket, our three raincoats and two umbrellas. We put on everything we can and then line up, facing first the rear and then the front, clutching our passports.

'*Ladies and gentlemen, we have landed at Santa Cruz Airport in Bombay. The local time is 4:00 a.m. and the temperature is 33° centigrade …*'

'Over ninety,' I whisper.

'It's been raining,' she says.

As we file to the front and the open door, I can feel the heat. My arms are sweating before I reach the ladder. An open bus is waiting to take us to the terminal. No breeze, s r o. The duty-free bag begins to tear.

I follow our beam of light across the tarmac. A man is sleeping on the edge of the cement, others have built a fire in the mud nearby.

'Tea,' Anjali explains.

Other thoughts are coming to me now: not the howling sand of Kuwait – *mud*. Not the empty desert – *people*. Not the wind – *rain*. I want to scream: '*It's four in the bloody morning and I'm soaking with sweat. Somebody do something!*' Even in the open bus as we zip down the runway there's no breeze, no relief. Anjali's hair, cut and set just before we left has turned dead and stringy, her sari is crushed in a thousand folds. This is how the world will end.

We are dropped in front of the terminal. Families are sleeping on the steps. Children converge on our bus, holding out their hands, making pathetic gestures to their mouth. I have a pocket full of *centimes* and *pfennigs* from this morning's stops, but Anjali frowns as I open my hand. 'They're professionals,' she says. 'If you must give to beggars wait at least till you get to Calcutta.' They pull my sleeve, grab Ananda by the collar of his raincoat, until a man behind us raises his hand. 'Wretched little scum,' he mutters. They scatter and I find myself half-agreeing.

We have come inside. Harsh lights, overhead fans. Rows of barriers, men in khaki uniforms behind each desk, desks laden with forms and rubber stamps. The bureaucracy. Behind them the baggage, the porters squatting, the customs, more men, more forms. Then the glass, the waiting crowd, the parents, the embraces, the right words, the corridors. *I'm not ready*, I want to scream, *turn this plane around*. I've stopped walking, the passports are heavy in my hand. I've never been so lost.

'Darling, what's the matter?' she asks, but she has already taken my hand, taken the passports, the declarations, and given me the flight bag in their place. Ananda stands before me, the beautiful child in his yellow slicker, black hair plastered to his forehead. I take his hand, he takes Anjali's, and I think again: *I'm not prepared*, not even for the answer which comes immediately: and if you're not, it says, who is?

Translation

1.

At forty-three, Porter, *né* Carrier, feared he was sick again. The warning came at night with a vision and an odour just as it always had. Debbie suspected nothing. She was mincing tuna for a week's supply of sandwiches. He loved the sound of a long silver spoon knocking the sides of an empty mayonnaise jar.

He said, 'For the first time in my life, I really know that I'm going to die. It's a profound awareness.'

She didn't look up. 'Am I disagreeing?' She'd been spending most weekends with him for the past two years. She would soon be thirty.

'It's the way you're looking in that bowl.'

'Philip, how do you *want* me to look into a bowl of tuna fish? Let me translate what you're saying. You're saying that you read in a paper today that someone who meant the world to you when you were fourteen years old just died.' She looked up, smiling wickedly for confirmation. 'You're the proverbial ear in the forest, don't you know? The one that actually hears every tree that falls? It's okay, Porter, it's okay to die.'

'You'll find more mayonnaise in the pantry.'

'If every man's death diminished me the way it does you – God, I'd disappear!' She licked mayonnaise off her knuckles. 'But you don't actually diminish, do you? You're no anorexic. I'm sure you grieve in your way, but it keeps you going.'

Much as Porter loved her most days, he knew the relationship was ending. Not because of her reaction, which was appropriate. It was ending because of the vision.

Dying had been a spectacle, something older people did for his pity or instruction. Death had been mowing down the radio greats of his childhood and the holdover politicians of the New Deal, then the actors his parents had thrilled to and the boys of his happiest summers when he'd been a child and they'd been in their prime. And now there was no gap left. He'd sung their songs, thrilled to their debuts, made love to them in his dreams. He'd been standing at the end of a long queue, bored by how slowly it moved, but now the soft shuffle of the quotidian had taken him to the ticket stand and the open doors of a darkened theatre.

'People I've loved are dying,' he said.

'Porter, dear, you have many lovable traits. But please don't tell me you know what it is to love.' She smeared two Ry-Krisps with tuna salad. 'Not that it matters.'

He'd heard it often enough. Until Amy, his first wife, left, Porter had thought himself a deprived, embittered man capable of great tenderness. She taught him he was a sophisticated lover from a privileged background, lacking none of the graces except a core of essential decency.

2.

His childhood dream had been of a glacier, or at least of something cold, mountainous and inexorable bearing down on him. He could hear and even see through its gelatinous distortions the grinding of boulders and forests, and he could smell the scorched, catastrophic swath of natural pavement in its path.

He would wake, often screaming. It moved a foot a year, and he couldn't outrun it. He always woke when the ice touched him with its scalding cold. When flesh met glacier they were fused, like a tongue to an ice tray.

His mother would be holding him and by then extracting the wooden spoon she kept at his bedside. He would bury his aching head in her breast, and she would hold him, swaying.

'The glacier again?' and he would nod. 'See, there's nothing out there.' He wouldn't open his eyes. After those attacks colours were too bright to bear, and the odours of the world all bordered on rottenness. It was as though life were offering a putrefied version of itself for his eyes and nose only.

Those were the attacks at night in sleep. In the day his nose would fill with a sweet, burnt odour, and colours would turn red like ageing film and kids would say, 'Hey, Porter, I'm talking to you!' Sometimes he'd find himself on the floor or on the ground, his muscles numb from supreme exhaustion.

But all of that ended thirty years before.

Why now should life suddenly turn perilous? He went to his doctor for the first time in three years. Since his last visit he'd cut down his drinking to a few beers a week, had gum surgery and three crowns put in and lost thirty pounds. He jogged twenty miles a week and in the winter lifted weights and swayed to calisthenics. The doctor declared him 100 per cent fit, a model of 1980s self-reclamation. America was seeing a generation of potential centagenarians.

'By the way,' he asked, 'what are you guys pushing for epilepsy?'

'Doing another story, Porter?' Porter had not been totally honest with his doctor. He'd never been honest with anyone. When he was forced into magazine writing between novels, he found the doctor an enthusiastic collaborator. He'd helped him with 'Mid-Life to Mod-Life', 'Toward a More Perfect Carcinogen', and his steroids piece, 'Higher, Faster, Stronger...Dumber?'

'I'd heard that epileptic medicine can slow you right down to idiocy. If they'd treated Dostoyevski – no *Crime and Punishment.*'

'No way,' said the doctor. 'Any new medicine comes on stronger at the beginning than it needs to be – look at the first birth-control pills, the Salk vaccine, the tranquillizers. The first generation anti-convulsants might have turned him into a zombie for a few weeks, but we'd have had him driving a car inside a month.'

'That's very reassuring. And now?'

'Designer doses, Porter. Tegratol, Dilantin, some phenobarb at night. We'd have nailed it. What are you writing?'

'I was thinking of giving a character a very heavy curse.'

'Diabetes is good,' the doctor mused. 'Mainstream, too, with lots of paraphernalia. Or what about Huntington's chorea? That can *really* ruin your day.' Porter's doctor conferred imaginary disorders with greater enthusiasm than ever went into their healing.

'Let me get back to you,' he said.

3.

One day Debbie was making tuna salad and inviting him to parties, and a few weeks later she was busy in Manhattan with her children. A month after that she announced she wanted to go to Europe for spring break, alone.

He wasn't even disappointed. In marriage most men are tempted early and often by other women. Porter loved women, but his great temptation was solitude. Amy had called him a libertine monk. Debbie left him in February. Snow was deep; he doubled his calisthenics and bench-presses and set August as the date for the delivery of his novel. After five earlier books of stories and two novels with child and adolescent characters, this was to be his wet-winged emergence into the adult world of marriage and poisonous self-knowledge. He was not unhappy, in his bitter, private way, that no one would be interfering with his ridiculous little schedules.

He lived in a cottage in Duchess County. Amy had kept their old house in Binghamton, their kids were on scholarship, and with a pasta diet, a garden and few vices, he could just about live on his writing. The nearest town was Poughkeepsie, where Debbie taught. He went into New York when he had good reasons.

According to many who knew him, Porter wasn't altogether sane. He'd been a professor, then had changed jobs, surrendered tenure, taken pay cuts and finally come to the conclusion – logical under the circumstances – that the remaining obligations were too strenuous, underpaid and insecure to keep at all. He taught for a while as an adjunct in metropolitan campuses with 'at' in their titles. The self-destruction had cost him a marriage.

During the February thaw, the dripping icicles and the hiss of wet tires on the exposed blacktop outside the cottage lured him into three days of bonus running. He valued the accretion of small details and the web of images that clung to him as he ran. He loved the things of this world, passionately. He loved activities like running that stimulated a disinterested scrutiny. Running was like writing a short story, a familiar habit begun in pain but ending breathless and exultant. Weight-lifting, so dramatically exerting, so ambitious, was like writing novels.

As he ran that first day looking at the early buds on the trees and hedgetips, he realized he couldn't name a single tree in English. He'd probably never known them in French – there hadn't been many trees in his life as a Carrier. They all existed in some abstraction of treeness. He was a writer, after all, and to name was to know. All he knew for certain was childhood in Pittsburgh and adolescence in Montreal, plus some articles aided by a doctor's vocabulary.

He smelled it again, a putrescence in the world, as though a winter's worth of carcasses had been shovelled to the roadside.

He took three days off for a trip to the city, uncharacteristically, to check out the movies and bookstores. When he got back to his typewriter, the novel was cold.

4.

Thirty years before when he'd been x-rayed at Pittsburgh General, the neurologist had termed his epilepsy 'trauma-induced', meaning that a childhood injury – a skull fracture at the age of three – was the probable cause. And with adolescence the skull might achieve adult contour, and he could be free of seizures for the rest of his life.

It had returned a day or two after the thaw. He'd been writing in bed – still his position for serious work – when he'd noticed a puddle of coffee on his sheets and the mug overturned in the blanket. The coffee was almost cold.

He'd known many people like himself – arrested cancer victims, one-time cardiac patient, recovered alcoholics – who'd mastered the etiquette of daily gratitude. They never planned, they never deferred. Gratitude had never been Porter's style, but he heard himself praying over the coffee stains, *Please, God, don't let it come back. Let me finish this one last book, that's all I ask.*

In response, God pinged him lightly a second time. Like mice and returned cheques, seizures came in clusters.

The medicine he'd taken all his childhood had made him slow. It hadn't been until his rebirth as Philippe Carrier in Montreal that the curse had disappeared. His high school had classified epileptics with the insane and retarded. There'd been a girl, Marie Bolduc, nicknamed *la tordue*, who'd been taken around to classes strapped in her wheelchair where she sometimes slumped and stiffened ten times an hour. Her neck was one enormous muscle. The sisters never caned her, despite her blatant disruptiveness and frequent inattention, though they were not above using her as an example of God's wrath, or His mercy.

She'd been the first death in his life, the first of his generation to go under. Laid out to her full length in the open casket, neck cushioned against the satin, she'd been a tall, pretty girl. Some of his classmates had snickered, half-expecting the coffin to give a sympathetic lurch. He'd snickered louder than any of them.

When he returned to his novel after that seizure and the memory of a distant funeral Mass (having epilepsy, he'd once written of a character, was like writing with a ballpoint pen that occasionally skipped), his arm was numb, his fingers cold and tingling, and he found it immensely hard to catch up with his thoughts. He remembered perfectly the gelatinous, unresponsive, mental fatigue of epilepsy. He remembered feeling like a human glacier, an obstruction, slow and brutish. In the depths of his brain he could smell fresh ironing, and he caught a glimpse of a woman in a bathrobe who disappeared before he could recognize her.

When he next looked at his novel, it was dead. He didn't recognize the writing, he couldn't even imitate it. He turned a page and wrote three sentences that had nothing to do with anything he'd ever written:

The sons of suicides bear a graceless burden. She let go of my hand as the bus approached. 'There's something I must do,' she said, and pulled away.

5.

And so it was not to be the novel that made Porter relatively rich and famous; it was *Head Waters,* an autobiography. During his years as a professor he'd often lectured on autobiography, calling it a maligned and poorly described art form that attracted more than its share of hacks. 'The self-biographers,' he'd termed them, those who saw their own lives as miniature histories, who began their books with the fatal words, 'I was born ...' as though life had not existed before them, and the glory and pain of self-consciousness – the true subject of all autobiography – were not finding the niche where one fit, but clearing a site for the shopping-mall of the self. Porter called autobiography the democracy of bafflement. Every success reinvented the form.

He refused all medication while he wrote. He was forced to spread pillows under his chair. He glued a strip of foam rubber to the metal rim of his typewriter, and he gave up trying to drive.

Because he even feared walking into the village for food (twice he'd fallen, spilling his groceries, and once he'd wakened to see tire tracks across his loaf of bread), he took in a woman. Her name was Petra, a Middle European who assisted in Vassar's Russian program. She was forty and had never married. Sex between them was infrequent and barely satisfying. Porter felt himself diminishing as a man, disappearing into his infirmities and literary graces. He made love like an old man seeking comfort. From one of those early encounters, Petra got pregnant. Porter counselled abortion (half-heartedly; his soul was deeply Catholic), and in their second year Petra and his daughter stayed weekends and came over twice a week.

Hannah was an old-fashioned little girl: wide-eyed, well behaved, Old World. Even as a pre-toddler she sat on the breakfast table while her mother cooked, playing with silverware and paper plates, never dropping them on the floor, never straying over the edge. Her isolation and intensity frightened him. He thought, 'Hanno Buddenbrooks,' and felt she was doomed, a dead end, the last Carrier, the last Simonovska. She had taken her mother's name. He'd resigned his role in this second family. He doubted he'd live much beyond her early schooling.

Petra never intended marriage or motherhood. Yet in some strange and uncharacteristic way, he had *courted* her. She had arrived as a companion, a cook, a driver; he had forced the issue. She mentioned that her previous experiences with men were less frequent than those with women, but her deepest drives were, like his, private, studious, uncommunicative.

He wondered if Hannah would grow up to reflect on the absurdity of her birth, that in a normal world she would never have been. She owed her life to his epilepsy. Would it shock her? Amuse her? She was a child of accident and calculation; she never cried, never whined, took delight in spoons and glasses and started violin and piano lessons before she was three. She stared at the world like an intent Anne Frank, with a face perfectly composed and adult. Even if he was forced to leave her early he could see exactly how she'd look twenty years down the line.

6.

Some time in his forty-fifth year Porter asked his body, 'Okay, what do you want? What are you trying to tell me?'

He'd been studying his face in the bathroom mirror. Of course he'd aged, lost weight, and his hair and whiskers were greying. But it was the cuts, the scabs, the myriad nicks and tiny bruises he suddenly noticed; like a drunk's. The dozens of small stumblings, the sprains and burns and confused looks from everyone but Petra that indicated to him he was having more episodes than he'd even suspected. The ballpoint pen was running out of ink.

An interviewer came over from Boston, and Porter must have blanked out in the middle of a question. When he'd come out of it the interviewer was saying to his sound man, 'We'll go back to where I ask, "Why did you leave Montreal and return to the United States?"' And to Porter he'd said matter-of-factly, 'Would you like a glass of water?'

Porter, still confused, had mumbled, 'Montreal can break your heart.'

But now his body was giving no answers, 'My head's shrinking, is that it?' The skull was closing in ever so slightly. There had to be a message in it. In rational, pain-free moments he caught glimpses of his disease like a shadow leaving the room the second he snapped on a light. He could almost catch it, almost smell it (the smell of ironed clothes turned sour), and once or twice alone in his cottage he heard himself shouting. 'Stop, you!' and his mind tried to lock on the shadow. It was *possession*, wasn't it, just as the ancients and the conjurers had always said – a devil to be cast out. At least that was one alternative.

Once in his teen years in Montreal, an orphan living with whores and working in a strip joint, young Carrier had dragged himself to a free clinic, complaining of fatigue, weight loss, stomach pains, bleeding and worst of all, *a sense of evil*. The nun had taken down the symptoms, pausing a while on *malaise globale*, but otherwise moved by his distress and orphaned state.

'Where do you live?' the doctor had asked.

'Around,' he'd answered, not wishing to compromise the janitors who let him sleep in basements and the girls who gave him food and a bed in their off-hour mornings. Those had been his *célinesque* years in Montreal, when the city had finally made sense to him.

The doctor was listening to his stomach. 'What are you eating?'

'Whatever I can get,' he'd answered. Waitresses would sneak it out. He was only seventeen.

The doctor seemed to be addressing the nun. 'I would say this young man is harbouring a serpent in his bowels.' Then he turned to Carrier. 'A worm, understand, young man? You may well have thirty feet of tapeworm swimming around down there – no wonder you're weak and bleeding. Its head is chewing into your stomach, and by now it's taking four-fifths of everything you eat. And it's *still* not satisfied. So we'll feed it a little something extra.'

Carrier's complaint was not uncommon in the slum clinics of Montreal in the mid-fifties. The doctor had free samples in his drawer, and the effects, he warned, would be dramatic.

'If you are in the habit of gazing fondly at your stool, I would strongly advise against it for the next three weeks,' he said.

Porter, remembering the chunks of the beast as they passed through him, thought again of purgation, and something in his deeply Catholic soul responded. *I've got you, you bastard.* He tapped his temple. *You can run, but you can't hide.* He put away his razor blade – no use taking chances – he'd let his beard grow out, white or not. He looked into his eyes so closely he could almost see the beast behind them.

Hiding, are you?

I'm taking you home, baby.

7.

Porter dreaded the Canadian border. The simplest questions of an immigration officer were the imponderables of his life: What is your name? Where were you born? What is your nationality? If Porter had a demon in his brain, taking it to Montreal was like poking a stick in its cage. He didn't have a passport and couldn't get one. Canada was the world for Porter; America was all there was for Carrier.

Head Waters had been a success in several languages. Philippe Carrier's *Les Sources de mémoire* had been a local best-seller for Éditions d'aujourd'hui. They'd wanted him to go on the talk shows in Montreal, but he'd refused. 'Ah, we understand, M'sieur Carrier,' the publisher had said. 'We're very small, and we can't afford to pay you well.' It wasn't that, but better they thought it was. The simple truth was that he was an illegal alien, just as his father had been, and sooner or later, given publicity, questions would be asked.

Often he'd had to rehearse his border crossings. He'd work on his accent, seeking to match it to his New York plates and licence. In his bus-riding years, he would go up to Montreal as fun-loving Phil Porter, and return to the States as humble Carrier, down to visit a cousin. He was always afraid the officer would ask him first, 'Where were you born?' instead of 'Where do you live?'

Phil Porter, in reality, did not exist. No such person had ever been born. 'Porter' had been his father's fiction, easily dropped when cornered (*coincé*, in fact, was his father's favourite word), but Porter had been trapped in it. Like any threatened faith, it now seemed all the more precious. He held an American social insurance card under one name, and a Canadian social insurance card under another. It was a complicated little drama, but one that suited him. For this trip in the summer of his forty-sixth year he'd flown in as Phil Porter, Expos fan, for a week of baseball.

This isn't my city, he told himself in the airport bus. *It was Carrier's city. It's all an accident.* Let it go. False intimacies can kill. Acknowledged attachments bring only bills and sentimental cards on Father's Day. Bills he willingly paid for the privacy they bought.

The infinite perversity of life – as the nuns would say – was that the sincere involvements undertaken with a dream of permanence, marriage and fatherhood, had deserted him. Only the coldest and most brutal, Petra and Hannah, showed any sign of lasting. And one other. One other chunk of flesh that inhabited his body and possessed his mind *still*. Porter, a man of few attachments, was haunted by unbearable intimacies. Even a French rock station listened to by a Haitian taxi-driver lit cells in Porter that were floodlights in Carrier's cave.

8.

He met Florence Lachance, the publicist for his publisher, in a small Lebanese restaurant in a remodelled area behind the Main. It was a hot day, and she wore a T-shirt and jeans, with the publisher's logo over her modest bosom. Across her back was a picture of his book. It didn't concern him.

'They've loved it,' she said, riffling through a packet of reviews. He was called, in a casual translation, not quite a cultural chameleon, more a ... what? Newt? Mud-puppy? Thanks a lot.

'They're calling you a new Kerouac,' she went on. 'There's a word they use at the university – *porterisme* – for a kind of special Quebec tragedy.'

He read a long review more closely. To its author he was an intermediate cultural life-form, not slimy by intention like Monsieur Trudeau, not a cultural chameleon like the Ottawa mandarins, but a permanent, arrested cultural larva with lungs for land and gills for water.

She watched him frown and reached across to tap his hand. 'Oh! Not *you*, M'sieur Carrier. It's the *situation* you describe. Ten years ago people would have said it's what happens when you're just a colony. They would have called you *vendu*. Now they see we're all like ... those things. I can't say the word.'

'Axolotls,' he said. He thought: I *am* my condition.

She giggled. She looked so chagrined he wanted to hold her. The role of publicist for a Quebec publishing house seemed so cosy and absurd, so *sincere* and guileless, that he felt light-headed with remorse.

Les fils des suicides supportent un fardeau sans grâce.

'Who's this Madeleine Choquette?'

Florence squinted and asked, 'Seriously? Madeleine Choquette?' As though he'd asked, Who's this Wayne Gretzky character?

'She begged us to let her do you. You'll meet her.'

'A writer, then?'

'One of the important writers. She's also very well known in France. People compare your book with hers all the time – maybe you don't like that? Do they ask you that – why you don't come back? Why you don't write in French?'

'All the time,' he said, lying graciously. No one in the States knew or cared that he'd had a double life. Most Americans couldn't really conceive of it, and most of those who did couldn't conceive of its being French-Canadian. They were talking in French, but his French, he wanted to say, wasn't good enough. It had once been a thin, elastic membrane, transparent and stuffed with words. Now it was a loose sack of familiar phrases, a duffel bag to drag along on trips to Montreal. *Fardeau* or *charge*? *Supporter* or *appuyer*? What's wrong with good old *porter*, 'to carry'? Hell would be having to make a conscious choice, like a translator, between dozens of perfectly serviceable likenesses for every phrase of every sentence.

He could tell, looking at her in her blue-tinted glasses, at her confused little frown and her nervous way with a cigarette, that she'd asked another question while he'd ducked under his unspeakable little cloud.

'Can I get you anything?' she whispered.

'Now you know something else about me. Not just an axolotl, but an axolotl with epilepsy.'

A familiar path doubling over. He wondered if he was doomed to enter a violent convulsive stage, as he had when he was eleven and twelve back in Pittsburgh. Would he be driven all the way back to the battering when he was three, was he doomed to repeat it all?

She recovered graciously. 'We have an interview with Corinne Carrier at Radio-Canada. You'll like her, and she knows Madame Choquette. She'll introduce you, M'sieur Carrier.'

Carriers and Smiths, thought Porter. Everything in Quebec was sooner or later connected, everyone eventually related. So much so that the names were interchangeable, like Changs. Only a fool or a foreigner would assume an actual, blood connection.

9.

In the buried years that Carrier had lived in his uncle Théophile's flat, his cousin Dollard, two years older, had been his window on an intolerable future. Dollard had dropped out of school at fourteen and worked at a series of manual jobs, digging and filling, until Théophile's political and church connections had gotten him on the city payroll. He was sent to work as a *fossoyeur* at Côte-des-Neiges Cemetery, the Vatican City of digging and filling. By that time, Carrier and his parents had left Théophile's flat and found a smaller one of their own a few miles west on Snowden. His father sold kitchen equipment in a restaurant-supply house on the Main. His mother had started substitute teaching in the Protestant schools all over the western parts of the island.

And then his father disappeared. Not exactly vanished – he first got in practice by making himself scarce. He would come home to sleep in the middle of the week, but wouldn't show up on weekends. Fishing, he said, or hunting, knowing that his wife didn't approve of either, or the men he did it with. Then he disappeared altogether.

Carrier and his mother moved into two rooms near McGill. She wanted him to transfer to a Protestant English school before his French Catholic allegiance cost him his soul, and her job. 'Before it's too late,' she always put it, but he fought her. He was sixteen; the brothers wanted him to go to Laval.

One day after school young Carrier took a trolley over to the restaurant-supply store. It was a Jewish place, but the men inside spoke every language on the Main. His father spoke a pretty fair Yiddish, perfect Italian and adequate Greek and Portuguese. He could even make Armenians and Lebanese feel at home. Carrier *fils* had won a Latin prize at school, and he wanted to show it to his father. But Mr Samelowitz said Carrier *père* hadn't been working there for months. Something unpleasant, but he wouldn't go into it. For as long back as Carrier could remember, people had spoken of his father in hushed, embarrassed tones. Where he had gone, no one knew, or would tell. That's how it remained.

He tried to remain faithful to both families, as much as Montreal etiquette permitted. They were now living on the English side of town – which Théophile equated with wealth and perfidy – though no one around them spoke a word of English or had a dime to their name. If his father was in touch with them, they never mentioned it. Nevertheless, he had attended Dollard's wedding three years later, in Longueuil. The wife, Paulette, he remembered as another small, squat, beetle-browed addition to a family already overrun with cultural clichés. At the time, she was three months pregnant. And there *had* been a daughter, he recalled, born the following spring, twenty-five years ago. And he remembered her name as Corinne.

Quebec might be twice the size of Texas, but its people were all one family. In a family of five million there are bound to be thousands of Corinne Carriers; hundreds, perhaps, with parents by the name of Dollard and Paulette. Still, it was possible. It was a culture made for coincidence.

* * *

One look at Corinne Carrier seemed to confirm an utter lack of common ancestry, for which Porter, ever on the lookout for new love, gave silent thanks. She was the right age for cousinhood – twenty-five – but too tall, too beautiful, with long, greying hair, a rectangular face with large green eyes and a generous mouth. The classic Carrier face was just the opposite: small features pulled chinward like a cod's. He associated her kind of charm with ageing stars of the French cinema – not quite beautiful, but so animated they turned nearby men into unwitting cameras. She wore a thirsty satin blouse and faded jeans with beaded moccasins. She moved and spoke with expensive, inherited grace. Her French was Radio-Canada International, without the pouting, asphyxiating gutturals of Paris. Her show was called *Quelques paroles pour l'après-midi,* or more familiarly, *Corinne t'en parle.* Bright tapestries from Asia or Africa were hung on her dressing-room walls. Interspersed were dozens of framed black-and-white stills taken from movies. *Her* movies. She took him on a tour of her walls.

'We were shooting in Cuba last year,' she explained. 'Those are from a documentary we made on child care in Cuba, Nicaragua and China.'

There she stood with Castro, same height, her arm on his shoulder, looking chic and committed. She was a serious woman – another blow against consanguinity. Quebec had a long history of turning out flirts and strippers and kitteny bundles of winter delight, but something on the scale of Corinne? He'd have to go to Scandinavia to find her equivalent. A Quebec girl going to China? To Cuba! The girls he'd known had been lucky to get to Plattsburgh.

Porter asked if she had children – he was old enough now for avuncular questions – and she tossed off an amused shrug that told him her interests were feminist and political, not personal. 'I'm only twenty-five, *please,* m'sieur!' In his Quebec, the only twenty-five-year-old unmarried women he'd known had been whores or nuns. One, in fact, Jeannine Jolicoeur, La Soeur Dure et Mure, had scandalized the eastern townships, stripping down to rosary beads from a nun's starched habit.

She took him into the radio studio, introduced him to Ree-shar, her sound man, a Gauloise-addicted, permed, tanned, but still pudgy man Porter's age, then sat him across from her behind a mike. They had a few minutes, but she was already in her interviewing mode, elbows on thighs, slumped forward, cleavage from the satin blouse as daunting as a *Cosmo* cover girl's. There was nothing on American television to touch her.

'I read your book last year as soon as it came out, of course, because of our connection. I thought it utterly remarkable. Frankly, I wasn't ready for those reviews, though! What did you think of them?'

What do I think of being a newt, an axolotl? He asked instead, 'What connection?'

'Oh, don't tell me! – you don't know? I didn't think I had to tell you –'

'Not Dollard's daughter?'

'Of course. I've been hearing about you all my life. My father's brilliant cousin in America! When I started publishing my novels I even thought of sending them to you, but I figured you'd think it presumptuous. What if you hated them? What if you didn't want to hear from anyone up here? After all, you called yourself Porter.'

'How could I think it presumptuous? If I'd known, it might have saved me.' Her *novels?* Her films? Dollard's little girl? 'I mean, I'm terribly out of touch.'

'Who wouldn't be? It doesn't matter, you're out of the woodwork now, and *I'll* introduce you, starting tonight.'

An old word leaped to mind, bringing a smile to his lips; *cousine de fesse gauche.* A kissing cousin. 'So, frog begets princess,' he said. How had any of this happened in just a generation? Mutations without a missing link.

'He wants to see you, by the way. He's alone – my mother's dead.'

'We'll see.'

'Where men still outlive women – that's backward,' she said. 'We've still got a long way to go. As you remind us, m'sieur.' That seemed to be her cue to begin.

'I have just one request,' he said. He tapped the glass, alerting Richard. 'Put this show on a two-minute delay, okay?' Corinne frowned; she was all spontaneity.

'In case my French is rusty,' he explained.

10.

Corinne lived off St. Denis near Carré St-Louis. When he'd last inhabited the area it had been a low, squalid slum, dismal and tubercular. Post-war immigration and the diaspora from the old Jewish ghetto had made the area an attractive no man's land of suspect ethnicity between the once-solid halves of a bilingual city. And now, with the rest of the English nearly gone, the fulcrum had shifted further east, and the area was young, upscale, arty and French. Soho *de chez nous,* thought Porter. If he were ever to return to Montreal, as he sometimes fantasized, he too would settle near St. Louis Square.

On a steamy night in July, Corinne and Richard threw a cocktail party in his honour. Alas, the pudgy little sound man in the tight polo shirt, jeans and gold chain was more than a sound man, and Porter had been slow in picking up the inflections.

Porter had been sipping beer in the kitchen, a lone, bushy-bearded, middle-aged man in shirtsleeves among men in abused leathers, cropped beards and baggy corduroys. Quebec was both chic and Third World at the same time; unlike New York, everyone smoked. The uncirculated summer air was dense and blue. It was like being in a Bogart movie, or something terribly earnest and existential.

He was the oldest male, but for two white-maned eminences from the upper levels of publishing. Richard came close, but worked at looking younger in his leather jacket, tight jeans, frizzy grey hair and tightly trimmed black beard. Culture matters, thought Porter; four hundred miles south of here and he'd look decked out for Fire Island or a cruise down Christopher Street.

He wondered why he'd let himself in for all this. Corinne was the only obvious reason, but Richard, if not older prohibitions, had blocked that possibility even before it arose. To meet his translator, perhaps. Or something older and more characteristic of him: to prove that even in a Montreal so utterly transformed he still had force, continuity. He didn't recognize any of the locally famous names, he'd read none of their books, he didn't know their films or plays or songs or the names of their publishing houses. He wanted to know if any of that really mattered. He wanted to prove to himself that he still had currency.

Richard had followed him to a small porch off the remodelled kitchen. They didn't seem to have much in common, beyond an obvious interest in Corinne.

'I listened very carefully to your interview this afternoon,' Richard said, in the French they had been using together, then looked up slyly and added in English, 'Right on, man!'

'Which part was right on?'

'Oh, the part about the perils of collective thinking. Or feeling a double loyalty and catching shit for not being loyal enough for either side. And not being able to explain *why* you feel so goddamned intense about your French-Canadianness when there's at least six million just like you in New England who don't give a damn.'

The man's English, at the very least, was remarkable. Not that it was unaccented, more or less like Corinne's, but that it was *noticeably* accented.

'And do you know what really broke me up? It was when Coco asked you such a simple little question as –'

'– *where was I born?* But that's not such a simple little question. I didn't know till I was thirteen, and it still gets me in trouble.'

'Man, you turned white! It made my own hands sweat. I know *exactly* what you mean.'

'Just where were you born, Richard?'

He snorted. 'Shit, can't you tell? I didn't speak a word of *French* till I was twenty-three years old – that beats you by ten years. Look, do I sound *strange* or something?'

'You sound,' said Porter, 'like you learned your English in New York City.'

'Well? You think *you* got identity problems? I grew up as Dick Goldstein in the Bronx. Came up here to dodge the draft, got a degree at McGill, got involved in anti-war stuff, then in PQ stuff, the independence thing, got married, had kids. Everybody's story.'

'Except that now you're Ree-shar and you live with Corinne Carrier. I'd call that life after death.'

'And I've got two Jewish kids who went to French schools because that was the right thing to do, and now one's a folksinger in France and the other's a lumberjack on the North Shore and they both refuse to speak a word of English except when they sing. Try explaining *that* to their *zeyde* and *bubbe*. I did my six months for amnesty so I can at least go back and visit them.'

'Have they met Corinne?'

'Sure. She freaks them out.'

Porter could tell they'd gathered a small crowd behind him; he could smell the smoke of discovery. He could even detect the fragrance of his left-cheek cousin just at his elbow.

Richard winked and slipped back into French. 'The Expos get back in town tomorrow, and I'm on the television crew. If you want to go, just get word to Coco.'

That seemed to be her cue; she turned Porter with a touch on his shoulder. 'M'sieur Carrier, there's someone here who's been waiting to meet you.' An older woman in a pastel dress stepped forward. 'May I present to you Madeleine Choquette, your translator? Madame Choquette, my cousin, Philippe Carrier.'

11.

Earlier in the evening he had noticed her, a stocky, grey-haired woman with youthful skin, and he'd assumed she was a publisher's wife. She had the assurance and the accessories that would have led anyone looking at her and Corinne together to think, 'Of course!': mother and daughter. They made sense together. Maybe there hadn't been a mass mutation of the provincial gene-pool; parts of the Montreal generations really did fit together.

A flashbulb went off. Corinne moved automatically to the middle; the party had suddenly found its focus. He felt his translator's arm tighten around him, and he knew she had come alone. A young man wanted to know what he'd thought of the translation. He had to admit that he hadn't yet read it.

She said to him later, 'Don't apologize, Mr Porter. Please, don't even bother reading it. In fact, you're the *last* person who should read it.' Just as Florence Lachance had said, her English was perfect.

'You're the first person in Montreal to call me Porter.'

'That's how I know you,' she laughed. 'And because you're no Carrier.' She held out two fingers and pinched them just under his nose. 'We're *this* close, you and me. But I'm on one side and you're on the other, and no one but you or me could tell us apart.'

'So what does that make me?'

'An American. A Franco-American. Like the spaghetti.'

Just when he was getting used to being a newt, an axolotl.

It was a warm night, still early. Corinne's apartment opened on a pedestrian mall lined with restaurants and bistros. Somewhere on these streets that were now closed to traffic, young Carrier had lived with whores, had slept on their sofas, gotten up at noon and made his way to the backs of unsanitary restaurants where part-time hookers, the sisters of strippers, the girlfriends of various petty gangsters and enforcers on the block, served him food. By afternoon he'd show up on Dorchester Street where he had a job sweeping and mopping at the Club Lido. Fifi Laflamme, *née* Jeanne Gobeil, had been a headliner, and there was Kitty Coulombe who worked with doves and Soeur Cerise, too outrageous even for Montreal. And every night there'd been a circle of men around the horseshoe stage slurping drinks and reaching up for a feel, whom Carrier zapped with imaginary death rays as he worked the reds and purples. He could remember it all perfectly tonight, the girls, the smells and the twisted alleys off rue de Bullion, the steamy nights of unscreened windows and the ice-etched glass of winter with pans of water on the rads, the girls waiting in front of the *casses-croûtes* for Americans dropped off by taxi-drivers.

He was seventeen and dreaming of purity, living in the midst of sin and disease. The girls had TB, they had social diseases ('Honey, I'd let you climb on 'cause I really like you, but I'm doing you a favour, see?'), they had little kids that Carrier would take to the park on nice days while their mothers slept.

Why *can't* I forget all this?

He'd written about those years. He'd squeezed it all out, but he was still tortured. It was all so Catholic, so medieval, he was a four-hundred-year-old man. He remembered trying to sleep on a torn sofa as Félice Gagnon stood under sixty punishing watts, not his forgiving reds and blues, ironing a dress. She'd stand there for hours half-dressed in a pair of black undies as he buried himself in the crooks of her sofa.

Tonight with his translator in Montreal he felt as though he'd been reduced to a burst of static and flung into space for thirty years, and only now, with this woman, finally captured. He wanted to trust her, this woman so close to him in fate but from the other side of the world. They had a small second dinner at a Greek seafood restaurant, fried squid, salad, retsina.

He'd often wondered, back in his married days, and in his years with Debbie, what it would take to make a healthy, vigorous, attractive man ever grow interested in an older woman. Even if he *ought* to. Even if it was the best thing for him, not to mention the right political thing to do? It just seemed unnatural. And now he knew that unblemished young women were merely the least complicated form of a polymorphous attraction.

Of course, he was no longer healthy, young or vigorous.

'I want to hold you,' he said.

'Of course you do,' said his translator. 'And you will.'

12.

These were dangerous streets for Porter, the steep downtown slopes between MacGregor and Sherbrooke – Peel, Stanley, Drummond, Mountain – for it was in a tourist room between Burnside and St. Catherine on Peel that young Carrier had last lived with his mother. After seeing Madeleine home (a woman of a certain age leads a complicated life, she reminded him; he could not visit her *that* night, but was welcome the next morning), Porter had walked back down Park from Outremont to the complex around Pine, then down the rest of the mountain to Sherbrooke.

It had been Peel Street in 1956, before Montreal joined the twentieth century. No Métro, no autoroutes, no democracy, no self-expression outside of stripping and skating. Carrier and his mother had two rooms. She still went by the name of Hennie Porter; otherwise questions would arise. In the winter, she would leave before dawn for her teaching assignment. He would take off in his coat and tie for the *collège* on Côte-Ste-Catherine across from the Oratory. And when he got back his mother would still be gone, and he'd change clothes and walk down to the Club Lido. His mother thought he was selling programs at the Forum. He remembered that year, even now, as a happy time.

She was fifty-two, an attractive woman with dark hair and bold, non-

Carrier features. She surprised people by her age. Education and travel kept her young, she said – she didn't know what people did in this life without memories of better times. She'd studied and worked in Europe and held responsible decorating jobs in Montreal before getting married. She should never have married, she said, though she didn't regret motherhood. That was her matrimonial refrain.

The schizophrenic twenties and thirties had formed her. She doodled flappers on the backs of envelopes, sketched Art Deco interiors, hung pictures of Shaw and Huxley. But she'd been in Germany for the rise of Hitler, been forced from the Bauhaus to Prague, from Prague to Warsaw, Warsaw to London and London finally to Montreal. Thanks to his mother, Carrier learned – long before he could ever use it in dead, repressive Montreal – that once upon a time there had been a human place of sublime achievement against which the accomplishments of North America were to be held accountable and owing.

She was also a gloomy reactionary, cynical and suspicious. She attracted men without much effort – Carrier was an expert, reading lust in the eyes of strangers – but her only friends were mannish couples of unmarried women. She had married in her early thirties and suffered his father's instability and constant infidelities.

In 1956, Carrier was living in three discrete worlds: that of his mother and a cultured, English-speaking world focused on McGill University; that of a scholarship boy at an elite French *collège,* and that of a janitor in a bilingual shrine to venereal veneration. He was choking on female intimacy. The celibate world of the *collège* was his island of relief from a sea of powders, creams and endless costuming. He led a life of pure disguise; if the brothers had discovered his job, he would have been dropped from school. If the Protestant school board knew he attended a French Catholic school, his mother would have been fired. If his mother ever found out where he worked, she would have died. If he'd acted on any of his passions, he would have been arrested.

He and his mother had evolved an elaborate sexual etiquette. In matters of modesty, she was not of this century. They neither spoke of sex, nor alluded to any of its forms. They kept all doors locked even during the mildest states of disarray.

Then one day he'd come home from school and found his mother in the bathroom with the door open. She was preparing for her bath. She stood before the mirror in her dressing-gown and was busy brushing out her hair. He made as much noise as he could, and she turned to face him. 'Hello, dear, did you have a good day?' she asked, perkier than usual, then unknotted the bow and spread her arms, and the robe fell open. He'd expected a joke to save him at the last minute, like the girls at the Lido, a slip at least, but her body had engulfed him, white, close, utterly, utterly nude. His legs went rubbery. 'I'll go –' he said, and she answered him, stepping out of the bathroom and moving towards him, 'No, it's quite all right. We're two adults here, aren't we? Why don't you put some tea water on?' and he ran for the kitchen cubicle while the rings of the shower curtain scraped against the rusty pole.

He stood in the kitchen watching the gas rings, hands moist and shaking, eyes burning from the vision. It was as though the gas had sucked all the air out of the room and the pounding of the water and the echoes off the bathroom tiles were in the kitchen with him. He could hear it all again tonight, nearly thirty years later, and his breath still came short.

When he had dared to turn, holding out the cup of tea, she was unwrapping herself from the towel in order to dry her hair. An alien being had occupied her body. 'Just put it down, dear,' she said, as she took a chair and finished drying her legs and thighs.

13.

One day in the winter of his sixteenth year, Philippe Carrier had been a scholarship student at Jean-de-Brébeuf with a bright future before him in law or the classics, and the next day he'd been clawed from the skies and dumped in the gutter with nowhere to turn. He'd been standing with his mother at seven-thirty in the morning on the corner of Peel and Dorchester where the buses came in. She wasn't going to work that day, but she'd wanted to walk with him to the bus stop. She'd been bright and witty, her twenties not her thirties self, full of brittle talk and saucy opinion – the side he preferred, but couldn't fully respond to. It was easier to be the son of her sour, schoolteacherly side.

It had been a mushy morning in late March, with the night's fresh snow already crushed to slabs of silvered sherbet by the pre-dawn ploughs and now the rows of backed-up buses. Twenty different bus lines circled Dominion Square; buses were lined two abreast in the street and bumper-to-bumper along the curb. It was the sign of late winter, his mother observed, the number of lone male galoshes poking up from the puddles, sucked off by slush.

His bus, an express, sent up a wave of brown, salted ice as it slanted to its dock. Carrier was looking down at his feet, making sure of his footing, when his mother took his hand and said, 'There's something I must do,' and then pulled away and dove for the right front tire. The driver slammed his brakes so hard he mounted the curb, but his mother had already disappeared under the bus in the slushy, black pool of gutter water. A woman screamed at Carrier, *'Qu'est-ce qui s'est passé? –* What happen'?' and he found himself pushed aside by policemen and drivers and some passengers who worked their way under the bus to pull his mother out.

At the inquiry it was determined that she must have slipped on the icy curb and been pushed forward by the surging crowd. Carrier did not dispute the finding, and for thirty years he'd accepted it. He concealed from everyone the letters she had left back in their rooms: a termination notice from the Protestant school board and, from the nearest town in Ontario, a notice from his father to file a Bill of Divorcement since Quebec did not permit divorces.

He was now standing at the spot. In front of him now was a six-lane Dorchester Boulevard and just down the hill the giant cheese-grater known as the Château Champlain Hotel. Windsor Station and the old Laurentian Hotel, profitable places for passing out peep-show leaflets, and the old Club Lido itself were gone, and Dominion Square was now an art park. The only survivors he could place from thirty years ago were the old grey mastodons: the Sun Life building and Marie-Reine-du-Monde. When he sat on the park bench the city fell away in bluffs and terraces down to the river. Cool air rose from the invisible water like a sea breeze, bringing the smell of fresh ironing.

Not the smell of ironing: the stench of it, the way all ripeness implies rancidness and rot. He could smell the stench of foul clothes right down to the sweat and sebum and the powders that lay against them. He could smell the scorch of cotton and, faintly, the odour of searing flesh.

Most children find the image of their parents' sexuality amusing if not ridiculous. Many children of older parents of his generation felt they were spawned in some awkward and accidental effort, never before attempted, never later duplicated. Porter had carried that feeling for many years.

But by the time he married and embarked on his own tenuous course, he began seeing his parents in heroic and tragic dimensions: his mother a frail Giacometti; his father a squat, fierce Rodin. He saw his father as the existential beast, his mother as the balance of restraining forces, consumed by contraries. He carried that image of their heroic decimation into his adulthood and into his writing. And his writing to date had been of himself, the adolescent yo-yo, the little rubber ball restrained by his mother's frail rubber cord, whacked by his father's paddle.

It was two o'clock on a July morning in the last fifteen years of the twentieth century. A different generation in a different city in a country he no longer recognized had taken over. The only continuity between that winter morning at this spot and this summer night were the defunct buildings and the diseased synapses in Porter's brain.

14.

She met him at the door of her apartment, dressed for summer in a wide straw hat and peasant skirt, Indian top and sandals. 'I thought we could drive up north,' she said, and she'd even packed a wicker basket with lunch and wine. They'd go to her mountain cabin near Ste-Agathe and spend the rest of the week in the cool air on a lake. In fact, she'd come back to town only for Corinne's party and to meet him. Friends had been using it; that's why he couldn't stay the night before.

Porter had walked over the mountain from Côte-des-Neiges and Camillien-Houde to near Côte-Ste-Catherine where she lived. It was a muggy day climbing to the nineties; the mountains were appealing, and a lake would be nice, but nothing could match a quiet air-conditioned apartment on a sidestreet on Outremont.

'Do we have to go?' he asked. And he followed her silently back through the living room into her bedroom where he lay on the bed and untied his shoes as she stood in front of the closet, slowly undoing her day's preparations. She laid the straw hat on a ledge, stepped out of the sandals and loosened the pearl earrings and placed them on the dresser. It was the slowest, most orderly undressing in Porter's long experience, as she took down the hangers, the hooks, for both their sets of clothes.

'Would you like to shower?' she asked, and yes, he said, he would. The serene lack of urgency was something new and unexpected, for last night, thinking of Madeleine Choquette as he lay awake in his tourist room, he'd all but phoned her at four in the morning, all but taken a taxi out and pounded on her door. Minutes later she slid the shower door open and stepped inside with him, and they stood wrapped together under the warm waterhead until it seemed to him that air and flesh and water were continuous and he had stepped out of his body altogether.

They were lying on the translator's bed, talking for the first time since last night. She'd been playing little translation games, confessing small confusions with English, even after twenty years of intimacy. 'There's a sign on the thruway going down to Albany,' she said, '"Trucks Under 40 Use Low Gear," and my first impression was, *How very old their trucks are!* Or last winter, the TV weatherman in Plattsburgh said, "Expect six quick inches of snow," and I panicked! What's a "quick inch"? Is that like a country mile? Even last night when you said you had to go straight back to New York, I first thought, well, I certainly hope he's not going to get *bent* first! You see what I mean? And then I hit sentences in your book like, "I spun my mental Rolodex and her name came up ..." How am I supposed to deal with that in French?'

He ran the palm of his hand up her body, resting it on her cheek, then back down. They had cooled off, returned to their separate bodies. 'Madeleine,' he said, 'help me.'

She pressed cool fingertips to his eyes.

'I'm lost,' he said.

'I'm here. I'm not going away.'

'I'm forty-six years old, Madeleine. By forty-six a man should have an ability to predict likely reactions. Utter ignorance should be pretty well eliminated. Total insecurity should be fairly unlikely ... you know what I'm saying?'

'Those are American expectations. I'm fifty-two and my life is exactly the same. I don't know anyone whose isn't.'

'My mother was fifty-two,' he said.

'Don't think I don't know. I was almost afraid to mention it.'

'My epilepsy has come back.'

'I know. I saw it last night at dinner.'

'I don't know how to treat it. Last time, the medicine slowed me down. I couldn't take that again. I don't know if it's a medical condition or ... a message, you know? My mind is falling apart. I haven't written in over a year. I have a new family, but I don't feel like I belong to them.... I feel like a monster, sometimes.'

He felt like a blind man, trying to assemble a thousand-piece jigsaw puzzle.

'You were a Quebec Catholic once,' she said. 'Remember the consolations of melancholy.'

She lifted her fingers. She crouched over him, a full, immense woman of fifty years, her breasts whiter than milk, nearly touching his eyes. She was a smiling haze above him, grey hair without striking features. Then she buried her face in his, her lips on his, and the long, erotic nightmare of his life began to build. He was conscious of the presence of sin in what his body was doing, impurities linked to the dusty hallways of his childhood and adolescence and the dingy lights of de Bullion Street and none of it mattered. He would have handed over his soul at that moment for just twenty more minutes like this, fifteen, ten, and when it was over and they were lying still in one another's arms, he fell asleep believing that no condition, moral or medical, could have survived those last eruptions intact.

15.

He had a very active profile, cutting in and jutting out, like an ingenious edge to a jigsaw puzzle piece. Ageing was just a process of thinning here and thickening there, getting shorter, or stretching out. His hands were comparatively huge – arthritic, Porter supposed – and his forearms bulged like Popeye's, but the neck was frail and the cheeks were sunken. Porter would not have recognized him, and no one would have placed him in the same century, on the same continent, with his daughter.

He limped now – again, the arthritis, Corinne had mentioned on the drive out – and he hadn't worked since Paulette died. He was on disability, which paid the beer and the rent on a second-floor flat in Ville d'Anjou. He wasn't yet fifty, but he'd lost out on things.

It was Madeleine who'd persuaded him: see your cousin. 'I met him when I was translating your book. He's a little sad, but he sincerely wants to meet you again.' Then she'd said, 'You know what he told me? He said, "Knowing Phillie gave meaning to my life." How's that, eh?'

Whenever Corinne visited her father, the neighbourhood gathered. 'Coco, Coco,' people shouted, and lined the sidewalk hoping for a glimpse. There should be a documentary in this, Porter thought: the New Quebec, built on the bones of men like Dollard. With Corinne and Richard, Madeleine and Porter all out on the front gallery and with a case of beer at his feet, Dollard Carrier was the soul of volubility. He reminded Porter of an artificial-heart recipient, an affable soul utterly confused by all the attention. Now he was waving down to the passers-by, toasting them with a beer at eleven in the morning, giving his daughter loud kisses and keeping one enormous paw on Porter's knee.

'Some times we had, eh?' he laughed, rolling a cigarette. 'Christ, this guy comes up from the States and steals my bed. Him and his parents, breezes into our little flat down in Hochelaga that was already jammed … goddamn, I hated him at first. Couldn't understand a word of English, of course. I must have made life hell for you, Phillie, I'm sorry. I never apologized. I'm not right sometimes. Stupid, that's what I am. No, no … you took it all like a man and surprised the shit out of me, I'll admit it. You were weak and twice as smart as anyone else, and I couldn't say it then but I'll say it now – I was damned proud of you.'

Corinne winked at Porter; Madeleine squeezed his arm. Richard asked. 'Did you hear him on Coco's show?'

'Naw, she knows about me. Can't understand her on the radio, speaks too high class for me to follow. Give me a baseball game or a hockey match.'

'I was sorry to hear about Paulette,' said Porter.

'She was a good woman,' said Dollard, dipping his head. He held up a new beer; he was drinking alone.

'Dollard –' and now Porter moved closer and put his arm on his cousin's shoulder. 'My mother, you remember, killed herself?'

Dollard crossed himself. 'Terrible thing. A tragedy,' he muttered.

'I wondered if anyone ever talked about it. One thing was, my father wanted a divorce. She was carrying the papers with her when she died.'

'We don't believe in divorce,' he said. 'Everyone else is getting a divorce nowadays. Not me and Paulette. Twenty-three years married, praise her soul, six good kids. Already two of the boys – Coco's brothers, there – they got divorces. You understand what's happening, Phillie?'

'No, I don't.' If he could have answered he might have said, twenty years of intimacy is too heavy a burden for the human heart. What he said was, 'I was hoping for word of my father. You're the only person I can ask.'

Until he'd come back to Montreal, Porter had felt comparatively young. Now he felt like the last of his generation, the last, along with Madeleine and maybe a few old priests and nuns, who remembered the bad, murderous and suicidal old days. It was a culture made for incongruities. Dollard and Corinne; Dollard and himself.

'Uncle Reggie,' said Dollard. 'My father always warned me about Uncle Reggie.'

'What happened to him, Dollard?'

'He was a restless man, Phillie. That's what my father always said.'

'Where is he?'

'It's a home – St. Justin's out in Laval. He's an old, old man. The sisters do what they can. Sometimes he must ask for me, and they come over and get me.'

'What does he say, when he asks for you?'

'Nothing. He forgets, or probably he never asked. They have to keep busy, too. I don't mind.'

'Does he ask about *me?* About his son?'

Dollard turned slowly and looked down at his beer. 'He doesn't have a son, not where he is.'

16.

They were lying in bed after another day of not making it past the front hallway of Madeleine's apartment. She had greeted him now three days running, freshly showered and crisply dressed, as though ready for tennis or a long afternoon in a rented punt, a picnic from straw hampers in a Impressionist glade. But she would close the door and move to her well-stocked closet and casually begin undressing. She scattered the hangers on the bed, and they hung up their clothes in silence. And they would lie together as though they'd already been out, taken their exercise and now were back for rest.

She made him feel he was on perpetual vacation in some tropical resort, passing his mornings in strenuous touring then stealing a few hours for drinks, sex and slumber while the rest of the tour was on a dusty bus visiting ruins. She was the oldest woman in his life; the only older woman in his life.

And then they would talk. About his parents, his childhood, her family, her children, his children; her adjustments to the States when her family had moved down there, his to Montreal; about her writing, his writing. Madeleine had left the States when her marriage failed ('Husbands can forgive their wives hating them, so long as they don't learn to love other men,' she said), but she'd gone to Paris and lived there ten years, working in publicity. She was going to stay, thinking that Quebec held nothing for her. She started writing in Paris. Quebec writers and singers were just beginning to catch on in France, after three hundred years of ridicule.

Her children were Americans, they'd stayed back in Boston with their English-speaking father. And why did she leave Paris? Something so small, really, but one of those potent moments that forced her to examine her irrelevance in France. 'A perforation in the fabric of indifference,' she called it.

'I was walking with my lover in the Bois de Vincennes, passing to the Parc Floral.' She named those places as though Porter had seen them, as though any cultured person knew them intimately. 'We had to take a subterranean passage under a stone bridge. There were unpleasant piss-odours, but that's not uncommon on the streets of Paris. No, it was the graffiti sprayed on the walls of the passage: *Mort aux juifs,* and *Violer les filles arabes* and *Purité aryenne,* and dozens of condoms, hundreds of them, slippery underfoot. My friend was roaring with laughter – he'd *brought* me there deliberately! It was all *funny* to him, you see. He was a very sophisticated, socialist lawyer, but he said he liked to come down there to "get in touch with his feelings."

'The obscenities weren't on the walls – they were in his politics, and I'd never appreciated that before. When I got upset he called me a typical reactionary Quebec cow. To him, the problem was I couldn't take a good joke.'

Porter had had no such moments, at least, none that he remembered. He envied people their moments of clear hate, knowing their own names and where they were born, their small perforations. He hungered for clear distinctions. What this visit had awakened in him was the realization of his fundamental Quebec Catholicism, the Jansenist belief that there is no end to the implications of a single act.

One day in Pittsburgh when he was twelve years old and living in utter harmony even with his epilepsy, his father went to work and learned he'd been fired without warning. 'My name was Phil Porter, my father was Reg Porter and we were Americans from Pittsburgh.

'Then in one moment my father hauls off and slugs the man sitting at his desk and runs from the store. I wake up the next morning without the parents I thought I knew, without the name I thought I had, without a city or a country or even a language I could speak! And because of that I become split down the middle, my mother kills herself and I'm sitting here in middle age and I'm still running.'

Madeleine ran her fingers over his shoulder, down his arm and flank. 'Why do you think you're epileptic?' she asked.

'I was battered by a baby-sitter's husband when I was three, in Cincinnati.'

'I know that's what you wrote.'

He gathered her fingers in a stunted bunch of carmine nails. 'Wasn't I?'

'Isn't it time to find out?'

'I don't remember any of it. The earliest memory I have is of sitting in the kitchen sink and being bathed. I remember Johnny Mercer singing "Don't Fence Me In" on the radio, and I sang along with him. And I remember sitting next to my father on the arm of his chair, and I fell off and broke my arm.'

'I'll tell you what I think, Philip. You're the one who's always so amazed by *mutations,* right? You keep looking at Coco and saying. "How did it happen?" like she's some kind of miracle. And you look at Dollard like he's a caveman or something –'

'A fish,' said Porter. 'I'm a mud-puppy.'

'Okay, whatever. But Philip, there's no such thing as a mutation here. Where's the transition between *your* father and *you?* It's your mother, right? and between Dollard and Coco – it's *you,* that's who. *We're* the transition, Coco's a transition, your little daughter who plays Chopin and Mozart, *she's* a transition. There aren't any permanent forms of *anything*, Porter darling. Where did you pick up that museum mentality? Listening to you is like going on a tour of Ste Anne de Beaupré or Lourdes or Brother André's Shrine – it's medieval! You look at life like it's some kind of before-and-after picture. Either it's totally damned or it's too good to include you. That's old Quebec Catholicism, darling. You're holding out for a miracle to come down and save you.'

17.

There are no permanent forms, except perhaps the styles of institutional Catholic architecture: schools, hospitals, convents, nursing homes. The muggy weather had begun to break when Porter made his way alone over the black river to the island of Laval. Maison St-Justin could be spotted from half a mile away, a battlement of yellow brick in the middle of unvarying fieldstone duplexes.

Grey Sisters ran the place; they made Porter nervous. St. Justin's seemed to be in a permanent state of renovation, like Olympic Stadium with its cranes, the result of insufficient public money beginning to supplant the church. Ladders and scaffolding, dropcloths, uncured drywall and brightly painted television rooms were jammed into dingy, cream-coloured corridors with varnished oak doors, set with stippled glass. The number of Greys thinned out on the upper floors; rough-looking orderlies with lips curled cruelly over hockey scars seemed to be in control. His father was listed on the fourth floor. Dozens of old men in striped hospital pyjamas lined the halls in wheelchairs. The opened doors of the wards showed only withered legs and bony toes pointing up at silent television screens.

He asked one of the orderlies for M'sieur Carrier's room. The young man snickered, but gave out a number. 'Reggie,' he winked. '*Reggie, l'américain!*'

And then there was no delaying it. He stood at the base of his father's bed staring the length of his father's body, from the bare feet up the shins and over the sleeping chest to the enormous nostrils, the flaring eyebrows, and the immense pink ears, caught by the pillow and spread out full. His mouth was open as he snored. The teeth were out;

his father had become all cavities, air was claiming him.

Over the bed hung a crucifix.

He took a chair at the head of the bed. The plastic wristband around the bundle of purple veins read 'Carrier, R.' He remembered his father as a snorer and heavy sleeper. He held his father's hand and gave it a firm tug.

'Dad?'

The eyes were open. Porter thought he read panic. He cranked up the bed. His father didn't seem strong enough to sit up straight. 'Dad, it's me, Philip.'

No recognition. He wanted his teeth; his eyes told him that. He slipped them in without any problems, then cleared his throat. This was as long as his father had normally gone without a cigarette. Such a drastic change as that – what had it cost him? When had he done it? Who had suffered through it with him?

The male orderly came to the door, accompanied by a nun. 'M'sieur Carrier,' she said, 'there's much to talk about.'

Fees? he wondered. He couldn't afford his father's care; didn't feel he owed it.

His father cleared his throat, smiled briefly, and fluttered his hand in the nun's direction.

'Sometimes we can't shut him up.' She repeated it louder, for his father's benefit. 'Eh, Reggie? He looks confused right now.'

'I thought, all these years ...' Porter began, 'he was lost. Gone. Totally out of my life.'

He felt his French deserting him. Fear of the nun, back to the time when he was learning the language under the unforgiving tutelage of Soeur Timothée. She'd had a nickname; that too had deserted him. He realized he had never spoken French to his father, despite the fact that his father's Frenchness had helped destroy his life.

'He did not list you among his immediate family.'

'That is nevertheless my father,' said Porter. If this was a Catholic home, he didn't want to jeopardize his father's care by too much disclosure. 'My mother has been dead nearly thirty years. I went to the States and changed my name.'

'That's your business, of course. If all the papers are in order, we can release him to you,' she said.

'I can't look after him.'

'So you came here for what? Curiosity? Will you sign papers attesting to your refusal, then? It is required, now that he is a ward of the province.'

Porter signed. Bless socialized medicine; forms, not bills. He used his proper name, Philippe Carrier, *fils.*

'Dad? Do you know who I am?'

'This is your son, Reggie,' she echoed, louder. She glanced down at his signature. 'Philippe.'

'He knew me as Phil. We always talked in English, so maybe, if you don't mind.... Dad, I haven't seen you in thirty years. I want to talk to you. I want to find out what you've been doing, where you've been.... Do you understand me?'

There were flickers in his eyes, as though he might have understood and then immediately suppressed it.

The orderly had worked his way to the head of the bed where he was untying the bow of the old man's gown and slipping it over his head. His father slumped forward a little, and the orderly took out the pillow.

His father was obviously starving to death. What kind of man lets his father starve to death? Porter wondered. He probably weighed well under a hundred pounds, and the dead white skin was marked with bruises, nicks, veins and scars that Porter had never seen.

He must bruise like a peach, he thought.

'You might help us here, Mr Carrier,' said the nun. 'We try to account for as much of the medical history of the patient as seems relevant. Your father has had quite an extensive medical involvement.' She traced the still-red scars of abdominal surgery, indicated more whorls of stitching in his groin – 'Hernia, we had to do that' – and then tipped him forward to show deep, smooth scars under the shoulder blades. 'A lucky man – lung-cancer operation, at least ten years old. We have a fairly complete record from your brother in Ottawa, but he couldn't tell us –'

'– my brother?'

'Yes, of course. He often visits, along with your sisters. They're much better than you've been, you'll forgive my commenting. Technically, your father should be moved to a more medically oriented facility – this is still for the ambulatory and continent, and you can see your father is not in that category.'

'I'll sign,' he said.

'And one more thing, just for our legal records. There's this scar on his back –' she tipped him forward like a slab of meat into Porter's arms and loosened the knot of his clean gown. 'What do you know of this?'

He had never noticed a scar; to him, his father was unblemished. His parents had never undressed in front of him, except for his mother that one time. And now, today. His father after thirty years smelled the same, the same powders, the same sweat, the same stale cotton odours, but with age the ripeness had turned putrid. My God, don't they bathe him here? Should *I* bathe him? He pulled his father closer, loosening the robe that melted from his dead-white shoulders. It was like baby's flesh rubbed in flour, red at the slightest touch, scabs clustered where his collar bone had nearly poked through. He knew even before he saw it what he would find.

It was an old, discoloured patch of skin, shaped like a shark's fin, a neat, purple parabola. It wasn't deep, but it was extensive, and it had withstood the shrinking of his body and the loosening of his skin. It looked like a decal ready to be pulled off.

'I don't think it gives him pain,' the nun said, 'but watch –'

She touched it with her ballpoint pen, and Porter's father lunged forward, hard against his chest. 'You see, there's sensitivity there – or maybe a memory of it, locked away. You could stick pins in the rest of his skin and he wouldn't feel them. His circulation is entirely gone – he can't move his feet, and they're like chunks of ice to the touch.'

'Don't you operate?'

'We must justify the expense, m'sieur. Your father is not likely to survive surgery – or live long enough to benefit from it.'

He could feel his father's breathing, his heart pounded fast as a bird's against his arm. He stared down his father's back at the patch of discoloured skin rising like a shark's pointed snout breaking water, and he felt a twist of terror.

'I think I know,' he said. 'It's shaped like an iron, isn't it?'

'What kind of man brands himself with an iron on his own backside? Your brother said he'd always had it.'

'A man like my father,' said Porter. 'A woman like my mother.' Then, savouring the words, 'My brother was always a particularly unobservant boy.'

He laid his father down, straightening the new gown and centring his head on the pillow. He could smell the ironed clothes, deep in his brain. 'My father remembers the iron, I'm sure, don't you?' He showed signs of wanting to speak, but again held back. Porter stifled an urge to ask for an iron and bring it close, and closer, to his father's face. Deep in the brain, the intruder ran from room to room, and Porter turned on the lights, chased, blocked the escape routes.

'That scar happened over forty years ago, when I was three years old. My mother was ironing clothes. My father was bathing me in the kitchen sink. And I started screaming. Why, I don't know.' But he remembered it vividly: the record playing 'Don't Fence Me In,' the water, and being lifted and dropped, lifted and dropped, and his head striking the porcelain partition between the sinks. 'I didn't remember it till this minute.'

The nun seemed not to notice.

He turned to her. 'Get me a sponge and some water, please.'

He gathered his father's head in his arms and pressed his lips on his forehead, his cheeks and then his lips. He stared into the grey eyes that gave nothing back, praying for just another sign of recognition, and then his father closed his eyes.

'Sleep, father,' he said. 'I have loved you all my life.'

18.

They met him in Poughkeepsie station and drove him home. He'd been gone just under a week, but they had news! Hannah had learned a new sonata that she wanted to play for Poppy that very night, tired or not.

'Have you learned some things, too?' Petra asked him as they cleaned the dishes later that evening.

'I'll see the doctor in the morning. He said he can dose me, so I'll let him try.'

'You didn't really believe in miracle cures, did you?'

'I'm afraid I did.' He took her into his arms. 'I've learned many wonderful things from many wonderful people, but I did not learn any miracle cure for epilepsy.'

She didn't struggle, as she often did. She even returned the hugs and lingered for a kiss. 'We've missed you. Well, Hannah's been too busy to really *miss* you, but I've missed you.'

When the dishes were dry, they moved to the living room and sat quietly as their daughter began to play.

Life Could Be a Dream
(Sh-boom, Sh-boom)

It's your *Brigadoon* moment, a fortieth reunion coming round once a lifetime to these cloistered Ohio hills. In the squealing voices, *'Forty years! It seems like yesterday!'* youth is restored, tempered by wisdom, taboos and barriers fall away, callowness is banished – what fools we were! *'One day I'm waiting in line for dinner, waiting for a sink to open up and the next minute – My God! Could that be –?'* How intolerant we were, how harsh our judgements. Past and future are blended, noble souls shine through clearly. It's a chance to correct our mistakes. Is this not beauty?

A girl who tormented your dreams now brushes her teeth in the sink next to yours. The shower stops, the curtain opens. 'Promise not to look, boys, I left my bathrobe in the room.' Your dreams made flesh, mad dash down your freshman corridor into a room once smoky from bull sessions and all-night study. Forty years ago, girls' dorms were fortresses of security entered on pain of expulsion. Now you're on the second floor sitting on the edge of a bed drinking beer with a girl you never dared to talk to, nor would she have answered, forty years ago.

'Girl' is not quite right, nor is it exactly wrong. She's already said it: 'My god, you haven't aged a bit! Okay, we're all a little grey or hiding it and most of the guys are bald, but look at you! It's like you went to sleep and just woke up.' And you've said the same to her, remembering your freshman Shakespeare and the many times you've used it profitably, *'Age cannot wither her/nor custom stale her infinite variety …'* Time, that sweet avenger, has wiped away baby-fat beauty. Canes and dentures have settled on the athletes. Scandals and divorce have humbled the frat boys, and bolsters of fat hang upon the sorority queens.

In the barely imaginable year of 2001, on my fortieth college reunion, I was invited back for an honourary doctorate. I live in Paris now and the invitation sparked a few rounds with my wife (if I remember

Salinger correctly, a 'breathtakingly level-headed' girl), a paragon of Huguenot parsimony. Try explaining to Lucy, the budget-minded descendant of provincial shopkeepers, that an otherwise sensible man of sixty must suddenly travel a quarter of the way around the world to spend a summer weekend at a school that nearly killed him, among people he despised. American nostalgia translates gaudily.

Lucy's is a nobler thing. When she was a child, coffee was strong and everything French mattered profoundly. Her comfort food is still leek soup glistening with goose fat. She can be moved to tears by a slant of sunlight after a night of rain. Her adolescent world dressed in black and sang soulful songs. It smoked like chimpanzees in a controlled experiment and acted out its existentialism without a trace of irony. In her twenties, the European Community took off; and she served her time in Brussels. She speaks the languages, except for English. But she can still amaze me. We're friends of Samuel Beckett, but she's never sat through one of his plays. When I think of the fifties, I'm back in Pittsburgh in the front seat of my father's Bel-Air, the radio blaring rock 'n' roll.

I'd been a high school success, with romantic notions of becoming a painter or a writer. The gene for self-expression, any kind of art – that came from my mother. From my father, I'm still trying to puzzle it out. It took me years to appreciate, or even acknowledge, that I had an exotic background for that time and place. My mother thought I could even be a singer, with the proper training. Singer, writer, painter! But one year in college taught me that a boy with self-regard should find a science. I looked into a future of endless labs and my eyelids grew heavy. I blew the chance for Phi Beta Kappa in my first semester.

Pam Weigl – Broadway-bound even before she emerged a few years later as Debby Wagner – had written: '*Charlie, I know it's futile to ask – why would any sane person leave Paris in June for three days in hot, sticky Ohio? – but it would mean a lot to me and to the school. We've got fifty-two self-proclaimed (I call them 'self-admitted') millionaires, a senator and four congressmen, all Republican. No surprises there – they gave off a raw stench from their first day on campus. I have believed for 40 years that you are the outstanding graduate of our class. I hope they're polishing your Nobel. Think about it, okay?*'

Pam called herself a street kid from Greenwich Village, a concept not even remotely imaginable to me, but for central Ohio in the late fifties she had certain untranslatable charms. Dark hair, pale skin, no make-up but mascara, all-black tights and sweaters. 'Street kid' did translate to a brownstone on West Tenth and a father on Wall Street. Fraternity boys and their girlfriends used to whisper, where she comes from girls like her give out blowjobs like Lifesavers. I wouldn't know.

I have my madeleine. It's not as succulent as leeks and goose fat, but in the summer of my freshman year it passed for the ultimate sophistication. There were flavours and textures that pierced my soul, a way to remain lean and fit for life on pennies a day. Pam Weigl had brought a yoghurt-maker to her dorm. Sprinkle a little crust of sugar on top, preferably unrefined. Some people – you know the type – like jam in the bottom. Go ahead, throw in some berries. Honey's good, too. Me, she said, I like it straight. She took a spoonful and made a scrunchy little face.

Here's my exotic little story. My parents were Canadian, or perhaps I should say, simply, from Montreal. My mother was German, my father French. I grew up with subtitles flashing across their chests. I translate, therefore I am. One night when I was twelve, we abandoned our large, shabby apartment in Montreal and moved to a smaller, shabbier one in Pittsburgh. That overnight drive broke and never quite remade my world. Gone were the streetcars, the cluttered back porches, the busloads of Harlem tourists (*'Free at last, free at last!'* they'd sing out, and then look for a boy like me to carry their bags), and the gaudiness of Ste-Catherine Street at night. Gone, too, was French, which registered to me not as a language but as a special code, a way of recognizing ourselves in the jungle, in the dark.

In Pittsburgh I learned to avoid the taint of foreignness in public, never speaking their languages, never answering them except in English. I sat in on a high school French class and didn't recognize a word; I took Spanish in high school, Russian in college. I'm the only American novelist with a Montreal sensibility threaded through a Pittsburgh needle's eye.

My father was 'dapper'. Dapper was usually followed by 'little', as in 'a dapper little man', then finally 'a dapper little Frenchman'. He was trim and moustached, and a sharp dresser. Sharp dressing went with being dapper. He had Charles Trenet records at home, and he could sing, but he modelled his English on the liquid baritone of Bing Crosby. My mother had come to Montreal in 1934, carrying a collection of cabaret music with her.

They divorced in April 1958, towards the end of the second semester of my freshman year. My father had sneaked into our Pittsburgh house after midnight, expecting to pick up a few clean clothes and ironed shirts, and was confronted by my mother. He slugged her. She filed. He liquidated the art-supply store they'd started five years earlier. She got the house against which the store had borrowed all of its expenses, sold it, paid the bills, and went back to her only relative, a sister in Ottawa, to start a teaching career. My father raced off to Mexico with his girlfriend and the store's full value.

So, gone were Pittsburgh, the free oils and pastel chalk, the acrylics, the canvas and stretchers, and the Pirates and the streetcars and the great calm of Carnegie Library and Museum. For the remaining month and a half of school year, my freshman dorm room was the only roof over my head.

The place I now knew best was this Ohio village of professors and churches, a bank, barber shop, haberdasher's, pizzeria and a drugstore. Montreal was a fading dream; Pittsburgh too painful. If I didn't stay enrolled, the army was waiting. My freshman grades made a scholarship impossible, but the registrar said a National Defense loan might not be out of the question. He said there had been fifty divorces among freshman parents. 'Seems like a lot of families stay together for the sake of the kids, then the kid leaves and so does the old man.' My father would have to countersign the loan, but I didn't know his Mexican address.

And so I stayed on in an empty spring and summer village of remembered winter dates, careless pizzas and between-class coffee in a crowded union. The union was closed. I hadn't made friends with any professor; there was no one who would take me in. The only job in town was on the campus grounds crew – mowing, pruning, replanting, turning mattresses, razoring old tape off the walls and windows, plastering nail holes, testing boilers, checking every light bulb and faucet on campus. By the end of the summer, I was the only boy in the class of '61 who'd been in every girls'-dorm bathroom, in every room and sat on every bed, and yes, I smelled the mattresses.

For a few weeks in June, when I had no money and no place to live, the summer stock cast of *Brigadoon* took me in. Five seniors plus Pam

Weigl were sharing a funky faculty-house. During the school year, the French professor who owned it wore a beret and a long scarf over a tweedy sport coat. He churned across campus under a Gauloise cloud, but in the summers he conducted mysterious research in Paris and left his house to the theatre crowd. The walls were filled with alpine vistas and French movie posters. Dun-coloured French paperbacks with their shaggy page-endings lined the bookshelves. Whisky crates held a huge collection of French and German records. Those were the songs I knew, Weill and Brecht, Trenet, Piaf and Juliette Greco; I started singing, and Pam's jaw dropped. I didn't know they were *recherché*, or that I had suddenly soared in everyone's estimation. I didn't know what life had already equipped me to know, which is, I suppose, the definition of being a freshman in college. We spent our wee hours with jug wine and pots of chili, mixing European songs to our old favourites. Every night a European cabaret, in central Ohio.

I'd sung before, so they gave me one rousing *Brigadoon* solo *('... and all along the green — I'll — go home with Bonnie Jean!')*. Pam called my tenor a good second lead, but I needed to work on my steps. In mid-June *Brigadoon* returned to the mists, new people joined the cast and my life-sustaining glimpse of Bohemia was over. They were doing *Godot*, then *The Glass Menagerie*. I was on my own again.

The hills were hot and sticky, the woods dark and deep, and buggy at night. I still ate with the actors and worked with the grounds crew, but now I took a blanket and pillow to the woods for every dreaded night of sleep. Ants and mosquitoes feasted on my body. One night, it came to me: all this madness is for a purpose. Where, in the history of the world, has Montreal crashed into Pittsburgh? Who in the world could describe it, who would want to read it, if it didn't kill me first? But it's me; I'm the energy-release. I'm what you get when a Montreal atom smashes into a Pittsburgh wall. A dream-voice speaking from deep in woods said, Europe's the only place for a guy like you.

After two weeks in the sodden woods a proper solution presented itself. I had my groundskeeper keys to the empty dorms, and a blanket. I was used to the dark. Who would ever know? The National Defense loan was arranged. I forged my father's signature. I'd be nineteen in the fall. By the time I graduated, I'd be a thousand dollars in debt for every year of my life.

Europe finally entered my life in 1970, when my fourth novel made a modest splash. I could live a careful year in Paris or three reckless ones in Mexico and who knows how many in Tangiers – but I blew it all on an unelectrified chalet overlooking a long, lake-filled Swiss valley. Deer in the meadows grazed on a carpet of wild flowers. I was enough of a *bricoleur* to paint and plaster, to landscape, to insulate and bring in power.

A narrow bicycle path strayed past my back door. Two kilometres west took me to a French-speaking village of baguettes and red wine. A kilometre east brought me to a German village for sausages and white wine. Summer nights, nostalgia would get the better of me and I'd lie in the meadow under the night sky dome, a polished black sieve riddled with stars. The English language was an unabridged dictionary kept high on a shelf, wedged between well-thumbed pages of foreign phone-books.

I spent three years in the Jura, typing on cold keys through woollen gloves. In the end, I had the atom-smashing book I'm still best known for, and when I sold the chalet to Italians, I had money for five years in Paris, maybe more. Nothing Swiss entered that book – it was set in Pittsburgh with a memory of Montreal. I'd travelled six thousand miles but I'd never left the conditions of a Montreal childhood and a Pittsburgh adolescence, however cosmopolitan I chose to play it.

In early July, the campus came alive again for the strange ritual of alumni return. *'Welcome Back Class of '17 and '18 for Your 40th!'* and *'The Heroic Classes of '17 & '18!'* the streamers read. Sixty-five percent of the boys had left school and joined the army in 1917; thirty had died. During the school year, I'd walked past their cenotaph every morning, slightly amused at their uniforms with the wide-brimmed hats and riding breeches. Now, I was assigned to restoring dignity to a statue defaced by generations of students scratching their names and fraternity letters and stubbing out their cigarettes and stuffing gum in those heroic brass folds. I sanded, filled and painted, and in the process memorized the thirty names. It was so biblical back then, with names like Asa/Ace, Micah/Mike and Isaac/Ike, just like the president. I went down to the VA hospital in Columbus and loaded up a college truck with spare wheelchairs. They shuffled along the brick paths, some of them still wearing their Class of '17 or '18 freshman beanies, others in their decorated World War I combat jackets. We were issued instructions: *Our visitors come from a different era. Treat them with respect and courtesy. They do not want to feel 'out of it' in any way. They were once exactly like you, and the education they received here helped them face and surmount the unimaginable challenges of the 20th century. You'll be coming back for your 40th and when you do – sometime in the next century – you'll appreciate getting the same reception.* We pushed them in their wheelchairs to breakfast and dinner, and engaged them in safe conversation if we could. Nineteen-seventeen seemed far longer than forty years ago. The year 2001 seemed closer than 1917. I'd even thrown away my '61 beanie from the fall.

They too had explored ways of sneaking into the fortress. Those wild, pre-flapper girls kept their windows unlatched and wedged matchbooks in the doors. Just imagine how hard it was, coming back to a Baptist college after a year in the trenches and another year in Paris. After a year in Paris, a boy don't settle in too comfortably with silly regulations. They turned around in their chairs. 'But I reckon you boys found a way around them too, haven't you?' Pursuant to instructions, I agreed. I'd have to be careful, sleeping in the girls' dorms with all the old-timers poking around. Usually, all the doors were left open at night; one closed door would look suspicious. I locked all the doors on my corridor.

Pam Weigl sits with me on my bed. We're like a high school drama class, acting old. It's just so much grey paint and pasted-on eyebrows. Her hair is dark, touched with grey, and she's dressed in black, as always. We're having a beer in my freshman room. Skin lies puckered on the tops of her hands, brown with spots. No bad make-up there. Her wrists are thin, with blue shadows between the bones. I ask her if she'll be my date to the 40th Reunion Mixer. Nothing too fast or unfamiliar for us old-timers. 'I asked you here, didn't I?' She turned her hands over, palms up. I was staring down at mine. 'It's not pretty, is it, Charlie?' Before the dance, there'd be a memorial service to attend 'for our fallen classmates', if we were up to it, if we had friends among those cut down prematurely. I did; my freshman roommate. His parents had divorced in his first semester. I'd taken him home with me to Pittsburgh for Thanksgiving, not knowing my father, even then, was spending his nights and weekends away. By his senior year he'd made his first million dollars, buying and rehabbing old airplanes and selling them to executives in Cleveland and Columbus. His will had endowed the new business administration building, which I did not intend to visit.

I heard fumbling at the door and thought: it's all over, campus security, the village cops. I'll be thrown out. The door popped open, and there they stood, three portly guys in shorts and beanies, one of them still holding a key off a steel hoop.

'Well, I'll be damned,' said the man in the middle. 'What have we here? I thought this was a girls' dorm.'

'I'm Charlie Ducharme, sir, and I can explain,' I said.

'French boy, eh? I'm Buzz C. Crawford, and this is Ace and this is Corkie. We're Ace, Buzz and Corkie, the A B C Boys of Nineteen Hundred and Seventeen.'

'You wouldn't be keeping a girl in here, would you?' asked Ace. He jiggled the keys.

I told him my story, as far as it went. Montreal, Pittsburgh, singing in *Brigadoon*, living in the woods, then here. A different room every night, pushing a mower, painting and plastering, no home, no parents, nowhere to go.

'Ah, to be young again,' said Corkie.

'Hell, Ace here spent a whole semester in the dorm, *in the winter,* hidden by the girls. He made a key to every room up here, and they still work!'

'Never know when they'll come in handy. Two years at the front, a year in Paris, and we come back here and can't drink, can't smoke a cigarette, can't take a girl out after nine o'clock. What did they expect?'

'And the girls hadn't seen a man in three years. It was molten back then. You boys wouldn't have the slightest idea.'

They took the second bed, three old guys perched like crows on a power line. 'Seems to me,' said Buzz, 'this boy's got some promise.'

'I was worried about gumption these days,' said Ace.

'Have you declared a major yet?' asked Buzz.

Ace jiggled the hoop and the keys jangled like a gypsy caravan.

'Pre-med all the way,' I said.

'That's not a bad life,' said Corkie. 'Pays the bills, but let me tell you, it's boring as hell. You get into med school, you got to play by the rules. This right here, tonight, this is the wildest thing I've done in twenty years.'

An old man in a beanie and shorts and a thin summer jacket; life suddenly seemed so terribly sad. He dug into his pocket and presented me with a can of beer. 'Let's see, how many rules have we broken? There's the girls' dorm, the break-in, the underage drinking, the alcohol possession –'

'– and the keys, Ace, you'd have a hell of a time explaining the keys,' said Buzz. They all had beers, maybe they'd been hiding them. After a few minutes of contemplative sipping, Buzz asked, 'So, how much do you need to tide you over?'

I must have looked confused.

'Five hundred? A thousand?'

All of my life I have accepted the kindness of strangers, and I have never felt guilty. The true mark of an artistic conscience, someone must have told me. They took out their chequebooks and assessed themselves three hundred and fifty dollars apiece to the Class of '17 Scholarship Fund, in my name.

'Accept my advice, boy,' said Corkie. 'You've got too much pepper in you for medical school. Don't do like I did. Go out there and let it burn you up.'

They stood as a group, and left their beer cans on the dresser top. 'The girls will think we died on them,' said Buzz.

'They'll get a kick out of the story,' said Ace.

'They'll think we're making it up,' said Corkie.

Our class seems fitter and younger than what I remember from forty years ago. No wheelchairs, and the women are still attractive. To my eyes, we're looking better than the stringbean boys we were, or the undifferentiated blond girls dressed alike except for Pam Weigl and a few of the theatre majors. My god, we're a distinguished bunch, senators and millionaires notwithstanding. I've come the farthest ('and gone the furthest,' quipped Pam), outdistancing all the Floridians and Californians.

On the way to the memorial service we pause a few minutes before the Great War Cenotaph, and I tell her the unfinished story of my incredible freshman summer. The night of the three ghosts, probably the most important night of my life. The night a mantle was passed, the night I became a man in some curious way. There is a Buzz Crawford on the base of the cenotaph, which surprises me – I thought the statue honoured the dead, not just the enlistees – and maybe the Asa was my Ace, but nothing resembles a Corkie.

The day has turned uncomfortably hot. Perspiration rolls down my back, making my skin crawl. The chapel is cooler, but the air stiller, more oppressive. The only breeze, it seems, comes from the organ notes themselves. Pam, in her Debbie Wagner persona as Class Voice, comes forward and sings the school anthem, then I, as Class Pen, say some words. I speak about my old roommate, but my thoughts are on the three ghosts who visited me, and saved me from a wasted life. We retire to our seats to listen to our senators, and then the roll call of honour, those among us who are with us in memory only.

We'd been handed the sheets on entering. I remember the early deaths, automobile accidents mainly, and a girl from our class dead from leukemia without anyone telling us, but now everyone's faces, the living and dead, come back to me as they'd been in our freshman guidebook, black-and-white high school graduation shots, four hundred and fifty white faces with flattops, Princetons, ducktails, bobs and ponytails. The names of the dead take up three columns, half of us have died; it is enough to make me reach for Pam's hand, just to say, 'Look, we've come through!'

'Yes, we have,' she says, and her finger slowly traces the columns of names, stopping at mine, then at hers. When she smiles, I can see all her teeth.

I take her hand. An ant marches slowly and patiently over the puckered skin. She hasn't felt it. I flick it away, but another emerges from her black sweater, and another, then dozens. When I lift her hand I see only a pool of ants and bones, my bones entwined with hers and ants pouring from my shirt, out the wrists and between the buttons across my belly.

The Belle of Shediac

My take on the complexity of all things Canadian, or perhaps only the mysteries of Montréal, developed rapidly in the summer and fall of 1970, in my first six months in Québec. I had arrived in the east four years earlier from Winnipeg to study Canadian literature in Ottawa. What I learned was that my proposed thesis topic, 'The Prairie in Post-War Canadian Fiction' was little more than my own life, with footnotes. *La thèse, c'est moi.* On the promise of earning an eventual degree, but the reality of having written and published a small novel while on my thesis-grant, I landed a lectureship at Sir George Williams University in Montréal.

With the province of Québec fast coming to a political boil in the summer of 1970, I spent three months living on the Poulain family's summer porch in Limoilou, a 'working-class suburb' of Quebec City, learning to speak French. Those were the years of passionate gestures. My most extravagant ambition was to remake myself like a northern Gatsby into the platonic conception of a complete Canadian. Eight years of mandated French in Winnipeg schools had left me with a cement-head ability to read Proust, but to stumble over ordering a meal. This time, I swore, it would work. None of the Poulains, or their neighbours, spoke a word of English.

A glazier by trade, Monsieur Poulain had recently quit what he called the 'putty-knife brigade'. He'd grown tired of being on call twenty-four hours a day, mopping up broken glass and cleaning up after hail and windstorms and events he called 'infamous acts', by which he meant drunken brawls and break-ins. He and his two sons had started a small window factory in their garage, working as subcontractors for the pre-fab housing industry, turning out metal frames and insulated sliding panels for a larger enterprise in Saint-Jean.

It was the beginning of an era. Every kind of independence was in the air. A generation earlier, a responsible family man like M. Poulain would never have given up job security for the risky adventure of self-respect.

To help with the transition, Madame had advertised for a quiet man to occupy the summer porch at a hundred dollars a week, meals included. That I was an English professor earned some respect, but the fact that I had nothing better to do than poke around the house with a notebook and tape recorder opened me up to levels of arcane euphemism far beyond the competence of any dictionary. I was the 'English fog', sometimes the drizzle. 'Front's coming in,' one of the sons would say, just as I appeared at the dinner table, 'grab your boots.' For three months I was the quiet gentleman in a bellicose family on a noisy street – there is no such thing as a 'working class suburb' – grateful for every precious word they fed me.

Take rhubarb. *Rhubarbe,* but I never heard Madame use the word. The first signs of spring were little pink shoots, *petites didinnes,* little pricks, bursting through the dirty old snow. Madame had a different word for every stage of rhubarb, the shoots, the tumescent red stalks ripe for stewing (*mon marié* she'd say, my bridegroom), to the last hard wooden stumps she called the nun's saddle. Freud could have learned the interpretation of dreams directly from her.

M. Poulain, the glass-worker, had dozens of words for nicks, scrapes, slices or gouges. The scars were whores, priests, bastards, bitches, oozers, seepers, tricklers and spurters; blood was wine, juice, pus, slime. Every scar told a story, like tattoos. To listen in on the father and sons was to learn the terse poetry of labour and survival, the gravity of sweet talk, what Gilles Vigneault meant when he called the Québécois *'gens de paroles et gens de causerie'.*

Thirty-five years later, there still are trees, flowers, fish, vegetables, anything to do with glass and windows and power tools that I know only in French, and forms of humiliation and aggression that seem shallow and petulant in English. An early mark of an educated man is the realization that sometimes, no matter how ideas and languages and experiences seem to bleed together in some kind of grand synthesis, it's still an illusion. I'd been looking for a pure moment of perfect equivalence, something I might be able to structure my life around.

One September morning, two weeks after returning from Limoilou, I was sitting in my office at Sir George in downtown Montréal, when history knocked. He was a tall, lean gentleman in his sixties, dressed like a banker in a white shirt, grey suit and striped tie, but with shoulder-length white hair and an uncombed beard that fell nearly to his waist. The effect was of a zealot and a hippie, a Victorian dandy with bohemian tastes. His card read 'Pierre-Paul Saint-Joseph', a saintly trifecta with a classy Outremont address.

A true Montrealer would have recognized the name – he smiled as if I had – and perhaps thrown him out. But coming from Winnipeg, I deferred with silence. 'I must congratulate you on your success,' he said. 'It is a fine book, well-observed, and socially conscious.' A translation? A movie offer? Did he know that the little book he was praising, according to its lone national review, was 'under the sunny evocation of a prairie childhood' something 'dark and dangerous'? If you had been one of the two hundred and forty-two to buy that book when it first came out, and preserved it, it would be worth about three hundred dollars today.

'Now, I have come to take you on a journey,' he said. 'The next step, so to speak.' And so I asked, Where? (Toronto? Paris? London?) 'Come,' he said. We jumped on the crowded escalator. I stood one tread above him all seven floors down to de Maisonneuve Boulevard. Students passing on their way up seemed to find him amusing, and giggled behind cupped hands.

It was one of those perfect Montréal September days, the air cool and crystalline, a bit of Indian summer after the first hard frost. Out on the sidewalk he asked, 'Are you familiar with the prison-complex called Bordeaux?' And I thought, *what?* My god, he's a Mountie! What have I done? What does he know about me? As the separatists say, *they're everywhere.* There's nothing dark and dangerous lurking in my book. I'm sunny, I'm innocent, I'm from Winnipeg.

'Vaguely,' I managed.

'The men who are incarcerated there need your help. They need to learn the finer points of self-expression; otherwise no one will listen to them. I offer you no pay, and the work is exhausting. Nevertheless, I sense that you will do it.' He raised his arm, as though signalling a taxi, but a black limousine crawled around the corner of Bishop Street and stopped in front of us.

2.

A brief history of the Cold War, picked up in a limousine on a late September drive in 1970, from Sir George Williams University to Côte Ste-Catherine Boulevard:

It was a foreign war, of course; we French Canadians were not involved. I didn't fight; Mr Trudeau didn't fight. Montréal was a neutral city surrounded by passions. It was a grand time and place to be in the flower of one's youth. We were flooded with exiles, we'd become a world-city by default. My family were exiles, too – my father was a painter who'd studied in Paris in the twenties and managed to stay on. We didn't come back here until the fall of Spain; he'd lost friends there. For the first time in his life he was glad to have Montréal at his back. He abandoned everything European, all that grandiose Expressionism, and started painting Québec landscapes and Montréal streets, those icy alleys behind the tenement blocks, under the back galleries, with kids playing hockey, home-made rinks banked with dirty snow. Urban Krieghoff, he called it, something he'd made fun of in Paris.

Montréal grew up suddenly, it became a city of many cultures, it could hold its own anywhere. We thought we'd put Lili St-Cyr and all that touristy honky-tonk behind us, and the Sainte-Anne-de-Beaupré, Brother André, crutches-in-the-oratory medieval Catholicism would just blow away. Of course, it was especially fine to have been part of a very small, privileged class of French Canadians, like my family, or like Monsieur Trudeau's. There were not many of us, we were a genuine elite, our families were intermarried, we courted the same girls, we went to the same college, then to the same foreign schools, our families lived in the same neighbourhoods, we kept ski lodges on the same slopes and fishing camps on the same rivers. We behaved the way elites always do, supremely confident of our own opinions with an exaggerated sense of our importance. We were accustomed to being listened to and to influencing events. We never doubted ourselves, nor was there anyone around us powerful enough or cultured enough to command our attention. I worry that my friend the prime minister continues that practice.

My young friend, we thought we were the future. We didn't know we were a dead end. If anyone had said the future of our people is to be found in Pointe-Saint-Charles or Verdun, or out by the refineries, we would have laughed in his face. Many of those boys, I grant, are simple voyous, but they are far more honest than I.

In those wartime years, while keeping up my social life, being seen in society, attending the openings of plays and exhibits, visiting the galleries, I had been recruited by the government as part of an international team to help build an atomic bomb. I was a chemist among physicists. I was a Canadian among Americans and British and a horde of Europeans. I was French among English. I saw a flaw in the American thinking – it had to do with the collection of heavy water, how the heavy isotope could be stripped by the means of chemical solvents. Let us say, I was taught that it was not the place of a Canadian to lecture Americans, or a French Canadian to know anything more, as they charmingly put it, than where to find a clean woman for the night. I have already explained to you that I was not one to accept corrections. Perhaps you have read about me.

(I hadn't.)

In 1946, a lowly clerk defected from the Soviet Embassy in Ottawa, Gouzenko was his name, bringing with him the names of Canadian collaborators. We had not known until that moment that our governments – the Soviets, and the Canadians – were at war. I had grown up with the notion that only the Communists stood against the evils of my youth, Fascism and the Church. The circle of artists in Paris was totally Communist. I was identified as one of the collaborators, along with many others. My heavy-water formulas were in Russian hands.

I suppose I'm very lucky. *He laughed.* I spent eight years in prison, but if I'd been American I might not have lived to see such a glorious day as today. And to make a long story short, that is why I became a social activist. I can no longer teach or do research. I recruit artists of conscience. I know the indignities of confinement. I survived because I could communicate. I concern myself now only with the welfare of inmates.

His was only the second French Canadian home I'd been inside, only the second Québec family I'd ever met. I must have thought the only wife for a self-confessed revolutionary would be a Rosa Luxemburg figure, someone nearly as inspiring of snickers as Pierre-Paul himself. Yet the woman who greeted us at the door was as beautiful as any woman I had ever seen, a beauty so obliterating it wiped out considerations of age. I thought I recognized her, perhaps from movies or television, but her name, Liliane Pelletier, was unfamiliar.

As she stood against the walls of paintings, I could imagine her as a one-time model, one of those legendary muses who had inspired, then married, the older man. I asked where she'd come from, thinking the ateliers of Paris. She was too fine even for the upper strata of refined Outremont society, and she laughed. 'I could ask you to guess, but we don't have all day.' She shifted her French from Outremont-international to something local, almost sub-local. 'I'm from Shediac, my dear. Do you know Shediac?'

I associated Shediac with those famous Atlantic salmon streams, like the Ristigouche or Miramichi, a long ways away, not even in Québec. 'New Brunswick?' I asked.

'Moncton was my Paris,' she said. It was a funny line, delivered earnestly. I didn't know if I should wince, or laugh. Moncton was the capital of Acadia, the other side of Frenchness, the poorer side with the worst accent.

'Her father was a doctor,' Pierre-Paul interjected. 'A very strict man with strict ideas of education. So Lilou came to Montréal with her mother in 1944 to play Juliet with José Ferrer. The most exquisite beauty Montreal had ever seen, the most beautiful French, the most delightful English! Seventeen years old and they were already calling her La Belle de Shediac! The next year, she made her London debut at the Royal Vic.'

When he'd mentioned José Ferrer, I thought of the little man on his knees, or the swashbuckler with a banana nose. Thank God I hadn't laughed.

'You forget, my dear, I opened in Paris after that,' she added, with a gentlest hint of a rebuke. 'There was still bomb rubble in the streets. People were starving but they beat the doors down to see Shakespeare again.'

It was beginning to sink in. I was in the company of stage royalty. Classic roles in two languages on the world's greatest stages in successive years, before the age of eighteen.

'I met her in this house, with her lovely mother, at a reception thrown by my mother. It was in this very room with a chamber orchestra playing. That's how it was done in those days. The old châtelaines got together and decided our fates.'

'With the war, many of the actors couldn't go back,' she said. 'There were famous names, great actors and directors from France and Germany and Hungary. Can you imagine, seventeen years old and coming from Shediac and being brought to a house like this, meeting people I thought were dead?' This house was the portal through which France had re-established contact with the New World. Chamber ensembles, the old painter's studio transformed into a rehearsal stage, actors staying on for the entire run of their plays or the *tournage*. She named the names, and I recognized not a one. My discomfort must have been apparent.

'I must apologize for my ignorance,' I said, and I silently vowed that I would never permit myself to emerge in society again, so preposterously ill prepared.

'Of course, it was a bit ignoble of them,' she said, 'how quickly they returned to Europe the moment the war was over. They spoke of their war-time banishment in Montréal. They were not always the perfect guests, were they, my dear?'

'Europe is doomed,' said Pierre-Paul.

She served chilled soup and quiche; she talked of music and literature. When her husband had been 'away' for eight years – her word – she'd gone back to films and theatre and television. She changed to her perfect English when she sensed I'd been manoeuvred out of my depths. As an enlightened embodiment of the St. James section of Winnipeg, I'd been a sophisticated rebel. Ask me anything, and I knew the answer. The trouble was, I'd been the one asking the questions, Winnipeg questions – of course I knew the answers! How shallow and pretentious I was! I felt I should be banished to the cultural mud room or a summer porch.

After lunch, Liliane asked, 'Would you object if I read your palm?'

'Some day,' said her husband, 'the book of Liliane's palm-readings will be opened, and we'll realize the world holds no surprises.'

'That's what I fear,' I said.

'You see this line, how deep and strong it begins?' she said. 'But there are discontinuities. There should be a parallel line, a partner-line, but I see you are alone now, and I don't see a partner until here, many years from now. Your future will be more interesting than your past. Let's hope you're not going out in the world to save it, we've had quite enough of missionaries. But look at these stars, how they radiate!'

She opened her own hand, drawing my finger over her lines, the deep partnership, her stars. 'You will travel far, young man.'

3.

Pierre-Paul guided me through the intricacies of Bordeaux security, the rings of bars and searches, the procedures I'd be following in the weeks to come. No one frisked us. Of the guards, he said in English, 'These aren't the brightest people in the world. You have to ask yourself, what kind of person elects to imprison other men for a living?' He seemed Tolstoyan to me at that moment, and I was feeling superior as well. What a day of perfect symmetries this had been: the lunch and the prison, the litany of grand events and immortal names and accomplishments – and this collection of anonymous wreckage, the tattooed arms, the collapsed young faces missing teeth.

A week later, with the city in an uproar over the FLQ kidnapping of the British trade commissioner, James Cross, the limousine took me out to Bordeaux Prison for the biggest adventure of my life, teaching my first class to the anglophone multiple murderers. It was a sunny morning in the brightest week of the Montréal calendar, when the low sun generated the purest light, pointing every brick with its own black shadow. The familiar streets of the city had been transformed. The army barracks had been emptied. Traffic was being directed by uniformed soldiers with their rifles at the ready.

The francophone killers were being taught by another of Pierre-Paul's recruits, a young writer named Gilles Lacroix. He was a tiny man, a little over five feet, frail and nervous. His hands trembled, his fingers and a drooping moustache were nicotine-stained (he was only my age, barely thirty; how long, how ardently, had he been smoking?) He reached out to shake my hand, but pulled back at the last minute. I didn't ask why, but I assumed it had to do with possible pollution from my language. That, too, was common in those years. I'd brought a copy of his latest novel for him to sign, but found myself sliding it into my pocket instead. This is the only contact, or near-contact, that I have had with the man who has changed my life.

I'd read that novel, *Siropicide – Candied Man* in my eventual translation. It was typically macabre, as it concerned an explosion in a sugar refinery and death by boiling syrup. The enemy, as always, was the spiritual captivity of a society by the forces of the S S, the *sois-sagistes*. Not the do-gooders, but something far worse: the *be*-gooders. They included the oppressive Church, the rotten politics, the historic poverty, the exploitative English, the imperialist Canadians and Americans, inherited habits of mind and soul. '*Sois sage!*' Be good, be quiet, be obedient. Bite your tongue.

'Gilles Lacroix is our future,' said Pierre-Paul. 'You have much in common, I think.'

His novels were set in a single neighbourhood, on streets that twisted their way down the gentle bluffs to the lower city and river *(les ondes de misère, ruelles qui tombent et glissent vers le fleuve comme des soûls marins …)* Their names celebrated confinement: la rue du Bon-Conseil, between rue de l'Acte-Gratuite and le Parc de la Puanteur with its Bassin des Malodeurs. His alter ego was an inquisitive child, Prospère Dugrandin, a snoop of seven who for half a novel could catalogue the contents of his mother's dresser drawers, his brother's closet, his father's tackle box, tying every wan souvenir to a moment of thwarted passion. The apartment was meticulously described, the nave and every apse, ending in the basilica of the back gallery where old furniture was stored: the old icebox, cases of beer, skates, fishing rods and old magazines, ending at the *lignes des linges* – 'clotheslines confessionals –' connected to another gallery across the alley. (He loves anagrams; what are they but shadows of alternative meaning?) He who worships at the gallery-altar is a *galérien*, a galley slave, an underground observer with a 'leeking soul' and a 'beeting heart'. (He loves puns; translator be damned.) His suggested licence plate motto reads *Le souterrain nous soutient* – forces of the underground sustain us.

We didn't see it then, but Lacroix is our Proust. He transcribed the history of his people in 'voluptuous escutcheons' of prose. Little Prospère Dugrandin faithfully recorded a stagnant world in the language of inherited piety. The parks were scary places, the ponds scummy and undrained; the fire-alleys were garbage-strewn in summer, hockey-violent in winter; no urban Krieghoff for Gilles Lacroix. He was a child born in the wrong time and place, confused and ignored, but blessed with vision, language and a mythic imagination.

As a teen, Lacroix had published poetry, like Emile Nelligan. At

nineteen, like Limoilou's own Marie-Claire Blais, Lacroix started publishing novels, and he'd continued to pile up the titles through his
twenties. New books seemed to be coming out every few months. We
were nearly the same age, but he'd already published a dozen novels.
None had been translated, and I'd never seen his name in any English
newspaper.

The English-speaking prisoners in my 'writing class' were my age or
younger. The small classroom had a catwalk overhead, permanently
patrolled by guards with their automatic rifles off safety. My students
were Canada's worst; killers on the outside who'd also murdered inside
the system. Many were Indian and Métis. They hated everything French,
starting with the warden, guards and trusties. They were self-styled
patriots and itched for the chance to kill a separatist.

Pierre-Paul left me with some advice. Don't get started with politics.
Don't ask why they're in, what they did, or if they did it. If the Indians
aren't able to write let them tell their stories. Watch out for the protected
prisoners, the rapists, snitches and child-abusers who would be killed in
any general prisoner population. They'll probably be the best educated,
the most articulate, the best writers and the most adept at currying
favour. Nothing they say or write will ever be acknowledged by the
general run of murderers. This was another conflict I was not to challenge; it is built into the etiquette of survival. Look on the bright side, he
said. If the prisoners ever decide to make a break, I'll be safe. First, they'd
kill the snitches and rapists, and then they'd go for me.

I'll always remember 'the single mythic moment', as Sartre once
called it, when the memory glimpses the contingencies and 'perpetual
rebeginnings' of a life. My life was on the line that day, although I had
conferred a certain exemption on myself. The prisoners loved me, I
loved myself, the separatists had overstepped in the kidnapping,
Trudeau had overplayed his hand by clamping the entire country under
martial law – but I was okay.

Jackie Jack, an Indian, was telling a story. Everyone respected, even
revered Jackie Jack. 'So, these two Americans from Chicago flies up and
hires me to guide. They tell me how many fish they want, what size they
got to be, how long a time they have to catch them and what they're paying. Sure, sure, I say, I can do all that. So we flies up a hundred miles,
launch the boat and they starts hauling in the doré and trout. At the end

of the day, they say they ain't paying, I didn't meet the promise.' I was about to break in, talk about plotting, the climax, how to build the scene, but I let him talk. 'So I says, must be the bait.'

A couple of snickers. 'Yeah, man, the bait!'

'So I asks the first dentist does he agree it's the bait? He gets all hot, says I gave bad bait. So I says you're the boss. You come flying up from Chicago so you must know more than me. What do I know, eh? So, we play it their way. Must have been the bait 'cause soon as we chopped him up, them fish started biting like hell, biggest fish I ever seen. The other dentist, he didn't look too happy no matter how many fish he caught. Caught so many I had a boatload, so I just pushed the other bugger over the side.'

'Now, that's the kind of story you don't read, professor! How're you going to improve on that?' We were all laughing, the student had bested the teacher; no way I could touch it, but now that we were all in a good mood, thinking of the Chicago dentists and 'must be the bait', I thought I could squeeze a few ideas across without appearing some kind of tight-ass judge.

As it turned out, I didn't have the chance. There was a ruckus in the hall and I turned to the door just as three soldiers burst through. 'Lacroix!' they shouted, 'hands out flat on the desk.'

I must have been slow to respond, maybe smirking or just smiling, seeking first to inform them of their error, when my arms were practically ripped from their sockets in the rush to handcuff me. My students were standing, and the overhead guards were shouting instructions, 'Lock down, lock down.' The prisoners hooted: 'Break in, break in!'

'I'm not La –' I tried to say, but the soldier whacked me across the mouth and shouted, his voice rising. 'Shut up. Shut the hell up.'

They pushed me out the door, into the hall where jumpsuited trusties were mopping floors and keeping their heads down, where soldiers were running through the halls, followed by prison guards. And at the far end of hall, just before I was turned and marched in the opposite direction, I saw the tall, elegant figure of Pierre-Paul Saint-Joseph, his arm around the shoulder of Gilles Lacroix, exiting through the rows of doors and metal detectors.

* * *

179

We were interned – an enforced sabbatical, in my case – in a former seminary off-island. There were thirty of us. I remained Gilles Lacroix and no longer fought it. We didn't know the charges against us, or who had brought them, and the War Measures Act suspended our rights anyway. No one seemed to know what to do with us. We were mostly teachers and unionists, with a few performers thrown in. We fashioned our own entertainment. We found old crucifixes on the walls and wrenched them down, but as one of the poets later wrote, the ghostly grime, the bathtub ring of martyred flesh, remained. And then we sang, or I should say they sang, because I didn't know the tunes or the witty variations on old hymns and the folk songs they were satirizing. Scandalous songs for a scandalous time, Marc Lalonde crooning a lullaby, 'Mon cher Pierre,' to the prime minister. Our guards watched and laughed. Lacroix's unsigned *Siropicide* was in my pocket and I retired to a corner to read it with all the intensity of having written it myself.

They asked, why are you reading your own book, Gilles? and I answered, I'm not Lacroix, which they took as profundity, an existential denial. We staged little monologues to keep ourselves sane and entertained; I did Jackie Jack's 'must be the bait' in English, launching Lacroix's utterly undeserved reputation for extraordinary bilingualism. Others sang. Gilles Vigneault and Félix Leclerc got a workout. A stand-up comic did his favourite Yvon Deschamps routines – amazing, under those circumstances, how deeply they cut. *Qu'est-ce que c'est le bonheur pour un Québécois?* ... how does a Quebecker define happiness? ... *c'est quand le policier frappe à ta porte en demandant M. Tremblay....* it's when the policeman knocks on your door looking for Mr Tremblay ... *et tu pourras dire c'est pas moé que tu cherches! C'est le Tremblay juste en face!* ... and you can say, I'm not the Tremblay you're looking for. You want the Tremblay across the hall!

I'm not the Lacroix you want – but are you sure? Am I sure?

Pretending to be the man I wasn't, a talent I didn't have, a language I didn't possess, among people with a spirit I admired but didn't share, drove me deeper into Lacroix's book, looking for ambiguities, as though it were dense and convoluted poetry and not a novel. I made out vague shapes heaving and turning in the depths, shapes that had been in my own small 'dark and disturbing' novel. Little Prospère Dugrandin was a beaten-down but still triumphant version of myself. I had visited all his perceptions, plotted the same escapes and I knew what was undisclosed in his book and in mine. We didn't have an easy word for it then.

Three days later, a beautiful, mysterious lady vouched for my identity (this is a very Canadian story) and I was free to resume my life, if I wanted it. I finished my school year at Sir George, but never returned to teaching or to the dreams of writing I'd once entertained. I'd been used, sacrificed by one traitor to save another. Gilles Lacroix had been able to walk out of Bordeaux that day, into a waiting limousine and be put on the night flight to Paris. He has continued to write, a book for every year of his life, now over sixty, and I exist as the translator of Lacroix, which feels, after so many years, like translating myself. I live in the East End near the refineries in the city's gay ghetto, hailing distance from the twisted streets of Lacroix's imagination, in the shadow of the big Radio-Canada building on what used to be Dorchester Boulevard but is now le boulevard René-Lévesque. Dwelling on irony is so déclassé. His Nobel Prize, and his rejection of the Nobel Prize, brought him fame and brought me a lifetime commission.

In France they arrange these things more sensibly. When Sartre refused his Nobel in 1964 ('above all, a writer must not allow himself to become an institution'), no one accused him of spiting France or the French intellectual tradition. In fact, his gesture burnished both ever more brightly. In the case of Lacroix, he was so unknown at the time that the French assumed he was Belgian. Eight of his sixty books have now appeared in English (twenty more are on the way), including *Les Sons* ('The Clamour' in my translation) his 800-page homage to Sartre's *Les Mots* – but none in Canada. He was forgotten in Québec, and unknown in Ontario.

A simple resident of Marseille, a frail man with white hair and a brown moustache and no telephone or computer, a man whose deepest passion is privacy, is finally uncovered by the enterprising Swedes after two days of searching and innumerable false leads provided by protective neighbours. He is living with a Tunisian boy in the Arab quarter above a halal butcher's on an alley called locally 'la rue des âmes sales.' He admits, yes, he is Lacroix, he writes books, he has no telephone, he grants no interviews, and he is not interested in their prize, which, he understands, is awarded to writers from authentic, sovereign countries, not from provinces, to a France or a United States, not some mythical Yoknapatawpha. He has never been to that perfectly charming country called Canada, although he is grateful to them for having expelled him into the world.

Une atteinte au Québec, blared the press in Montréal. *A Spiteful Renunciation,* wrote the Toronto papers. We're the only G-8 country without a Nobel Prize-winner. We might be the only country in the world with a written language not to count a Nobelist. 'We have all moved on,' opined progressive opinion in Québec. 'M. Lacroix is late to the banquet, a bit *rétrograde,* but we still invite him home.'

Home? he asked. *The alleys of the casbah are crystalline in their logic compared to Montréal.* It is safe to assume he will never return.

Acknowledgements

A number of the stories included here have been previously published: 'Eyes', 'A Class of New Canadians', 'Extractions and Contractions', 'Words for the Winter' and 'Going to India' appeared in *A North American Education* (1973); 'I'm Dreaming of Rocket Richard', 'At the Lake', 'Among the Dead' and 'He Raises Me Up' appeared in *Tribal Justice* (1974); 'North' and 'Translation' appeared in *Resident Alien* (1986).

Several of the stories were included in the following magazines or anthologies: 'North' in *Saturday Night* and *New Press: Canadian Prize Stories;* 'Eyes' in *The Fiddlehead* and *Narrative Voice;* 'A Class of New Canadians' in *The Fiddlehead;* 'Extractions and Contractions' in *Student's Choice, Story So Far* and *Tri-Quarterly;* 'Among the Dead' in *New American Review;* 'Life Could Be a Dream (Sh-boom, Sh-boom)' in *Michigan Quarterly Review;* 'The Belle of Shediac' in *Threepenny Review*.

Clark Blaise has taught in Montreal, Toronto, Saskatchewan and British Columbia, as well as at Skidmore College, Columbia University, Iowa, NYU, Sarah Lawrence and Emory. For several years he directed the International Writing Program at the University of Iowa. Among the most widely travelled of authors, he has taught or lectured in Japan, India, Singapore, Australia, Finland, Estonia, the Czech Republic, Holland, Germany, Haiti and Mexico. He lived for years in San Francisco, teaching at the University of California, Berkeley. He is married to the novelist Bharati Mukherjee and currently divides his time between San Francisco and Southampton, Long Island. In 2002, he was elected president of the Society for the Study of the Short Story. In 2003, he was given an award for exceptional achievement by the American Academy of Arts and Letters.

Clark Blaise: The Selected Stories

1 Southern Stories (2000)
2 Pittsburgh Stories (2001)
3 Montreal Stories (2003)
4 International Stories (2005)

Mingling new pieces written especially for each collection with
several older, 'classic' stories, the series is an unprecedented event
in the history of Canadian literature. Never before has such a
large body of work been re-collected in such a way. Never has a
writer been so quickly and so completely 're-presented' to us. The
strength of the project is its ability to foreground the complexity
of Blaise's geographical imagination. The series takes what was
previously a more subtle tension between individual locales in
individual stories and individual collections and magnifies this
place-to-place comparison into a much more striking volume-to-
volume juxtaposition. [...] The series illustrates, more clearly
than ever before, that there is something remarkably original
about Blaise's work. Blaise is more than just a local-colourist who
ferrets out the curious details of 'marginal' communities in order
to delight cosmopolitan readers. Rather, if we consider the full arc
of his work, we see that for nearly fifty years he has been challeng-
ing the way that we understand the concept of place in contempo-
rary Canadian and American literature.

– Alexander Macleod, *Essays in Canadian Writing* (Fall 2002)